AMERICAN SPIN

A
Fake News
Mystery

By Gary Engler

Cover by Frank Myrskog

RED Publishing

203 32nd Street West, Saskatoon, Saskatchewan, S7L-0S3

WALTZ

1.

The Sun was setting, that was obvious. But exactly how long did he have until it disappeared?

The *Vancouver Sun* and the Vancouver sun.

Sitting on a Beach Avenue bench staring west over English Bay, waiting — that's one feature of journalism he wouldn't miss — Waylon Choy couldn't help the hackneyed metaphor. The namesake of the newspaper he worked at was about to paint its nightly naturalistic masterpiece.

Of course any comparison was ridiculous. The return of the life-giving celestial orb every morning was as close to guaranteed as anything on this planet, but the likelihood of printing another year's worth of the *Vancouver Sun* had become a favourite subject in a newsroom full of amateur oddsmakers.

On the other hand, he now embraced change, didn't he, so why worry? Ever since his marriage to Helena had begun to break up he had understood that feeling comfortable was dangerous, a sign something bad was about to happen. And he was definitely comfortable in his job. Everything about it was easy. He had been at the same newspaper for almost 24 years, the same beat — if you could call it that — for 15.

Should he take the buyout the company was offering? If he left the paper, what would he do? Reporter at the *Sun*, it was the only job he'd ever had. It was — if he was honest with himself — who he was.

The buyout would give him time to write a book. He had a few ideas. But what was the likelihood of earning even a half decent living from that? He had two kids to support. Go back to school and get a PhD?

Those who still can, do; those who have given up, teach.

Become a corporate or government flack?

Sell out.

Take advantage of the overheated Vancouver real estate market and sell his house, then use the money to stake a career as a professional poker player?

Another gambling addict in the family.

Now that he had finished restoring his 1965 AMC Ambassador 990 convertible perhaps he had enough experience to open a business? Become a broker? Maybe some sort of online network linking automobile restoration enthusiasts? WeAreARE.com?

Catchy name but the truth is I wouldn't last.

Restoring a car was one in a long line of infatuations that demonstrated how much of a dilettante he really was. 'A good journalist always has a little of the dilettante about him.' Who told him that? Someone who retired before newspaper journalism began its tortuous, agonizingly painful, death by a thousand cuts.

Three weeks left to decide whether or not to take a buyout.

Uncertainty and fear had become the sort of constant companions you hope never become friends, but you hang out with, nevertheless.

Pathetic.

A new job and a new relationship? His love life was even more pathetic than his career prospects.

I'm not ready to look for someone else.

Helena had moved on so there was no reason why he shouldn't, but the thought of all the hassle, getting to know someone new, finding the right person, or at least someone he could be comfortable with …

A soft clear voice interrupted his existential crisis.

"You're not Chinese."

Choy heard the words before seeing their source. He looked to his left, but then felt someone sit down close by to his right.

"You're Waylon Choy?" said the woman, momentarily obscured by the intense orange orb hovering just above her shoulder.

He nodded.

"You're not Chinese," she repeated.

He shrugged, as he had done dozens of times before when facing the same response to the juxtaposition of name and lack of 'oriental' physical features. "How do you know? And who said I was?"

Still unable to actually see the source of the voice that he recognized from the phone call earlier that day, he was caught completely off guard when she pressed her lips to his. As she pulled away, he shifted forward so that he no longer looked straight into the sun.

"You kiss every guy you meet like that?"

She was absolutely, stunningly beautiful — short tomboy black hair, a crisp white sleeveless sundress that glowed in the late evening light. Slim but curvy in all the right places and she was most definitely Chinese.

"Just the ones I want to like me. And I assumed from the name."

"I get that a lot," Choy said, inhaling a faint scent of a perfume that seemed the perfect complement to a gentle summer evening Pacific Ocean breeze. "My great-great-great-great-great grandfather came from California to B.C. during the Cariboo gold rush and married a Scottish-French-Cree woman. He was the only Chinese in my family and all I inherited from him was the name."

Of course that's almost certainly not true.

"I doubt that's true," she said, almost at the exact moment he had the same thought.

What is she after?

Only in fantasies do women act like this. "You need a Chinese reporter because?"

"It would be preferable."

"There's some cultural sensitivity involved?"

"One could say that, but it wouldn't necessarily be true."

She was sizing him up.

"It's more a question of believability."

"Because you have a story about Vancouver's first Chinese-Canadian police chief you think it should be written by a Chinese-Canadian reporter?"

"Something like that."

"Something like that, or that?"

After a moment she nodded, then glanced from side to side and quickly turned to scan the block of high-rises across the street behind them.

"Walk with me," she said, standing.

He would have preferred to dance. They would be the perfect cool couple, waltzing across the floor, everyone watching, wishing to be them.

But a walk will do, for now.

He stood up beside her as she continued to scan around them. In another surprising turn, she took his hand in hers, as if they were lovers out for a walk. He glanced down.

A kiss and now this?

"If someone is watching I want him to think we're a couple," she whispered.

She certainly had his undivided attention.

"I know this must seem strange, but things have gotten weird since ..."

"Since your father, the former police chief, died?"

She pulled her hand from his. "How ... "

"Why would a family friend be the one to contact a reporter when he has children?"

"My father was very careful to keep his family out of the news."

He tried to look cool but couldn't help his triumphant smile.

"Would you want a reporter who couldn't even figure out who you are?"

She stared at him.

"You'd have been blown off as another crazy, if I hadn't figured it out."

He smiled and she half returned it. Then she led him, not overtly, across the grass down towards the beach, all the while subtly checking for anyone who might be watching. If there was, her repeated intense glances at his face, the very slight 'I'm-in-love' smile and intertwined fingers would have been convincing evidence of romance. But she said nothing until they stood on sand made damp by a retreating tide.

"Okay," she said, moving her face so close to his that he thought she might be kissing him again.

He wouldn't have complained.

"Stare into my eyes."

He followed her order quickly and convincingly.

"I know how this must seem, but I am being followed."

"How do you know?"

"My father was a cop for 30 years. I'm a software engineer and I have a good friend who is an expert in surveillance. They're following me, both electronically and in person."

"Who?" said Choy, mostly focused on the face that filled his entire frame of vision.

"Someone connected with the business that killed my father," she said and quickly kissed him, before pulling away and smiling. "Sorry, but these men must think I'm just a ditzy young woman having a fling with a guy of absolutely no interest to them."

He returned the kiss and joined in the smile. "Happy to oblige."

"Listen carefully and do exactly what I say."

"So now I'm Chinese enough for you?"

"Yes. Please listen."

She moved even closer.

"My father didn't commit suicide. He was murdered and I want you to prove it."

She pressed her breasts against his chest and held them there. He stood perfectly still, enjoying a moment that should have felt weirder.

"After he retired from the force, he was working for a company. He put some files in a storage unit in Bellingham and the key to that is in our Birch Bay cabin. Someone must get the papers before they do and then figure this out."

"You must know some cops."

She pulled away.

"No police! You'll understand once you look at the papers. And I can't take the chance they will follow me there, so will you do it?" she said then kissed him again, this time a bit longer. "Please, I promise it will be a good story."

If the rational side of his brain had been engaged rather than other parts he might not have nodded yes, but in that moment it seemed the only possible response.

"There is a piece of paper in the pocket on the right side of my dress," she whispered, looking down towards her breasts "Put your arms around me and pull me tight. Take the paper out of my pocket as you touch my breast, pretend to whisper something in my ear and I will create a distraction so you can discretely put it in your pocket."

He followed her instructions and immediately after touching her breast she pulled away and playfully slapped his face. His surprise was so genuine that he almost forgot to hide the paper. She giggled as if they were discussing something intimate, then spun around like a lover enjoying the moment. She once again threw her arms around him.

"Did you get it?"

"Yes."

"And you promise to look at my father's papers?"

"Yes."

"What's your cell number?"

"Do you have a pen?"

"I'll remember."

He pulled her close and whispered his number.

She nodded and kissed him on the cheek.

"There's a phone number on the paper as well," she said, " but only call once you have uncovered the truth or if you have absolutely no other choice. They will be listening."

Before he could respond, she kissed him again, then ran away quickly, a half dozen steps on the beach, over the bike path, up the hill and disappeared across Beach Avenue between two apartment buildings.

He turned back to look across English Bay. This was definitely the strangest introduction to a story he had ever experienced.

How can I not at least check it out?

2.

Choy needed help but thought it best not to tell the two guys he had in mind the whole story, or really any of it at all, just yet. Better to treat them like he treated editors, saying what was necessary to get them on his side and be available in case they were needed. After all, he wasn't sure there was a story and if there were, what it was. No point in blowing your credibility by pitching a piece before you have a handle on it.

"I'm thinking about the buyout and want to get your opinion about some stuff," he had said. "Come take a spin with me down to Birch Bay and Bellingham. I'll buy you lunch. We'll cruise Chuckanut Drive in the 1965 AMC Ambassador 990 convertible I finally finished restoring. We can talk to some Americans about Donald Trump."

Neither needed more selling than that. Most Canadians were curious about what their southern neighbours saw in this caricature of the Ugly American who had just captured the Republican nomination for president. Both had heard Choy talking about restoring this car for the past four years and, like everyone else who knew him, neither had believed it was possible for an artsy-fartsy, bookish, bicycle-riding nerd to teach himself how to rebuild a car, let alone actually complete the job. Both were also enjoying a summer vacation just hanging around town, so relished taking one of the most beautiful short road trips in a part of the planet endowed with outstanding natural splendour.

Choy had considered his invitations carefully, just in case Celeste wasn't suffering from a nervous breakdown induced by the suicide of her father. If someone really had murdered the former Vancouver chief of police, the story would be well beyond the boundaries of his journalistic experience.

Despite his annoying habit of being too serious about everything, Doug Tait was one of the best hard news reporters Choy had ever worked beside. He had spent 20 of his over 30 years at the paper covering crime before taking a buyout five years earlier and moving over to teach journalism. He was tough and not intimidated by threats against his personal safety, as proven by a period of almost two years of police protection during which he continued to write about local gangs who murdered dozens of people in a bitter fight to control the Lower Mainland drug trade.

Dominic Donicelli was a former *Sun* entertainment editor, a former TV reporter and one of those journalists who was cynical about everything and claimed to be left wing, but who sucked up to powerful people wherever he went. He was the best bull shitter Choy had ever known, and absolutely fearless when it came to having an adventure, from bluffing his way into parties thrown by complete strangers to convincing the son of a former prime minister that it was a good idea to challenge a senator to a three-round boxing match. Two years earlier he had left the newspaper and gone over to the dark side of public relations and marketing, setting up his own company called Cultural Hegemony, which he claimed was inspired by Italian Marxist theorist Antonio Gramsci. Strangely, it seemed to be successful.

While neither was a particularly close friend, both had offered important advice to Choy as he went through his three-year long slowly dissolving marriage that ended in divorce two years earlier. Donicelli, who had been married and divorced three times, had been the one who told him: "Divorce is an opportunity to learn from your mistakes, to become a better person, and to make your ex see she was the problem, not you." Words that captured a personal zeitgeist. Tait, who lost his wife of 25 years to breast cancer, after which he took up the violin and joined a folk music society, had suggested new hobbies as a way of getting out of the ruts that trapped him, and meeting people. "Prove to yourself you can be whoever you want," he had said. That discussion led to finishing the restoration of his convertible and recovering old dreams of ballroom dancing.

"This is some ride Waylon," said Donicelli as they headed down Highway 99 towards the border. "Never thought you'd finish it."

"Cost me tens of thousands of dollars, all my spare time and delayed my taking up ballroom dancing for three years, but it turned out pretty nice, didn't it?"

"You're still thinking about competitive dancing?" asked Tait, sitting in the back.

Donicelli turned to repeat exactly what Choy had said. A convertible with its top down, driving on a freeway is not exactly the best place for a conversation, but quickly enough they were in a 100-metre-long line at the Peace Arch border crossing.

"So, if you take the buyout, what are you going to do?" said Donicelli, as the car slowed to a crawl and then a stop. "You're not independently wealthy. And you must be 20 years away from the big "r".

"How old are you?" asked Tait. "Forty-seven?"

"Forty-six," said Choy.

"You started right out of Langara College, didn't you?" said Tait. "I still remember the look on Griffin's face when he actually met you."

Choy smiled. The good old days when newspapers were hiring.

"Andrews, the AME, was in his office a half hour later and Griffin is all nervous and says, 'we hired him because we need more Chinese reporters, but he damn well doesn't look Chinese. What are we going to do?' Andrews thinks about it for a moment then answers, 'well, we can't get rid of him just because he doesn't look Chinese. I mean, if that ever got out, could you imagine the shit storm?' Griffin looks horrified at the thought. He hated controversy. Mr.

Congeniality, always wanted people to like him, probably the worst managing editor we ever had. Then Andrews says, 'so long as we never give him a column and put his picture in the paper who will know? The by-line is all that matters and that's Chinese. Besides, I'm told he is part Asian.' 'Let's hope it is the best part,' says Griffin. And he never spoke about it again. You never would have lasted a week if it had been a TV station."

Choy chuckled at a story he'd heard dozens of times before. Sure there was an underlying racist assumption that "minorities" were only hired because of some sort of affirmative action program, but he had long ago proven he was the best feature writer at the *Vancouver Sun* and besides, which part of his Chinese-Cree-Finnish-Scots-Punjabi-Russian-Jewish-French-Cherokee-African-Ukrainian-Chilean-English-German-Canadian identity was supposed to be offended?

"So, if you take the buyout, what are you going to do?" Donicelli repeated as the car inched forward.

"I don't know," said Choy. "That's why I invited you two along for the ride. Journalism is dying. The newsroom and the newspaper are shrinking, the company has been bleeding red ink, every quarter the ad revenue declines more, their digital strategy is going nowhere, the journalism we do is turning to shit, but what are my options? Stay and see how long the business lasts or the union stays strong enough to resist big pay cuts? Take the buyout and then what? One hundred and fifty thousand dollars won't last long, not with child support, a mortgage and this car. Newspaper journalism is all I've ever done. No experience on TV or radio. That leaves only three other things I'm qualified for: Writing books, teaching, or going over to the dark side."

"Public relations and marketing, which is where I come in," said Donicelli.

"You want me to sell you on teaching?" said Tait.

"Tell me about it, that's all," said Choy. "I could use the buyout to go back to school. Get a PhD in journalism or communications or whatever else universities call what we do."

"Those who can, do, those who get tired, teach," said Donicelli.

Tait and DD, as he called him, often fought when the two worked at the paper. Their relationship had particularly soured after a drunken argument at a going away party in which Tait called Donicelli "editor of the toy department" who was "in charge of sweetening the coffee the newspaper brewed for readers every morning." To which Dominic had retorted: "Bread and roses are what I'm fighting for." They sounded ready to take up where that conversation left off.

"Are there jobs and how much do they pay, that's primarily what I need to know," said Choy, trying to head off an inevitable argument that would be more palatable when the wind once again made it difficult to hear what his fellow travellers were saying.

"If you get a PhD and find a job as a professor the pay is not bad," said Tait. "But you'd be well into your fifties by the time you got your doctorate and there's already a lot of competition —a lot of experienced journalists have turned to teaching."

"Sounds grim," said Choy.

"There's at least twice as many public relations professionals as there are reporters — some say the proportion is closer to 4 to 1 — and that's not counting marketing or advertising," said Donicelli. "We've got you surrounded."

"And you think that's a good thing?" said Tait.

"It's a reality I accept and attempt to use to create an alternative cultural hegemony that subverts the ruling class while you hypocritically complain, all the while accepting and participating in the very system that creates this reality."

"What on earth are you talking about?" said Tait.

"You stick your nose up at what I do, what most of your students will end up doing."

"How can it be a good thing to have four people spinning the news for every one real journalist?"

"I reject your distinction between public relations and 'real journalism'."

"A flack, like a prostitute will do anything for anyone who has enough money," said Tait. "A journalist is paid to tell the truth."

"A journalist is paid to complete whatever assignment his boss gives him."

"A good journalist can't be bought. A good journalist is fair and objective. A good journalist always searches for the truth, regardless of what his boss wants. "

"Then a good journalist gets fired."

"What do you know about good journalism?"

"Reporting on what he says, she says and he says — fair and objective — that's good journalism?" answered Donicelli. "That's being spun. A computer running the right software and employing a not-so-complicated algorithm can do a better job of that than any human. Personally, I'd rather spin than be spun. Create the message, not just report it. That offers the real opportunity for subversion."

"I'm a journalist, not a subversive."

"And therein lies the problem," said Donicelli.

"Real journalists help people filter out the spin. We present all sides of a story, not just the one someone rich and powerful enough to afford a PR team wants us to hear. A good journalist is in a fundamentally antagonistic relationship with you guys."

"You actually teach this naïve crap? What do you tell them to do when confronted with the reality that their jobs are dependent on advertising dollars?"

"Do the best they can to seek the truth in whatever circumstances they find themselves," said Tait. "What would you tell them? That we're all part of some gigantic propaganda system, so we might as well just do what we're told and make as much money as we can, while pretending to be some sort of revolutionary?"

"I'd prepare them for the real world. Tell them that everything is someone's spin."

"Everything is someone's spin? There's no truth? No facts versus lies? No 'this is what actually happened' not that. No this is what he actually said and I have it on tape."

"Your glorification of a pointless search for objective truth is ridiculous."

"Pointless?" said Tait. "The Enlightenment, the scientific method — pointless as well?"

"The best your sort of journalism can do is describe what's going on," said Donicelli. "The point should be to change the world, not describe it."

"Can we please get back to what I want to talk about?" said Choy. "Before we cross the border."

They were two cars from the front of the line.

"Get a PR job with the government, a university or another big institution if you want stability and decent pay," said Donicelli. "With over 20 years at the *Sun*, you'd get hired somewhere. Maybe I'll hire you."

"If you're willing to give up truth and objectivity," said Tait.

"He's spent most of his career in the 'toy department' anyway," said Donicelli. "You know the place, where they add sugar to your bullshit objective liberal news. Is that so different from public relations?"

As Tait was about to answer, they pulled up beside the border guard.

"Passports?" said the stern-looking, overweight 50-year old, as he perused Choy's pride and joy. "Nice car. American Motors, right?"

"1965 AMC Ambassador 990," said Choy as he handed over the documents.

"Never seen an AMC convertible," said the guard.

"This was the first one," said Choy. "And they only made 3,499 of them."

"You restore it?" said the border guard as he barely paid attention to what came up on his screen while scanning the passports. "How long did it take?"

"Five years and the rest of my life," said Choy.

"I hear you," said the guard, who then remembered his job. "Where are you headed?"

"Bellingham. I'm taking my friends on a spin down Chuckanut Drive."

"Perfect ride for a vehicle like that. Perfect ride," said the guard, returning the passports. "Have fun. Wish I could come."

Choy smiled.

As the wheels of the car rolled over American pavement, Donicelli looked around and sniffed. "No scent of anything different," he said.

"No fascism in the air?" said Tait.

"Can't smell The Donald at all," said Donicelli, who then undid his lap seatbelt and half stood up, shouting. "Are there any Republicans around? Any Donald Trump supporters? No one willing to admit it."

The three men laughed as they headed south.

3.

"What exactly are we doing here?" asked Tait as they drove along a gravel lane towards a one-and-a-half story, medium-size, older, cedar-clad cabin on a three-acre lot with a view over Birch Bay.

"I'm picking up a key," said Choy. "To a locker in Bellingham. Doing a favour for a friend. There's some stuff she wants me to take a look at."

"You're going inside?" said Donicelli.

"Ya, the key I'm after is supposed to be on a hook in the kitchen."

"Good, cause I really need to use a bathroom," said Donicelli.

Choy couldn't help scanning the cabin and the property for any sign of ... he wasn't exactly sure what. Something suspicious. But nothing stood out. After he opened the front door, then punched in the code to the security alarm, the three men entered the cabin.

"A little stuffy," said Donicelli. "The bathroom?"

Choy shrugged.

"You better make sure the water is on before taking a crap," said Tait. "People often shut off the water if they know they won't be back for a while. I worked with this guy who went away on vacation and came back to a flooded house after a toilet on the second floor cracked. Spewed water for two weeks they figured. Almost a hundred thousand in damage."

"The water is on," Choy shouted after turning on a kitchen tap.

Donicelli had gone upstairs by the time Choy re-entered the living room with the key to the storage locker.

"Who is your friend?" said Tait, who had a framed photograph in his hands.

"Daughter of former Vancouver Police Chief Victor Wong," said Choy without missing a beat. "After her Dad's suicide she finds it too depressing to come down here, so she asked me to retrieve stuff from his locker."

"They found him hanging from a tree somewhere on this property," said Tait, as he stared at the picture. "I interviewed him dozens of times. Never struck me as the sort of person who would do something like that. Just goes to show depression can strike anyone."

"Ya."

"What's your friend's name?"

"Celeste."

"Wong never talked about his kids. He was always worried that some bad guy would, you know ... "

"Abduct them?"

"Ya, or worse. Especially back when they were going after those Indo-Canadian gangs really hard. It got very nasty. Ever talk to Celeste about that?"

"I actually don't know her all that well, although I'm hoping to get to know her better."

"Did you see a telephone? Need to call a Vancouver number. If the phone is connected here, I can avoid U.S. roaming charges."

"Kitchen counter."

Choy picked up the picture of Wong with his family. It was news to him that Celeste had a twin, but here was hard evidence. Two three-year-olds who dressed and looked the same. Even as toddlers, she, they were beautiful and extremely identical.

The thought of how easy it would be for identical twins to fool people bothered Choy as he drove south to the storage facility just off the I-5 in Bellingham, while Tait and Donicelli continued their argument about the true nature of journalism. Was the person he met really Celeste? How would he know? How would the person watching, assuming Celeste, or whoever, was being followed, know which twin it really was? And the meeting itself, was it a set-up?

What if there was something illegal in the storage locker that who-ever he spoke to didn't want to cross the border with? What if ...

"Even history is spin," Donicelli was telling Tait as they walked down a very long hallway. "It's mostly the study of what famous people said. Do you think famous people — politicians or govern-ment officials or rich people — were any more honest 200 years ago than today? Of course not. Yet today, we understand most things they tell us are what they want us to hear, to put what they do in a positive light. Spin."

"You're saying flacks write history as much as the journalists who cover politicians?"

"Exactly."

Journalism was definitely in trouble when Donicelli's view of it seemed closer to the truth than Tait's. Choy tried to empty his mind of thoughts that only led to paranoia. Focus on what might be in the locker. A few months after retirement from the VPD Celeste's father had taken an important job with a hedge fund that specialized in buying out small and medium-sized firms to create the biggest security company in the world. They were going after all kinds of security work, from software to hardware to guarding construction sites to boots on the ground in war zones. It was such a great idea that papers from the *Wall Street Journal* to the *Financial Post* to the *Vancouver Sun* had done stories on it. If Celeste was right, the hedge fund must be connected to her father's death.

If she really was Celeste.

Given the circumstances of the meeting why would she men-tion having a twin? It wasn't relevant. So why did it feel like it was?

Choy fiddled with the key to get the lock open.

"What does history tell us about the American revolution, for example?" Donicelli rambled on. "You really think it was about the rights of man or freedom or democracy or anything like that? All spin. It was about defending slavery when the British looked like they might abolish it, about speculators wanting to sell Indian land in the Ohio Valley when the British were preventing them and all kinds of businessmen and farmers trying to avoid paying their debts to Scottish and English merchants."

"If that's true, that's what a good journalist should have been writing at the time," said Tait. "The truth, not the spin."

In the centre of the locker there were a dozen file storage boxes, three each on the bottom two rows, two each on the next two rows and one each on the last two rows of a tower.

"But the point is, they didn't. That's not what was written. It was the spin."

The three men looked at the boxes.

"Will they fit in the trunk?" said Tait.

"With room to spare," said Choy.

As they were walking the boxes on three borrowed dollies down the long hallway, Donicelli suddenly stopped. "Shit."

"What is it?" asked Choy.

"My sunglasses. I think I left them back in that cabin. In the bathroom. I remember opening them so they'd hang over the rim of the bathtub while I was washing my hands and then ... "

"You haven't had them since we got back in the car," said Tait.

"Shit."

"No worries," said Choy. "We can stop back there on our way home. Do the Chuckanut, then back up the I-5 and we'll be back in Birch Bay for lunch."

"I hear there's a really good seafood place," said Donicelli.

"Get your sunglasses, then ... what's the name of the place?" said Choy.

"CBs or some other initials Beach House."

"Okay, we can ask after we stop at the cabin."

The spectacular scenery and the wind from the ocean kept the arguing to a minimum on the 20-mile Chuckanut Drive that was the perfect place to show off his pride and joy. Then, back on the I-5 he really couldn't hear what his two car-mates were saying as he encouraged both to sit in the back seat as if he were their chauffeur.

Their arguing and angst over issues only journalists cared about continued until Choy steered the car around a bend and up the hill to the entrance of the Wong family property. Police cruisers and other official-looking vehicles lined both sides of the road. Dozens of cars and pick-ups were also stopped, with people bunched together in a few groups.

"What the fuck!" said Donicelli.

Choy pulled over behind the last car, the three men got out and headed to the first clump of people.

"What's going on?" said Choy, to no one in particular as he got within a few feet of the circle.

"An explosion," said a fiftyish woman. "The cabin blown to pieces."

"They think it was the propane tanks," said an older man.

"Thank God no one was there," said the woman.

"Thank God the cabin is on that ridge in the middle of three wooded acres, so the blast didn't damage anyone's else's property," said the older man.

"The owner died a week ago — a suicide just a few feet away from the cabin — and the family hadn't come back to properly shut off anything," said another woman.

"You can hardly blame them for not coming back," said the first woman. "Can you imagine how hard that would have been?"

"They think there must have been a gas build-up, then with all this hot weather, something ignited it," said the second woman.

"He was Chinese," said the older man.

As Donicelli and Tait looked at Choy he gave them a very slight shake of his head.

"When did it happen?" asked Choy.

"Little over two hours ago," said the first woman.

Again Tait and Donicelli looked at Choy. That was only fifteen minutes after they left.

This is getting both weird and scary.

"Did anybody see anything?" Tait asked.

"People on boats in the bay saw the cloud," said the second woman.

"Everyone for a mile around heard it," said the first woman. "It was a huge explosion."

"Two seven-year-old boys staying at the next acreage over were the only ones who claim to have seen anything," said the youngest man in the group. "According to them there was a swarm of giant flying spiders a few minutes before it blew."

Apparently this was some sort of 'in' joke as all the locals in the circle chuckled.

Choy considered what to do next. "Can we get close enough to see anything?" he asked.

"The police won't let anyone on the property," said the first woman.

"Haven't seen you three around before," said the second woman.

"No," said Choy. "We're just down from Vancouver looking at property."

"It's normally very quiet," said a man, dressed like he might be a real estate agent.

"I'm sure it is."

"You have an agent?" asked the man as he pulled a card from his shirt pocket.

"Thanks," said Choy. "Well I guess we better get going. Nice talking to you. See you."

He motioned for his two friends to follow him, but then stopped and took a few steps back towards the group of locals.

"You going to ask them about Trump?" said Donicelli.

"Right," said Tait.

"Where would you suggest we eat?" Choy said to the first woman.

"Purple Fin," she said.

"Bay Cafe," said the second woman.

"CJ's Beach House," said the first man. "Best seafood."

"That sounds great. How do we get there from here?"

After getting directions, the three men walked back to the car.

Once they were far enough away that the locals couldn't hear, Donicelli said: "What the fuck? We've got to tell the police we were in that place just before the explosion and there was no gas."

Choy shook his head.

"Come on. If they find out later ... "

"I don't think that would be a good idea. At least not yet."

"There's something you haven't told us, isn't there?" said Tait.

"Yes, there's actually quite a bit I haven't told you."

"Shit," said Donicelli. "Fuck."

"I'll buy you new sunglasses," said Tait.

Donicelli shook his head, but after a few seconds smiled. "A sense of humour. Didn't think you had one of those."

Tait stared at Choy. Donicelli joined in.

"Let's go somewhere private where we can talk."

Judgment

The email appeared to be some sort of religious scam so he read only the first few words, clicked on the 'mark selected messages as junk' button and forgot all about it.

Dear WaylonChoy@yahoo.com,

The Day of Judgment is nigh. Will Thou be amongst the Elect? Or art Thou not of the chosen people and therefore will be damned?

Consider: YHVH is the one and only true and living eternal God (Isa. 44:6); the God of our fathers Abraham, Isaac and Jacob (Exo. 3:14-16), the Creator of all things (1 Cor. 8:6) who is omnipotent, omnipresent, unchangeable and all-knowing; the Great I Am who is manifested in three beings: God the Father, God the Son, and God the Holy Spirit, all one God (Deut. 6:4).

Art Thou a believer?

Please contact the sender to receive more information about the Word of YHVH God.

BOLERO

1.

"We could have been killed," said Donicelli, as they climbed back into the car. "I could be dead. Blown into thousands of tiny unrecognizable pieces."

"Every cumulonimbus cloud has a silver lining," Tait said, dryly.

"My heart is pounding like that time I went up with the stunt pilot at the Abbotsford Air Show," said Donicelli. "Please tell me what the fuck is going on."

"I second that motion."

"Let's go to that restaurant, get some takeout and find a secluded spot where we can take a look at what's in those boxes," said Choy.

"What have you gotten us into?" said Tait.

"I'll tell you what I know," said Choy then quickly described his meeting with Celeste.

As they pulled into the restaurant parking lot, Donicelli said: "That's it? Somebody you never met before says people are following her and her father didn't commit suicide and asks you please go get some boxes in a storage locker that will prove this company he was working for did something or other?"

"It's called a lead DD," said Tait. "Good reporters in search of the truth follow them to see if maybe there's a story worth pursuing."

"I was never asked if I wanted to pursue anything," said Donicelli.

"And I'm sorry about that Dominic," said Choy. "I didn't say anything because I wasn't sure if there was anything to her story."

"It seems like there is," said Donicelli. "There's no way that was an accidental gas explosion."

"I agree," said Tait. "And if that cabin exploded within fifteen minutes of us leaving, whoever caused it was likely nearby when we were there."

"No one was in there when we opened that door," said Donicelli. "The air was completely stale and I have an excellent nose. I grew up in a family of superb North Burnaby winemakers."

"No one cares about your father's or your nose DD," said Tait.

"I'm just saying ... "

"We know what you're saying and we agree, right Waylon?" said Tait. "There was no one else in that cabin when we were there. Which means ... "

"You think someone followed us?" said Donicelli.

"No one followed us," said Choy. "I was watching the whole way."

"Maybe they were watching the cabin, saw us go in and then entered after we left," said Tait.

"Maybe they have a tracking device, so they can stay out of sight," said Donicelli.

"Very unlikely," said Choy. "I know every inch of this car and went over everything last night to make sure she was in running order."

"Maybe they followed us by helicopter," said Donicelli.

"You don't think we would have noticed that, DD?"

"How about a drone? You wouldn't notice a drone following you."

"Do you know how far away from the controller a drone can fly?" said Tait.

Donicelli shook his head.

"Commercial ones only a few kilometres and they are not very fast. They certainly can't keep up with a car, not even one built in 1965."

"How about military drones?" said Donicelli. "You said this company was into all aspects of security."

"What I don't understand is why they would blow up the cabin after we left," said Choy. "To send us a message?"

"Maybe they didn't know we were there," said Tait. "Maybe the timing was a coincidence. Maybe they simply arrived after us. Maybe they blew up the cabin because they thought something might be in there."

"Like those boxes in the trunk," said Donicelli. "What if there's something that might be evidence in a criminal case? Maybe we should go back to the cabin, or what's left of it, and tell the police what we know."

"Which is what exactly?" said Tait. "We don't know anything."

"A much preferable state of being than knowing something and having whoever blew up that cabin know that we know something," said Donicelli.

"But how do we know they know we know nothing?" said Tait. "Consider that DD. They could be looking for us right now because they think we know something. Or maybe the explosion was just an accident and a coincidence. Maybe Waylon accidentally broke off the propane connection when he went into the kitchen and didn't notice."

Choy shook his head.

"Or maybe the seven-year-olds had it right and it was a flock of flying spiders that descended on the house, snuck in after we left, turned on the gas, and then lit a match," said Donicelli. "Just for fun, because that's the kind of thing flying spiders do."

"The point is we need to look at what's in those boxes in order to have any chance of figuring out what happened," said Tait. "And if we find something that could be evidence in a criminal case, maybe we do drive back there and hand it over to the police. But how do we know if we don't look?"

"You're playing reporter," said Donicelli. "And it's going to get us in trouble."

"I am a reporter following a lead," said Choy. "The legal owner of the cabin gave me the key and I entered it under her instruction. I took possession of the boxes, as she told me to. And we can look at what's in them, also following her instruction. How is any of that going to get us in trouble?"

"You skipped over the part about returning to the cabin and it looking like a Baghdad market after a suicide bombing."

"The police don't know that," said Tait. "They probably don't even know we were in the cabin in the first place. It's not as if there's anything to connect us with the place and if there were, it all went boom."

"Someone could have seen three men, in a very distinctive car, drive onto the property and leave just before the explosion," said Donicelli. "You don't think it's better for us to be the ones informing the police of our presence?"

Tait looked at Choy as if to say, he may have a point. "And I did make that phone call from the cabin. If the cops check the phone records ... "

"Who did you call?" asked Choy.

"A friend, but there was no answer."

"A woman friend?" asked Donicelli.

Tait shrugged.

"Did you leave a message?" said Choy.

"No."

"How well do you know this friend?" said Choy. "Would she think of you if the cops asked her who might have called?"

"Not a worry," said Tait.

"But the cops will know someone was in there just before it blew up," said Donicelli.

"If they check the phone records, which they'll only do if something makes them suspicious," said Choy.

"You're a feature writer, not an investigative reporter," said Donicelli. "So don't pretend like you're Robert Redford talking to Deep Throat in a dark parking garage. And I guarantee your editor doesn't know anything about this so-called story and you certainly don't have her permission."

"I'm on vacation," said Choy. "I was contacted on my last day of work and didn't know if there was anything to it so I never said anything to my editor. But in the course of checking out the story, on my own time, the cabin of the former Vancouver police chief was blown up a few minutes after we left it. This happened after the former chief's daughter told me she was convinced he did not commit suicide and that someone was following her. I say that's the making of one hell of a good story. I say that under the circumstances the editor in chief himself would tell me to look in the boxes."

"The editor in chief doesn't carry a gun," said Donicelli. "Washington State police do."

"DD is scared?" said Tait.

"DD prefers not to piss off guys packing heat, unless he has a very good reason."

"I'm starving," said Choy, frightened as much as Donicelli, but determined to be a real reporter like Tait. "Let's order something, find a quiet, secluded place and look through the boxes. I have a responsibility to do that, even if we do decide to speak with the police."

2.

Anybody driving by on the narrow gravel road in the state park would have seen three men having a summer afternoon picnic.

"DD, what does your excellent winemakers' nose think of this Riesling?" asked Tait.

"Global warming and a desire for higher and higher alcoholic content is killing Alsace whites," said Donicelli, after making a sour face. "Invest in north Okanagan and south Thompson wineries. That's where the next great whites will come from."

Each of the three men looked through a box stuffed with files.

"What am I supposed to be looking for?" said Donicelli, to no one in particular.

"Just look at every page in every file," said Choy. "

"Former police chief Wong was certainly busy with ZZZFund, speaking all over Canada and the United States," said Tait. "Seems mostly to groups associated with police benevolent funds or retired cops."

"His job was selling investors on ZZZFund," said Choy. "From chief of police to salesman. Must have been a letdown."

"I'm sure $350,000 US per year, plus expenses, plus bonuses more than made up for any loss of prestige," said Tait.

"What kind of name is that anyway?" said Donicelli. "ZZZ, put you to sleep fund."

"It's supposed to suggest sleeping soundly," said Choy.

"The companies they own provide security — people with no worries sleep soundly," said Tait. "And the fund itself is a sound investment, so people sleep soundly."

"I get what they're after," said Donicelli. "But ZZZFund doesn't do it for me. Too kiddie like. Doesn't sound 'sound' or institutional enough. There's an art to naming companies."

"Something you're an expert at of course?" said Tait.

"It is one of my specialties."

"Well, the name didn't seem to be a hindrance to investors climbing on board," said Choy, holding up a piece of paper. "Listen to this — from speaking notes at a pension fund presentation — 'we've invested over $1.6 billion in small firms in all areas of interest and plan to spend hundreds of millions more over the next few months.' ... 'this is an incredible growth opportunity in a sector that regularly provides returns in the 30 percent range'"

"Wow," said Donicelli. "If true, you can see the attraction for investors."

"You'd know because you are also an expert in finance," said Tait.

"I've run my own business for two years, which makes me more of an expert than you."

"Touché," said Choy.

Tait mimed being stabbed by a sword as he continued reading a piece of paper. "He was even speaking to retired military officers," he said. "Convincing them to invest in the fund. Cops and soldiers."

"It's going to take hours just to go through this one box," said Donicelli.

"Investigative reporting is hard work," said Tait.

"And no fun," said Donicelli. "That's why it never interested me. Or Choy, until the former police chief's daughter got into his head. We prefer playing with toys."

"Did you say something DD?" said Tait, looking up from his box.

"This is dry, boring work for humourless people who take themselves too seriously," said Donicelli. "You know the real reason why I never cared for investigative journalism? The Importance of Not Being Earnest. Reasonable people never take themselves too seriously. You can't trust someone who is earnest. They're either naive or a little stupid, usually both. Small minds, who actually think the system works the way the system tells you — whatever system you're talking about, politics, business, journalism ... "

"You know DD, sometimes words come out of your mouth and I think 'the person who said that must be very thoughtful and progressive, someone who seeks to make the world a better place' but then I realize, no, you're just the most fucking cynical bullshit artist I ever met," said Tait.

"Cynicism," said Donicelli. "A journalist's best friend. "

"Are you guys paying any attention at all to what's in your boxes?" said Choy.

All three looked silently through the material for a few minutes.

"Well, this is strange," said Tait, holding up a file. "The fund bought George Mason, the company founder, houses in Seattle, Portland and San Francisco and spent $29 million doing it."

"Must be some houses," said Choy.

"Look at this," Donicelli said as he studied a piece of paper. "Holy shit, I told you!"

"What?" asked Choy.

"What did you find?" said Tait.

"ZZZFund invested $60 million in a Seattle company developing miniature drones," said Donicelli. "The swarming spiders that the seven-year-old boys saw."

Chow looked over Donicelli's shoulder at the piece of paper.

"A logical investment for a fund dedicated to security," said Tait. "There's nothing untoward about that."

"Nothing untoward, a logical investment and a good explanation for what those boys saw," said Donicelli. "Prototypes of some miniature drones that can get into a place through the chimney or whatever, scout the interior, puncture a fuel line, put a few pieces of paper into a toaster and turn it on before flying away."

"Wow, DD, that's like from a half dozen different movies," said Tait. "Impressive."

"Wouldn't be the first time life imitates art," said Choy.

"You're actually taking him seriously?"

"It doesn't seem more fantastic than other stuff that's happened the past two days."

"It's a plausible explanation, if you use your imagination," said Donicelli. "If you have one."

"If you wanted to blow up a building but make it look like an accident, it's not a bad way to do it," said Choy.

"If it's even possible," said Tait. "Just because there was an investment in a drone company doesn't turn DD's fantasy into reality."

"Maybe," said Choy. "But it's worth checking out. We could drive down to Seattle. It's only an hour and half from here."

"You mean now?" said Tait.

"It's the best lead we have," said Choy. "And we could also take a look at the house the fund bought Mason."

"Hold on," said Donicelli. "You're saying we should drive down to Seattle and talk to the people who maybe blew up that cabin a few hours ago? Wouldn't that be dangerous?"

"I could tell them I'm a reporter from Vancouver doing a feature about the drone craze," said Choy. "They've been in the news a lot lately. Just last week they had to stop fighting a fire in the Interior because a drone got in the way of tanker planes."

"Hello Waylon," said Donicelli. "The red light is flashing. Danger! Danger! Danger! People who blow up buildings might also blow up people."

"Kill a *Vancouver Sun* reporter?" said Choy. "I don't think so. That would really get people digging. Bad guys wouldn't want so much light shone on them."

"Are you scared DD?" said Tait.

"I'm worried that Waylon is getting involved with something he has absolutely no clue about. He doesn't know who these people are, what they are capable of and he has absolutely no experience as an investigative journalist."

"That's why I need you two," said Choy.

"I never covered crime or anything remotely similar to this," said Donicelli.

"But Doug has and you are creative. Always willing to try out something new. Always looking for adventure, especially if it makes a rich and powerful dude look bad."

Donicelli stared but said nothing.

"I invited you two along to talk about the buyout and because if there was something to Celeste's story, I knew you could help. You're two of the best journalists I know."

Why was he pretending to be all gung-ho about doing this? He wasn't sure he even cared for journalism anymore — after-all the craft seemed to be abandoning its practitioners. Dominic was right, he wasn't an investigative reporter and he was scared. The idea of pursuing dangerous people made him more than a little uncomfortable. But, that was precisely why he had to do it.

I finished rebuilding the car when no one thought I could. I've been learning to dance despite Helena's claim I have three left feet. I can do this.

"Doug's got the background of covering this kind of stuff and you're always looking for something exciting."

"Even if there's no danger, why would we want to let them know we're on to them?" said Donicelli, whose body language now suggested interest.

"If drones blew up that cabin and this company was involved, there's a pretty good chance whoever is behind it already knows about Waylon," said Tait. "You did say this Celeste was paranoid about being followed, right?"

Choy nodded.

"So maybe she isn't paranoid. Maybe she just knows how capable they are. You got to admit, if they can use a drone to blow up a cabin they could just as easily have used one to listen in on your conversation."

"What's your point?" said Donicelli.

"My point is, if there's danger it already exists and we shouldn't worry about letting them know we're on to them. The right play is to shake the tree and see what falls out."

Choy smiled because it occurred to him investigative reporting was not that different from ballroom dancing. Chasing this story so far had a slower Latin beat, the Bolero maybe. Kind of sexy, kind of foreboding. Fun and dangerous.

"You could say you're doing a piece about what drones will be like five years from now," said Donicelli. "That would be the reason to ask about what they're capable of doing today. You could ask about how small they can make them, what their capabilities are, everything and it wouldn't be suspicious, unless like Doug says, they already are."

Tait nodded.

He'd convinced both partners, but not himself.

"It could be an interesting escapade and it has been a while since I've been to Seattle," said Donicelli.

"I've always believed in a reporter following his instincts, so if you feel this is a good idea, I say go for it," said Tait.

"The only problem I can see is none of us brought a change of clothes, or toiletries and we're going to need a place to stay tonight," said Donicelli.

"We can buy a three-pack of underwear and some shirts at J.C. Penney," said Tait. "And I have a friend who lives all by herself in a four bedroom house not far from Seward Park. If she's home I'm sure we could stay there."

"I say we put these boxes back in the trunk, drive to Seattle, get set up at Tait's girlfriend's place and then resume looking through this stuff," said Donicelli, looking ready for an escapade.

"She's not my girlfriend," said Tait. "Just a friend."

"A divorced friend though, right?" said Donicelli.

"Fuck off, DD," said Tait.

"Is she a typical American?" said Donicelli, smiling. "We could talk to her about Trump."

"She plays folk music and lives in Seattle," said Tait.

"So you're expecting she's a big fan of The Donald?"

"Right."

"Okay," said Choy, pretending to be certain this was a good idea, despite his doubts. "We have a plan."

"I'm going on an adventure with the most serious journalist I ever met," said Donicelli. "And having a sleepover."

"Fuck off, DD," repeated Tait.

The three men were smiling as they returned the boxes to the trunk.

3.

They woke up early to visit George Mason's house in ultra-exclusive Hunts Point, but a for-sale sign greeted them and a gardener said the owner had not been around for months, so it was only 9:30 when they pulled into a parking lot across from the "research facility" of the drone developer in Renton, close to the municipal airport. It was one of those cookie cutter industrial/warehouse complexes with rows of offices on two floors at the front and warehouses or workshops at the back. It was a gorgeous late July day; the top was down and the three men sat staring at the building.

"Are you going in?" said Donicelli.

"I don't know," said Choy. "Maybe I should look around first."

He was thinking about the meaning of Mason's house being for sale and also about the previous night. Donicelli was right, Diane, who Tait said he knew from his time in the Vancouver Folk Music Society, was more than just a friend. They clearly had a thing going. She had been a wonderful host. She went on a long anti-Trump tirade as she barbecued a salmon, then provided a musical dessert by playing a fiddle in her back yard that had a view of Lake Washington. But Choy had spent a mostly sleepless night repeatedly laying down and getting up from an unfamiliar bed. Each time he failed to sleep, he returned to the files. Even though he went through the motions, he mostly thought of the exploding cabin, his son, daughter, divorce and death, rather than the contents of the boxes.

Almost two years after the divorce was finalized, he still wondered if they had done the right thing. While kids shouldn't hear their parents fighting all the time, they do need stability and Helena's parade of live-in boyfriends couldn't be doing them any good. Of course 'parade' was an unfair characterization, but there had been two, and Samantha was already showing signs of teen-age rebellion.

Benjamin was quiet, always reading or playing video games, so inside himself that one day he was bound to explode. Maybe it would have been better to stay together, providing a parental presence that may have been angry at times, but at least was something they could count on. Kind of like his parents.

But what was the point of even thinking about his marriage? There was no going back to Helena — she had left him and he had left her years before the divorce. They had departed by different means; his vehicles of choice were absence and avoidance; hers were anger and affairs. The divorce itself, when it came, was mostly a relief.

The twin bed he slept on reminded him of Sam and Ben and events of the previous day caused thoughts of what would happen to them if he were killed. Was it really good idea to tip off whoever was behind the mysterious explosion by trying to interview someone at the drone facility? Not that they knew it had any connection whatsoever to the big boom. The point was doubt had found a hiding place in his brain.

Perhaps the very expensive house for sale meant nothing, but it could be a sign that the founder of ZZZFund was in need of cash. Or about to liquidate his belongings for some other purpose.

Do I really want to do this? Risk my life for a story? Doing anything is a risk to your life.

"I'm going to get out and look around," Choy finally said.

Just do it.

He needed to ask Dominic who had come up with that Nike slogan. It brilliantly captured a thought that occurred to everyone at some point in their lives.

Isn't that in some movie? Focus.

The geography of the neighbourhood made any pedestrian stick out so he walked quickly as if aiming to get somewhere. He followed a road between two buildings to the interior of the complex where he knew there would be loading bays and staff parking. Maybe people would be out back taking a smoke break and he could chat them up. Pretend he was looking to lease some space and ask about what sort of businesses were nearby. Sure enough there were a couple of middle-aged women standing at the bottom of the stairs beside a loading dock, but just as he was about to approach them a red Audi convertible drove past to a parking spot beside the second loading dock.

The woman who got out was Celeste!

Choy froze, but after a short moment of what appeared to be long distance eye contact, she exhibited no sign of recognition, barely pausing before climbing up the stairs to enter the building.

The twin? Who else could it be?

Did Celeste's twin have some connection with the drone company? Or was it possible that Celeste was here, pretending not to know him? That didn't make sense. But neither did Celeste not mentioning a twin who was somehow involved.

His fear about doing an interview about drones with people who might have blown up a cabin to destroy evidence disappeared, curiosity about this beautiful woman, or her twin, killing that particular scaredy cat. He had to go inside.

"Hi, I'm Waylon Choy," he said as he walked towards the only desk in a small reception room. "I'm a reporter from the *Vancouver Sun* newspaper, in Canada. I'm working on a story about the future of drones and I was told by a professor at the University of Washington that you guys are at the cutting edge of miniaturization. I don't have an appointment but is there a manager or a salesman I could interview? I just need a few quotes."

"Mr. Choy?" The middle-aged woman stared at him as if she desperately wanted to say, "you're not Chinese" but thought it impolite to do so. "I'll have to check if there is anyone who can speak to the media. Please, you can wait over here."

She stood up and led him down a short hallway to a room that contained a couch, a dozen or so chairs surrounding two tables, a coffee maker beside a sink on a small cupboard, a fridge and a vending machine.

"Help yourself to coffee," the receptionist said. "It may be a while."

Time passed quickly as he contemplated the meaning of what he had just witnessed. Two questions played over and over. What possible explanation could there be for her or her twin sister entering this building? What had Celeste gotten him into?

"I am sorry to keep you waiting Mr. Choy," said a thirtyish man in a white lab coat. "We don't usually get unannounced visits from reporters. I understand you're from the *Vancouver Sun*?"

Choy held out his card. "Yes."

"Hari Sharma," said the man, as he shook Choy's hand. "I'm the research director."

"May I ask you a few questions?"

"You may, but I'm not sure how much I can answer."

"It seems pretty quiet around here."

"We've been conducting field trials so there's only a few members of our team here this week."

"On your latest model?" said Choy. "Field trials?"

"Yes."

Choy put his digital recorder on the table in front of him and turned it on. "You don't mind? I take notes, but this helps ensure accuracy."

"Like I said, I'm not sure how much I can answer."

"I understand you specialize in miniatures. How small is your latest?"

"I am afraid that is proprietary information."

"Oh." He made a show of writing on his notepad.

"There's not much about our development projects that we care to talk about. I'm sure you understand if you've spoken to any of our competitors. It's a very secretive industry. One could say we're paranoid, but the entire value of this company is our proprietary technology. Other companies, countries even, are interested in the answer to your question."

"I'm not really after the specifics of where you're at today. I'm writing a piece about where the technology is headed. For example, looking five years or ten years out, can you see drones that are the size of insects? Like a spider for example?"

Sharma could have been thinking about how best to word his answer, but Choy sensed there was something more to his silence and the quiet tapping of his right ring finger on the table.

"Yes. Drones that small are already being tested. The technology exists. It's only a question of cost and improving battery life."

"Perfect. Exactly the quote I needed."

Sharma looked at the clock on the wall.

"Can you understand that some people might be worried about such technology? The potential for abuse by governments or corporations?"

"We're engineers and scientists here; we have no one who specializes in ethics."

Choy wrote down the answer, circled it and then looked back up at Sharma.

"Who are the clients for your technology? I don't mean company names or which governments, but in general, who is interested?"

"Anyone who thinks we might make a profitable breakthrough. Anyone who can imagine a use for miniature drones."

"What capabilities will these miniature drones of the future have?"

"Anything a full size drone today can do a miniature drone of the future should be able to do and more."

"Including weapons?"

"Weapons systems are not part of our expertise. Bulk remains important in the realm of explosives and projectiles."

"So, would it be fair to say that military and police interest in drone miniaturization would be more in stealth or surveillance applications than in weapon systems?" Like any experienced reporter Choy knew there was always a way to get the answer you wanted. And sure enough, he received a reply that would allow him to write a story with the words "military and police interest in drone miniaturization is primarily for stealth and surveillance applications, said Sharma" and have the words on tape to prove it. That is, if he were to write the story he claimed to be working on.

"More, yes, that would be fair to say. But there's also a broad range of non-military, non-law-enforcement applications. The people who design manufacturing systems, for example, have a huge interest."

"You're talking about drone robots on assembly lines?"

"Working in ultra clean environments manufacturing computer chips and circuit boards for example. We're not all about Big Brother and spying."

"I see. That's a great quote. I'll make sure it gets into my story."

Sharma nodded, pleased by his interview performance. "Any other questions? I'm very busy today."

"No, I think that will do," said Choy, standing. "Except for one other thing. Do you have any pictures or graphics of the products you're working on or have already developed that you wouldn't mind sharing with the readers of the *Vancouver Sun*?"

"We may. But I'd have to consult about that upstairs."

"And one more thing I almost forgot," said Choy, employing the 'oh and one other question I forgot' tactic he often used on reluctant interviewees. "I promised one of my business section colleagues that I'd ask about ZZZFund. I understand they now own a majority of shares."

"We're a private company. We don't comment on our ownership or financing or other such matters."

"But you would agree that a $60 million investment from ZZZFund is definitely a sign that you're doing something right?"

Sharma looked perplexed again.

"I'll tell you what Mr. Choy, even though I cannot answer your question, I have someone here today who can. A representative of ZZZFund, who is looking in on us — would you care to put that question to her?"

"That would be great."

What the fuck! Her? A representative from ZZZFund? Celeste's twin?

He waited at the table as Sharma slipped out of the room. He turned the recorder off, but other than that, time passed with barely a thought other than an endless loop of what the fuck is going on? Her?

When he looked up, Choy was both surprised and not surprised.

"Mr. Choy? But you're not Chinese."

It was exactly the same look Celeste had given him.

He shrugged and said: "I was adopted."

"I understand you're a reporter from the *Vancouver Sun*?"

He passed a card to her.

"You'd like to ask me a question about our investment in drone miniaturization?"

Absolutely no sign of recognition. She must be the twin sister.

"Yes," Choy said. "But first, can I get some background? What is your name and title with ZZZFund?"

"Ertha Wong," she said.

Ertha and Celeste. He couldn't tell them apart.

"I'm Vice-President, Technology and Marketing," she continued. "Now, what was it you wanted to ask?"

Choy felt like an adopted child who had just been told he had "real" parents in another part of town.

Judgment

Once marked, every message from the same sender went straight to the junk folder.

Dear WaylonChoy@yahoo.com,

Do you really want to know what's going on? To understand the Truth?

The entire Bible, both Old and New Testaments, as originally inspired, is the inerrant, supreme, revealed Word of God. The history, covenants, and prophecy of this Holy Book were written for and about a specific elect family of people who are children of YHVH God (Luke 3:38; Psalm 82:6) through the seedline of Adam (Gen . 5.1). God chose unto Himself a special race of people that are above all people upon the face of the earth (Deut. 7:6; Amos 3:2). These children of Abraham through the called-out seedline of Isaac and Jacob (Psalm 105:6; Rom. 9:7) were to be a blessing to all the families of the earth who bless them and a cursing to those that curse them (Gen. 12.3).

Have you blessed the chosen people? Or art thou cursed?

Please contact the sender to receive more information about the Word of YHVH God.

VIENNESE WALTZ

1.

"This is getting weirder and weirder," said Donicelli. "I like it."

"You're sure it was Celeste's sister?" said Tait. "Wong is a pretty common name."

"She didn't wear the same perfume, but other than that I couldn't tell them apart," said Choy.

"Maybe it actually was Celeste," said Donicelli. "That would be an even better story."

"There's no way. This woman never saw me before. There was not even a faint sparkle of recognition in her eyes. I suppose she could suffer from dissociative disorder or be a really good actor, but what would be the point?"

Choy's heart was beating at twice its normal speed and his hands were sticky wet. He grabbed the wheel of the car and held tight. He needed to breathe slowly, to calm himself and recover his wits.

"Why would Celeste not tell you about a twin sister working for the company she thinks may have killed her father?" said Tait.

"Maybe she doesn't know," said Donicelli. "I've got a brother and we never speak. He doesn't have a clue what I do."

"That's because you're an asshole, DD," said Tait, smiling.

"Maybe this Ertha is also an asshole," said Donicelli.

Choy imagined he was floating. Warm, calm water in a dark pool. A mineral water spa, floating in silence.

"If you wanted someone to prove your father did not commit suicide and you thought the real reason for his death had something to do with the company he worked for, you'd mention your sister was a vice president of that company," said Tait.

"We didn't talk long," said Choy. "Maybe it didn't seem essential, given how much time we had."

"This raises the question of motivation. Celeste may have another reason for getting you involved."

"To investigate her sister?" said Donicelli. "Maybe she thought you were more likely to have sympathy for a daughter pining over a dead father than for a sister who hated her twin. Maybe there's something in those boxes that incriminates Ertha."

It occurred to Choy that his compulsion to please a good-looking woman had once again led him astray. He'd always been a sucker, right back to high school when he took the blame for cheating after Lisa LaChance copied his answers on a physics test. Then Helena.

"But how does this fit in with someone blowing up that cabin?" said Tait.

"Maybe that was Ertha," said Donicelli. "Maybe she thought the boxes were in the cabin, full of incriminating evidence."

"What exactly did she say?" Tait asked.

He was too easily taken in. Pretty things and pretty people made him feel good. He believed pretty people, saw the best in them, and they took advantage.

Pretty things too. I need them and they know it.

They were also the reasons he gravitated to the newsroom's toy department. Real journalism was too ugly, too heart-breaking.

Not true. I ended up in the toy department because I have an imagination.

But that wasn't true either. He ended up in the toy department because he was assigned there and found it easy. He was good at writing features, especially creative ones with clever ledes and off-kilter angles that surprised readers. That was his speciality and, after writing lots of them, everyone assumed that's all he could do.

"Choy? What did she say?"

Concentrate.

"I can't remember," he said, his heart finally slowed. "She threw me off. I wasn't hearing."

Helena is right. I am pathetic. Like she says, the meek inherit nothing.

"I don't know why she had such an effect on me. How can identical twins be so different? I only spent a few minutes with both of them. I liked Celeste. This one looked the same, but, wasn't, inside. It's hard to explain the completely different vibes."

"Did you record the interview?" said Tait.

"The first guy, yes, but I turned it off when he left the room and didn't turn it back on."

Very unprofessional.

"The memory has got to be in your brain, somewhere."

"Is that her?" Donicelli pointed at a thirtyish woman wearing sunglasses and expensive clothes, driving a red Audi, about to turn onto the street.

Choy nodded and shrank himself into the bucket seat. His partners did the same.

"She is hot," said Donicelli. "And there's another one exactly like her? Wow!"

"Where is she going?" said Tait. "Maybe we should follow her?"

"In a 65 Ambassador convertible?" said Donicelli. "This is a car made for being followed, not for following."

"She's going to her office in Portland," said Choy. "She told me."

As he said this, the entire conversation came back to him.

"She told me she grew up in Vancouver, but now lives in Portland and was in Seattle because the family cabin in Birch Bay had blown up in a gas explosion. She had gone up there early yesterday evening and then spent the night in Seattle before stopping here this morning. Said she used to read the *Vancouver Sun* and even claimed to remember my name from some concert reviews. Said she was really into music when she was 15. An East Van girl."

"ZZZFund has an office in Portland?" said Tait.

"Said she went to school at Stanford. Engineering."

"A gorgeous, well-dressed, East Van, Chinese, groupie engineer corporate big shot," said Donicelli. "I could see falling for her, and her twin sister."

"She's Vice President, Technology and Marketing."

"An unusual combination," said Tait.

"I'm pretty sure that's all she told me." Choy felt like he was finally out of his state of shock. Like after his bicycle accident, when he woke up the next morning and realized how crazy he had been to walk to the doctor's office instead of calling an ambulance. Something about all that adrenaline pumping through your body makes you stupid. Some older, more primitive part of your brain takes over from the rational, clear thinking part.

"I didn't tell you about the drones," said Choy.

"What about them?" asked Donicelli.

"The guy in there said the technology exists today to create drones the size of spiders, but he wouldn't admit whether or not his company actually made them," said Choy. "Said the industry is very secretive and there are spies everywhere."

"Drones the size of spiders," said Donicelli. "What did I tell you?"

"Spies? Makes sense in an industry aiming their products at the intelligence community," said Tait. "And it raises even more questions about what's going on."

"I've always loved that term, 'intelligence community'," said Donicelli. "Not 'intelligent community' because they are anything but. I've always wanted to write a spy thriller with the main character being a sort of Inspector Clouseau."

"It's been done before, DD. Remember *Get Smart*?"

"There's a great story here," said Choy, mostly to himself. "I know it."

"I've got an idea," said Donicelli. "I have a friend who lives in Portland who used to work for *Vancouver Magazine*. He freelances and I'll bet he would be interested in doing a front-page feature about the daughter of the first Chinese-Canadian Vancouver police chief who went into engineering and ended up vice-president of this big hedge fund by the age of … what … 29?"

"Almost for sure he could sell that. There's a serious market for success stories," said Tait.

"We could get him to ask questions about her father's suicide, her twin sister, pretty much anything because the story is this intimate, exhaustive 5,000 word feature," said Choy, nodding. "And we could check out Mason's house in Portland while we're there."

"Very good, DD. Not a bad idea at all."

"Adam is probably thinking of coming back to Canada now that Trump has won the nomination," said Donicelli.

"Along with millions of other liberal Americans," said Tait. "Can you imagine if he were to actually become president?"

"Maybe that's why Vancouver house prices have gone so crazy," said Choy.

"The foreign buyers are betting on a Trump win?" said Tait.

"Those Chinese investors are smart businessmen," said Choy.

"You realize what this means?" said Donicelli. "Another couple hours south and another day at least on our short American spin."

"Summer time and the living is easy for a journalism college instructor."

"Like I told you, I have three weeks of vacation," said Choy.

"Okay then, the road trip continues," said Donicelli. "Can this old beauty take all the extra kilometres?"

"I assume you're talking about the car and not me or Waylon?"

"This old beauty has had more care and attention than the three of us put together."

"Okay then?" said Donicelli.

Tait shrugged. Choy nodded.

"First we need to go shopping," said Donicelli.

2.

Choy decided that learning about a twin sister who was vice-president of the company he was supposed to check out was enough of an emergency to call Celeste.

While Dominic and Doug went shopping for clothes and toiletries, he called the number he had been given. It rang seven times.

"Hello. Celeste? It's Waylon."

After a few seconds of silence there was a woman's voice — possibly, but not definitely Celeste's — that very weakly said: "Hello?"

"Celeste? It's Waylon. Waylon Choy. Celeste?"

"Yes?"

"Is this Celeste?"

"Yes. Hello Waylon, how are you?"

It was definitely her voice. Celeste. Or possibly Ertha. How could he know for sure?

"Remember what I told you?" she said. "Before we talk again? How I need to be sure there's not someone else?"

She was talking in code again. In case someone was listening. Why did he find this so damned attractive? It was like kids dressing up and playing make-believe. He had always loved make-believe. It was the reason he'd played with neighbourhood girls more than boys. Even though he was definitely not effeminate or gay, it was the reason he hadn't played many sports. He preferred freedom of imagination over the physical reality of competition.

Play her game.

"I remember," he said, after a few moments.

"Well, I'm not sure it is just us. I'm worried there's someone else."

"I'm sorry you feel that way, but we still need to talk," said Choy.

"Imagine my surprise when I met your sister. Why didn't you tell me you had a twin? An identical twin."

There was a short silence.

"Why do you care about her?"

"If our relationship is going to work don't you think we need to know everything about each other?"

"My sister and I don't get along."

"Why?"

"If you spent any time with her you already know the answer. Did she flirt with you?"

How was he supposed to answer that?

"No," he said, probably too tentatively.

"She did, didn't she? I knew it!"

"I thought she was you." The words dribbled from his mouth, like water drunk immediately after dental surgery.

"She has never been me and I have never been her!"

This was too strange, even for Choy.

"Celeste?"

Silence.

"You need to trust me and I must trust you, if this thing we have is going to work. Do you understand?"

"Yes."

"If we are to move forward it's necessary to take some risks."

"Say what you have to say," said Celeste.

Choy paused to shape his thought.

"She's always been my enemy you know," Celeste said before he could ask his question. "She always made sure our father liked her best but was never loyal to him. Not as a child and not as an adult. But he never saw it. Do you understand what that's like?"

"Did he get her the job with ZZZFund?"

"Yes," she said quickly.

"Is she part of the problem we discussed? The problem your father had?"

"Yes."

"Then why didn't you tell me?"

"She has stolen everything, everyone I ever had. I don't like talking about her."

"But ... "

"She turns my friends against me. Did she do that with you too?"

"No."

"I need to know the truth."

"We didn't talk about you at all. We discussed the cabin blowing up and her job."

"She loves to talk about herself."

"Maybe we can take advantage of that. You knew about the cabin? The explosion."

"My mother told me. Did you ... "

"I'm fine. Everything is fine. I was surprised about your sister, that's all."

"I'm sorry."

"I'll be gone a few more days, but I know you want it exactly perfect. Is there anything else you didn't tell me?"

"Lots and lots and lots," said Celeste. "Isn't that what makes getting to know someone so delicious?"

Beyond the weirdness of talking like this to a stranger, she had a point.

"Yes," he finally answered.

"Come back as soon as you can."

"I will. Good-bye, for now."

"Good-bye."

As he pressed the "end" button on his phone, Choy felt like he'd landed on his head after falling off a bike. Talking with Celeste was like dancing the Viennese Waltz, always circling. If there were someone bugging her phone, the conversation would have been confusing. She certainly had an imagination and that was one of his top-3 attractive qualities in a woman. As he contemplated her strange behaviour the two Ds returned.

Dominic dropped a bag on his lap after entering the front passenger seat. "Underwear, three shirts and khaki short pants."

"Thank you."

"Don't thank him until you see the colours and style."

Choy looked in the bag.

"Just kidding."

"Let's go to Portland!" said Donicelli.

"Portland!"

"The Rose City, here we come," said Choy as he put the car in gear.

"Maybe we'll find a Donald Trump supporter there," said Donicelli.

"Unlikely," said Tait.

"Why the hell did the Republicans nominate someone so unpopular?" said Choy.

"He doesn't need any votes from the Left Coast," said Donicelli.

"There's no way Trump is going to win," said Tait. "No way."

3.

It made absolutely no sense that Adam Wainwright was Donicelli's friend. While Dominic was loud, opinionated, cynical and somewhat of a sexist pig, the first thing Choy noticed about Adam was how much of a church mouse he was. The second was his sexual preference for men. The third was he had a hopeless crush on Dominic. Fourth, he learned that Adam earned a good living as a freelance writer.

Adam's sexual preference made Choy a little nervous — not that he was homophobic or anything — but the first trait diminished any perceived threat to the sexuality status quo: Adam was very easy to ignore. Not that ignoring him was Choy's intent; in fact the man's fourth aspect was of prime interest. Could earning a living from freelancing be a realistic option? A way of supporting himself and his kids? Here was a man who claimed to earn a minimum of $60,000 per year writing "this and that" — could he be a role model? Choy intended to pick his brain.

After a long discussion about Donald Trump, and the impossibility of his actually becoming president, Tait left to visit a friend and Donicelli disappeared somewhere as well so Choy and Wainwright had the files spread out in the living room of Adam's ground floor apartment just a few blocks on the other side of the Willamette River from downtown Portland. The three journalists had decided it was best to tell Adam everything and bring him into their "excellent adventure", which was what Donicelli had taken to calling their road trip.

"Tell me the secret to earning a decent living as a freelancer," Choy said, as he continued to methodically go through the files page by page.

"The key is knowing your market, who pays enough to make the work worthwhile and then focussing on those publications," said

Wainwright as he checked out a file folder stuffed with at least a hundred pages. "You've got to develop a reputation with the right people; they've got to trust you to work fast and deliver exactly what they are after. Only difference from breaking in at a big city newspaper is there's no guaranteed pay cheque."

"Pretty big difference."

"Not one you notice once the ball gets rolling. I've got more or less the equivalent of a "beat" — stuff I do regularly for the same customers. That's more than half my work and produces enough income to live on. The rest, the kind of thing we're doing now, is the gravy — the difference between a vacation and staying home all year."

Wainwright closed one folder and picked up another.

"I've gotten too comfortable at the *Sun*, but the uncertainty of the freelance life scares the shit out of me. Another eight years and both my kids will be in university."

"It's not for everyone. A lot of people think freelancing means working for yourself and having freedom, but the truth is, if you're successful, you have 20 or 30 bosses making demands on you, not just one."

"So, why do you do it?"

"Couldn't find a job I wanted after I quit Van Mag but started getting projects and voila, it's eight years later." He smiled, as if deciding something important about Choy. "Once you get used to it, freelancing is okay, but if it scares you, I wouldn't take the buyout. Keep your job until it disappears or you don't want to do it anymore. I mean that's assuming you still like it."

"I do, most of the time. There's bullshit and more pressure now because of all the cutbacks, but they still mostly leave me alone to come up with whatever story I think is worth telling. For how much longer? Even the question scares me. Journalism as we knew it is disappearing."

"I hear you," said Wainwright.

"And I worry that in the next round of cuts they will be laying people off, not offering buyouts," said Choy. "Maybe it's better to get out now with $150,000."

"That's what they're offering?"

"It's what the union bargained years ago during one of our strikes."

"That's a lot of money. I can see that would be tempting."

"But?"

"The paper offers something you value, security, and if they still let you write what you want … Freelancing, you're pretty much stuck with what sells, so maybe you should keep the job as long as it lasts but start writing books on the side. Dominic tells me you're a brilliant feature writer. If you can write long features, you can write a book."

"I've often thought of writing popular history, creative non-fiction."

"Sounds interesting. Write a couple of books that sell in the 10,000 copies range and you'll be well positioned if your job disappears."

"'Eighth Generation Chinese-Canadian'. What do you think of that as a title?"

"Good," said Wainwright, but something in the files had caught his attention.

"I'm thinking a personal history of my family since my great-great-great-great-great grandfather came to Canada during the Cariboo gold rush. The history of a dozen ethnic communities in one family. About people who never fit any neat racial or ethnic category, except mongrel-Canadian. Hey, you think that might be a better title?"

Wainwright ignored the question as he placed a half dozen pieces of paper in a row on the floor. Then he grabbed the folder he was previously looking through and pulled some more papers to add to the row.

"Take a look at this row of papers and tell me what you see."

Choy traded places with Wainwright and looked down. At first, he saw nothing, but then noticed each piece of paper had numbers highlighted either by a pink or yellow marker.

"Someone has highlighted numbers on each of them?"

"The former police chief, I'd wager. He noticed something in these numbers."

"What?"

"That's for us to figure out."

"The numbers in yellow all seem to be revenue — people, institutions buying into the fund. Maybe they were shorting him on commission."

Wainwright shrugged as he grabbed another folder and began quickly looking at the pieces of paper in it.

"Let's go back through each folder on the floor here and look for the same pink and yellow highlighting of numbers. Pull any paper that has it and put it on top of the folder. Don't look for anything else; don't even try to read the words. Just pull all the highlighting before we actually look at them. Then maybe we'll see a pattern."

It took over an hour to pull papers with pink or yellow highlighting from one box worth of files.

"Calice, tabernac, this is like assembly line work," said Choy.

"You want to know the real secret to making a decent living as a freelancer? Not having a life outside of work."

"You find it fun?"

"Doing anything well is fun."

"A positive attitude."

"I was tormented as a child and dreamed about suicide pretty much every day as a teenager," said Wainwright. "I was seeking social validation through my relationships, which is pretty common of course, for kids and teenagers, but my obvious homosexuality made that difficult. Then I discovered work, where you were valued for what you produced and people mostly ignored who they thought you were. I found that addictive."

"You found work addictive?"

"The more detail oriented the better. I was a ruthless editor. In fact, that's how I got my start in freelancing. I was the absolute master of quick turnaround editing jobs. Long hours of concentration with relentless attention to detail. Sometimes I still get problem manuscripts — usually supposedly written by someone famous who the publisher has paid big money — and you wouldn't believe what they pay to fix them quickly."

As Wainwright spoke he moved from file to file, kneeling, looking at the highlighted papers on top of each folder. "My life gets its meaning from work. They tell you friends and lovers are what count in the end, but I don't buy it. What you've done in your life, that's what matters. I don't give a good goddamn how many people are at my funeral, but in the hour before my last breath, I want to look back and think to myself: 'You accomplished a lot. People noticed your work.'"

"Assuming you have meaningful work. Many people don't."

"Maybe that's the explanation for all the drug abuse, alcoholism, depression. If it were up to me, meaningful work would be considered a fundamental human right."

Wainwright stood up. "I've got it."

"What?"

"The yellow highlighting is for revenue and the pink is expenses and assets. Whoever did the highlighting was looking at money coming in, money going out and money in the bank. He must have noticed something wrong, but exactly what, I don't have a clue. Yet."

"Something with the accounts though?"

"Oh yes."

"Conjecture?" said Choy.

Wainwright looked at Choy, walked into the kitchen and poured himself a glass of water. "Former Vancouver police chief gets a job with this hot hedge fund, finds out someone is cooking the books and commits suicide. What would that suggest?"

"That maybe it wasn't suicide. Maybe someone hung him on the tree beside his cabin because he was about expose some financial skulduggery."

"Or he did commit suicide because he thought himself responsible for what he uncovered?" said Wainwright.

"Like getting a job for his beautiful daughter Ertha who then somehow became involved with whatever is going on?"

"Maybe she's the one doing the financial skulduggery."

"The father learns about it and blames himself," said Choy. "I could buy that."

"Something to keep in mind when I interview her tomorrow morning."

"I'm dying to hear what you think of her."

"There's something else that's just occurred to me."

"What?"

"During our conversation, I'll get her to set up an interview with her boss."

"Mason, the founder of the hedge fund?"

"Yes. "

"Did we tell you that we went by his house in Lake Oswego before we came here?" said Choy. "It's for sale, $4.4 million."

"Must be nice."

"It is and it's also newer and bigger, but in not such a great area as the one in Seattle he has for sale for $11.2 million."

"Two houses for sale," said Wainwright. "Interesting."

Choy nodded.

Progress.

"According to these files, the company also bought him a very expensive place in San Francisco," said Choy. "And you'll want to interview him in person, right?"

"Talking on a phone is not a real interview. You need to see a person as they speak, read their body language, look into their eyes. Lying is too easy on the phone."

Hard to argue with that. "Have you got one of those garages around here where you can rent a bay? I should take a look under the hood and change my baby's oil before we head further south. Maybe take another look for tracking devices as well."

A short American spin was becoming quite the road trip.

Judgment

Dear WaylonChoy@yahoo.com,

To what tribe do you belong? Have you accepted the Word of YHVH God?

The descendants of the twelve sons of a Jacob, called "Israel", were married to God (Isa. 54:5), have not been cast away (Rom. 11:1-2), have been given the adoption, glory, covenants, law, service of God, and promises; are the ones to whom the messiah came (Rom. 9:4-5) electing out of all twelve tribes those who inherit the Kingdom of God (Rev. 7:4, 21:12). The White, Anglo-Saxon, Germanic and kindred people are God's true, literal Children of Israel. Only this race fulfills every detail of Biblical Prophecy and World History concerning Israel and continues in these latter days to be heirs and possessors of the Covenants, Prophecies, Promises and Blessings YHVH God made to Israel.

Please contact the sender to receive more information about the Word of YHVH God.

SLOW FOXTROT

1.

The rain required the soft top to go up and finally facilitated conversation.

Choy was dying to hear how the interview with Ertha had gone, but Wainwright had insisted on sitting in the back seat and writing on his laptop after they had picked him up from the Beaverton office of ZZZFund. So, when the rain started near Eugene, Choy immediately pulled the car over to protect the upholstery and to satiate his gnawing curiosity. "Tell me what you thought of her."

"A few more minutes," said Wainwright, his fingers continuing to dance on the laptop's keyboard.

"You've already had an hour."

"Give the guy a break, Adam, he dreams about this woman," said Donicelli.

"That's never earned me a break," said Wainwright, continuing to type.

Tait looked at Donicelli and smiled.

"Pleeeease," said Choy.

"Pleeeease," said Tait, joining in, then Donicelli followed suit.

Finally Wainwright stopped typing. "Okay, okay, I'm ready to talk. What do you want to know?"

"Everything," said Choy.

"She's a real femme fatale," Wainwright said in a flat voice. "Exactly my type."

Tait smiled and put his hand on Donicelli's shoulder in the front seat. "Maybe you should be jealous."

"Adam and I have an understanding," said Donicelli. "I don't hassle him about who he's attracted to, so long as he doesn't give me a hard time about who I fall in love with."

"I want to hear about the interview with Ertha!" shouted Choy.

"Okay," said Wainwright. "But there's no big revelation."

"What did you talk about?"

"The usual business profile stuff. I've done enough of these to know they're all full of themselves. And she was no different."

"Tell me the secret to your success," said Tait in a poor imitation of Wainwright's voice and then raised the tone an octave for the answer. "Hard work, commitment and reading absolutely every word Ayn Rand ever wrote."

Wainwright smiled. "You've done this interview as well?"

"Worse, I've had to grade a hundred of them," said Tait.

"Poor dear."

"The business world is infected with these stuck-in-adolescence, chip-on-their-shoulder, nobody-understands-how-great-I-am-so-I had-to-prove-it-by-building-my-own-company, self-centered pricks and prickesses," said Tait.

"So I'm gathering she never told you her daddy got her the job?" said Choy.

"Is that true?" said Wainwright.

"It's what her sister says."

"The crazy one Waylon is in love with," said Donicelli.

"Ertha said it was the other way around. Said she was already working for the fund when her father retired and she told Mason he would be a perfect representative to sell the fund because (and I quote) 'he's a former police chief and Chinese and all these racist cops think Chinese are great with money.'"

"She said that?" asked Donicelli.

"She did."

"What else?" said Choy.

"Lots of the usual stuff about always dreaming of going into business for herself, how tough it was being a woman in engineering and how much she owes her boss, George Mason, who 'believed in her' and gave her a chance. 'He's the most brilliant man I ever met,' is an exact quote."

"Anything else about her father?"

"Ya, we got into that quite a bit. I'd have to say she seems genuinely broken up by his death. In fact, she blames herself for pushing him into the job. Says he suffered post-traumatic stress from an incident early in his police career and this led to anxiety and depression. She was the one who convinced him to retire early and take the job as vice-president of marketing. Thought it would be a figurehead position, mostly public speaking, which didn't bother him, but he took the job too seriously and tried to sell, which he didn't find easy. He was successful at first, but then things slowed down and he felt like a failure. She thinks that's why he committed suicide."

"Two sisters with two very different stories," said Tait.

"Did she say anything about Celeste?" asked Choy.

"Said they are very close," said Wainwright. "'We're so close that we always know what the other is thinking,' was the exact quote. But she did say they are also very different. Celeste has more of an artist's temperament and is very creative."

"Creative," repeated Choy. "That's for sure. Overall, was she believable?"

"She came across as genuine, to a degree, but there's something not quite right."

"What?" said Tait.

"Can't put my finger on it. An undercurrent of stress maybe, like she was worried I wasn't going to believe her. A faint look of fear that she tried to hide, when I asked her about what it was like to work for George Mason, a discomfort when talking about Celeste and then a small stumble when I brought up the explosion at the family cabin. It was like she had rehearsed everything, but still was uncomfortable talking about that."

"So the bottom line is we don't know which sister is telling the truth?" said Tait.

"Maybe it's neither of them," said Donicelli.

"She also admitted the company was building prototypes of miniature drones," said Wainwright. "Said 'it was among the most exciting technology that the fund was involved with.'"

"I knew it," said Donicelli.

"Plus we have Mason's two houses for sale and the highlighted numbers in the files," said Choy. "The father was definitely concerned about revenue and expenses."

"We need to go over all the boxes more closely," said Wainwright.

"According to reports this fund had brought in almost four billion and that was more than a year ago," said Tait. "There's a lot of room for hanky-panky."

"Love, money and jealousy — the motivations for most serious crime — and we've got all three," said Donicelli.

"We've got a lot more work to do," said Tait.

"And a lot more driving," said Choy.

"The sky is clearing and the rain is over," said Donicelli. "Who votes for taking the top down again?"

"Who votes for confronting George Mason with what we know already?" said Choy.

"Which may provoke him to do something else, if he really is the bad guy," said Tait. "Only this time we'll be the targets."

Of course that was a danger but the investigation so far seemed like a slow dance while Choy wanted it to be a jitterbug.

"Send those drones after us," said Donicelli. "What sort of weapon system do you think they have? Miniature machine guns, firing itsy-bitsy bullets?"

"More likely a tiny mechanical stinger that injects a single drop of untraceable deadly poison," said Tait, who poked his finger at Donicelli's neck.

"You guys confront Mason if you want, but not until after my interview," said Wainwright.

"That's all you care about?" said Tait. "One more stupid 'titan of the business world' feature is more important than exposing murder, arson and some sort of business scam?"

"It's not 'all' I care about, but I do want to get paid."

"You really do take this freelancing seriously," said Choy.

"I spoke to the editor of Van Mag this morning," said Wainwright. "He's willing to pay two thousand and the piece is half done already. I got a great picture of her. It's easy money. Some of us only get paid when we work."

"The real face of journalism today," said Donicelli. "'I only get paid when something sells.'"

"There's always been magazine mercenaries," said Tait. "Don't blame journalism."

"Magazine mercenaries?" repeated Wainwright.

"You know what I mean," said Tait. "Somebody has always written the mindless, formulaic shit. I mean I know you do other, real journalism as well."

"Formulaic shit?" said Wainwright. "'Other real journalism?'"

"I didn't mean …" said Tait. "I know you're very good at what you do."

"Which is formulaic shit."

"Taiter thinks everything not what he used to do is formulaic shit," said Donicelli.

"Don't distort what I said," said Tait.

"You used the words," said Wainwright. "'Formulaic shit.'"

"Okay, okay, I take it back," said Tait. "How about this? There's the kind of journalism that important people go out of their way to encourage, the sort of thing that takes people's minds off how they're being screwed by politicians and corporations. We all know what I'm talking about. And then there's another kind of journalism that makes important people nervous. I respect one more than the other, because it requires more courage, that's all I'm saying."

"He's an intellectual snob," Donicelli said to Wainwright. "The only real journalism is that which reveals something he calls the truth and makes people uncomfortable. Anything that simply makes you think or entertains or allows people to survive their shitty lives is mere candy that melts in your mouth."

"Come on guys, let's get back to Celeste and Ertha and Mason," said Choy, who had not stopped thinking about the possibility he had been set up and what to do about it.

"I'm enjoying this," said Wainwright. "Haven't had the 'what is journalism discussion' in years."

Choy did his best to tune out his friends as he noticed the entrance to a rest stop a few hundred metres ahead. This was the most adventure he'd had in years. It was fun being a real investigative journalist even if it was a little scary. Every reporter's instinct told him the story was good and likely to get better. Plus it could be his last story for the *Sun*, or even his last work as a journalist, if he took the buyout.

Might as well go after something people will remember.

"I'm going to pull in here and take the top down."

2.

As they neared Redding, Wainwright received a call on his cell. "That was weird," he said, putting the phone back in his pocket. "The interview has been changed to Reno, day after tomorrow. At the university."

"Reno?" said Choy, who had been looking forward to visiting the Bay Area.

"Why is that weird?" asked Tait.

"The secretary also said, 'Mr. Mason recommends you stay overnight in Redding. She said it like he knew where we were."

"Whoa!" said Donicelli looking at Wainwright and then Tait in the back seat.

"How would he know that?" said Tait.

"A tracking device," said Donicelli.

"Or maybe Ertha told him when you left Portland and he can easily figure out how far you get in six hours," said Choy.

"That makes a lot more sense," said Tait.

"I looked around this morning after changing the oil and there's nothing," said Choy.

"If these guys can make drones the size of spiders, they can make tracking devices you can't find," said Donicelli.

"I built this car, piece by piece," said Choy. "I'd notice anything new."

"Anybody know anything about Lassen Volcano National Park?" asked Wainwright, as he looked at his telephone screen. It's on the way from Redding to Reno."

"I've read about it," said Tait. "Supposed to be like Yellowstone, only without all the tourists."

"'A hidden gem of our national park system,'" read Wainwright. "Perfect. You guys interested in stopping there?"

"Why?" said Tait.

"Another story," said Donicelli. "Right Adam?"

"Freelancers must manage their time and make the most of opportunities," said Wainwright. "Travel pieces sell."

Donicelli smiled.

"'Lassen Volcanic National Park is home to steaming fumaroles, meadows freckled with wildflowers, clear mountain lakes, and numerous volcanoes. Jagged peaks tell the story of its eruptive past ...'"

"You can walk right through an area with steam coming out of the ground, if I remember correctly," said Tait. "We ran a piece on things to do in northern California about 10, 15 years ago."

"Sounds cool," said Donicelli, "in a hot sort of way."

"'The remarkable hydrothermal features in Lassen Volcanic National Park include roaring fumaroles (steam and volcanic-gas vents), thumping mud pots, boiling pools, and steaming ground'," read Wainwright. "'Super-heated steam reaches the surface through fractures in the earth to form fumaroles such as those found at Bumpass Hell and Sulphur Works.'"

"Bumpass Hell?" said Donicelli. "What a great name!"

"'Bumpass Hell is the largest concentration of hydrothermal features in the park. Bumpass Hell was named after an early settler who severely burned a leg after falling into a boiling pool. The hydrothermal features can be reached today from a well-marked 1.5-mile trail that starts from a parking area opposite Lake Helen. A visit to Lassen is not complete without a stop at Bumpass Hell.'"

"I'm sold," said Tait.

"Me too," said Wainwright.

"Why did Mason change the interview location?" said Choy.

"Because that's where he's going to be," said Wainwright. "A meeting at the university."

"But Reno …" said Choy, disappointed.

"I've been to San Fran at least 20 times," said Donicelli. "And this Bumpass Hell at Lassen Volcanic National Park sounds interesting."

"I've never been to Reno," said Tait. "There's a journalism school there at the University of Nevada."

"And casinos," said Donicelli. "Blackjack, craps, roulette, poker, free booze."

"Very expensive free booze," said Choy, thinking about his father's gambling addiction that had caused the family so much drama and grief. Since his mother died the gambling had gotten completely out of control. He had recently considered having his dad barred from casinos in B.C. but decided that would only cause him to drive across the border to Washington State Indian casinos or fly off to Las Vegas.

Why have I never told any of these guys about my Dad?

Because they knew he too liked to gamble. Or at least play poker.

"The Reynolds School of Journalism. I'm pretty sure they have a graduate program," said Tait. "You could check it out Waylon, if you're serious about going back to school."

"I'm serious about heading to the craps tables," said Donicelli. "It's such a cool game."

"I'm serious about confronting Mason," said Choy, shifting the subject away from gambling. "He's got to be at the centre of all this weirdness. There are too many strange things associated with the man. Maybe it's all coincidence, but what are the odds?"

"What are the 'too many' strange things?" said Wainwright.

"The suicide of Vancouver's former police chief, his files with highlighted numbers that point to some sort of financial hanky-panky, the daughter who insists her father didn't commit suicide, the daughter who works for Mason; the explosion, the possibility of miniature drones flying around a few minutes before it went boom, the fact Mason has invested in a company that makes them, the fact two of his houses are for sale," said Choy. "It's like this dance, a slow foxtrot, is happening all around us, but we haven't figured out the steps yet. Something is going down. I feel it."

"Feelings don't cut it," said Tait. "We need a story that can be proved, a narrative with actual evidence backing it up."

"Or Mason could be playing us," said Choy. "Let's say he has done something illegal, some sort of financial scam. He hears about journalists sniffing around. Wouldn't it make sense for him to throw us off the scent by … "

"Agreeing to an interview about his young protégé?" said Wainwright.

"Blowing up the cabin, to scare us," said Choy.

"Make us wonder if he has a tracking device or a microphone in the car," said Donicelli.

"You're the PR man," said Tait to Donicelli. "What would you say to the head of a billion dollar company if he came to you and said: 'I've got these journalists on my tail who think I've done something wrong.'"

"'Have you?'" said Donicelli. "That would be the first thing I'd say."

"What if he'd done something illegal and needed your help covering it up?" said Tait.

"I'd tell him he was asking me to commit a crime," said Donicelli.

"What if he was willing to pay you a lot of money?" said Tait.

"Honestly?" said Donicelli. "My advice would be to get a good lawyer."

"What if he already had one?" said Tait. "What if he said he was coming to you for advice on a media strategy. He wanted ideas about dealing with journalists sniffing around and he was willing to pay a lot of money. What would you say then?"

"How much money?"

"After you had agreed on a price, what would your advice be about the journalists?"

"Be friendly, but that he was under no obligation to tell the journalists anything. I'd ask him how much they knew and if he didn't know that, I'd suggest he find out."

"Maybe by agreeing to do an interview?" said Choy.

"Maybe," said Donicelli. "But given the business he is in, maybe he'd just bug the car the journalists were driving."

"And after he told you the journalists didn't really know anything yet, what would be your advice?" said Tait.

"Do your best to keep it that way. I'd probably say journalists often sniff around, but if they don't find something quickly their editors usually ask them to work on something else. I'd tell him that the best way to keep journalists away from a story was to control all possible sources of information."

"Like by blowing up the cabin where one possible source of information might have kept his files?" said Choy.

"Yes, but I wouldn't advise him to do that specifically because it's illegal."

"Like having that source killed, but make it look like suicide," said Choy. "Then have his daughter followed to see what she might know."

"Again, this would not be my specific advice, but I see your point."

"What else would you advise him to do?" said Tait.

"I'd say one of the best ways to get journalists off your tail is to divert their attention," said Donicelli. "Give them another, easier story and chances are they'll forget about you."

"Maybe that's what's going on," said Choy.

"And I'd say prepare a strategy, just in case the story did come out."

"We can assume Mason's had similar advice," said Wainwright.

"Being a flack is all about how best to manipulate the media, right DD?" said Tait.

"I'd use the word manoeuvre rather than manipulate. It's like being a lawyer. Every client, even a guilty one, has the right to the best defence possible. That's how the system is supposed to work. I have a clear conscience."

"Of course you do," said Tait. "You're just doing a job."

"Exactly."

"The banality of evil," said Tait. "I couldn't do what you do, that's all I know."

"But you don't have any problem at all training young people to do what I do. You already admitted that."

"The system is fucked up and everyone who lives within it bears some responsibility," said Wainwright. "Either for what we do or don't do."

The four men sat in silence for a minute or so.

"Are we stopping in Redding for the night?" said Choy. "Or driving closer to the volcano park so we can visit first thing tomorrow morning?"

3.

The high country landscape of Lassen Volcanic National Park was stark, but eerily beautiful as the mists were evaporating from the warmth of the early morning sun.

"This place is awesome," said Tait, as Choy drove the car slowly down Lassen Volcanic National Park Highway.

"It's exactly what the road to Bumpass Hell should be like," said Wainwright.

"Spooky, with fingers of fog," said Donicelli.

"It's great we got up early to experience this," said Tait. "Does anyone else notice the altitude? I'm definitely feeling the thin air."

"You should be used to it," said Donicelli. "You're always feeling the thin air at your rarefied intellectual heights."

After about 20 minutes of driving on the parkway Choy noticed the sign he was looking for and pulled into the parking lot. Because of the hour there were only a few other cars. The four men stretched their legs then headed up the wood plank pathway to Bumpass Hell.

The walk, the tangy mountain air, and the conversation were invigorating. The steaming mud vents were incredible, a sulphurous burping of Mother Earth. It was like strolling around at the bottom of a volcano just before an eruption, both frightening and fascinating. They hung out for almost an hour as Wainwright took photos and tapped notes on his cellphone screen for a travel piece that might earn him a few hundred dollars. While Choy joked with Tait and Donicelli about the workload of freelancers, he grew more certain that a life where you always had to be on the lookout for story angles, even on a trip to Hell, was not for him.

Why would I give up the life I have now for that?

As they made their way back to the parking lot, they came to a point of high ground above a gorgeous alpine lake when they heard a helicopter nearby. As the noise generated by whirling rotors grew louder Donicelli yelled: "Maybe someone fell into one of those bubbling mud pits."

"It's not an ambulance," shouted Wainwright.

"That thing is so out of place in these surroundings," said Tait.

Choy was getting one of his bad feelings as the helicopter touched down on a meadow beside the pathway and three very large men wearing identical black trousers and white shirts quickly jumped out as if they were soldiers exiting a gunship in a battle zone. As the security detail took up defensive positions and the engine shut down, another large man wearing a suit stepped out and unfolded stairs from the open cabin door, which soon produced a casually expensive dressed, medium-height, sixtyish guy who carried himself with a slight military demeanour.

"Must be some sort of VIP," said Wainwright to the other men who stared at the scene about 50 metres away. Two of the three guards began moving quickly towards the pathway.

"Rich guy putting on a show for the masses," said Tait.

Wainwright nodded.

"A politician?" said Donicelli.

"Very few voters to impress up here," replied Tait.

The not so tall important person returned to the helicopter after taking a quick look around and helped a woman down the stairs. She was blonde, taller than her escort and wearing an overly sexual — for an 8,000-foot elevation parking lot or a national park — skimpy sort of pantsuit that revealed the entire area from three inches below her belly button to the foothills of her breasts.

"Ooh la la," said Donicelli.

"At least we know who he is trying to impress," said Tait.

"The $2000 an hour he is paying impresses her enough," said Wainwright.

"Are you saying that lady is for sale?" said Donicelli. "Is that what a high-end hooker costs these days. And why, may I ask, are you familiar with the price list?"

"I'm editing a book called VIP, Very Important Prostitute," said Wainwright. "It's a memoir by a woman who claims to have been one of the top call girls in the world. Billionaires, Fortune 500 CEOs, politicians, spy agencies — she worked for them all."

"I'd read that," said Donicelli.

"Of course you would," said Tait.

"What the hell are those guys doing?" said Choy as he watched two of the security guards reach the pathway.

"They're preventing that couple and their kids from coming this way," said Tait.

"So the rich guy can take a private walk with his 'escort'?" said Wainwright, shaking his head. "Incredible."

"You're sure they're not cops?" said Tait. "Or secret service?"

"There would be markings on the helicopter," said Wainwright. "No, these guys are private contractors. Former military, by the way they act."

"Assholes," said Tait, as the four journalists walked closer to the guards.

"Come on," said Donicelli, picking up his pace. "They can't stop people from walking on a public path in a national park."

As Tait and Wainwright followed, Choy was getting an even worse feeling. He had never enjoyed physical confrontations and since childhood had sought to avoid them. That was why he became a loner for many of his teen years — he experienced a few too many testosterone-charged gatherings. Not that he was afraid of confrontation or being part of large groups, rather it was a question of reward versus utility. Mindless, pointless clashes were what really bothered him. Hostilities with a definable purpose, on the other hand, were okay, or at least not to be avoided at all costs. The difficulty was distinguishing one from the other.

Choy hung back a few steps behind his friends as they walked aggressively towards the security guards.

Donicelli reached the two beefy men first then quickly moved to his left, off the path and straight towards the helicopter.

"Hey!" shouted the guard nearest him. "You can't go down there."

"Why not?" said Wainwright as he also left the path to follow Donicelli.

Their flanking movement caused one of the guards to chase after them.

"Excuse me, are you preventing movement along this public pathway?" said Tait, stepping to within a few inches of the remaining guard.

While one of the guards remained with the man and the woman near the helicopter, the man in the suit hurried towards Donicelli and Wainwright, who were skipping across the meadow.

"Excuse me," repeated Tait, as the guard, whose large chiselled face was level with his, said nothing, but continued to stand in the middle of the path. While the journalism professor matched his height, the bodybuilder bodyguard outweighed him by at least 50 pounds.

Donicelli and Wainwright joined hands and began dancing like 1960's flower children as the man in the suit confronted them.

"Gentlemen, please stop," he said.

Wainwright and Donicelli circled around him, then broke away towards the helicopter.

"You can't go down there," shouted the man in the suit, who was joined by the security guard who had left the pathway to chase Wainwright and Donicelli.

"Gentleman!"

The security guard who remained near the helicopter pulled a pistol from a holster. Wainwright and Donicelli immediately turned away and retraced their skipping steps back up towards the pathway.

The gun increased Choy's stress to panic level. He was relieved when he saw his friends returning.

"This is a public park," said Tait to the security guard who remained motionless on the path. "By what right are you interfering with people going anywhere they want?"

The young couple with their kids looked uncomfortable and unsure of whether or not to continue towards Bumpass Hell. Wainwright and Donicelli were dancing their way back towards Choy, followed by a security guard and the man in the suit.

Tait continued to stare at the meaty security guard on the pathway as his two friends began dancing around them.

"By what right?" repeated Tait.

"By right of being bigger and tougher than you faggots," said the security guard.

As Wainwright heard these words, he stopped dancing and stepped closer to the security guard who had voiced them. The man in the suit followed immediately behind.

"What did you call us?" said Wainwright, as Choy took up a position beside him.

"You heard me," said the security guard.

"Yes I did," said Wainwright. "And I want you to know I take exception. I am the only faggot here, unless of course any of your colleagues are also of the homosexual persuasion."

"Tom!" said the man in the suit. "Stand down."

The security guard's eyes were the sole giveaway that he had heard.

"Fall back," said the main in the suit.

Tom finally took a step backwards and then followed the man in the suit back towards the helicopter.

"You guys alright?" Tait asked the young family.

"They said we had to wait," said the mother.

"And stay at least a hundred yards behind the people from the helicopter," said the father.

"They had no right," said Tait.

"Hired bullies," said Donicelli, as he joined the clump of people on the pathway.

"They said there had been threats against their employer and they were just making sure everything was safe," said the young father.

"They don't have a right to prevent anyone from walking on a public path in a national park," said Wainwright. "No matter how rich their boss is."

"Are you guys going to see Bumpass Hell," said Donicelli to the two kids. "It's really cool. What do you think of a place called Bumpass Hell?"

The little boy laughed and his big sister said: "It's pronounced 'bump-ess'. Right Mommy?"

The woman nodded.

"Well I did not know that," said Donicelli.

"Me neither," said Tait.

"You're pretty smart for your age. How old are you? Eleven?" teased Donicelli, knowing she was younger.

"She's seven," said her brother. "And I'm five."

"Well, why don't you go see it now," said Wainwright. "It's an incredible place, however you pronounce its name."

"Bum pass," said the boy. "Bum pass."

"Rory!" said his mother.

"We're from Canada," said Donicelli. "Where are you from?"

Choy smiled to himself as his companions chatted playfully with the two kids. He thought of some things Helena had said years ago in the middle of an argument over their arguing. "We'd be back in the stone-age if there was never any conflict, because it produces progress" and "there's two sides to every fight — the right and the wrong." In Choy's experience that was seldom true. Most often he saw good and bad on both sides. And rather than being fights between moral extremes most conflicts were about one group attempting to impose its will on another.

Expressing this ideological predilection angered Helena further, but he prided himself on trying to understand all sides of a dispute. It was a gift, not a limitation. It was what made him a good journalist. People talked to him because they knew he would listen and give their views a fair hearing.

Of course this application of fairness to all presumed a willingness to respond in kind. Nothing ended his effort to be impartial quicker than someone taking advantage. Some people understood being fair as a weakness, as an opportunity to use him to further their own ends. And they might even get away with it, for a while, but he really hated being manipulated. Really, really hated it.

For some reason he thought of Donald Trump.

Judgment

Dear WaylonChoy@yahoo.com,

The cucks and the race traitors have no shame and no future. The Man Adam is father of the White Race only. As a son of God (Luke 3:38), made in His likeness (Gen. 5:1), Adam and his descendants, who are also the children of God (Psalm 82:6; Hos. 1:10; Rom. 8:16; Gal. 4:6; I John 3:1-2), can know YHVH God as their creator. Adamic man is made trichotomous, that is, not only of body and soul, but having an implanted spirit (Gen. 2:7; I Thes. 5:23; Heb. 4:12) giving him a higher form of consciousness and distinguishing him from all the other races of the earth (Deut. 7:6, 10:15; Amos 3:2). As a chosen race, elected by God (Deut. 7:6, 10:15; I Peter 2:9), we are not to be partakers of the wickedness of this world system (I John 2:15; James 4:4; John 17/9, 15, 16), but are called to come out and be a separated people (II Cor. 6:17; Rev. 18:4; Jer. 51:6; Exodus 33:16; Lev. 20:24). This includes segregation from all non-white races, who are prohibited in God's natural divine order from ruling over Israel (Deut. 17:15, 28:13, 32:8; Joel 2:17; Isa. 13:14; Gen. 1:25-26; Rom. 9:21). Race-mixing is an abomination in the sight of Almighty God, a satanic attempt meant to destroy the chosen seedline, and is strictly forbidden by His commandments (Exo. 34:14-16; Num. 25:1-13; I Cor. 10:8/ Rev. 2:14; Deut. 7:3-4; Joshua 23:12-13; I Kings 11:1-3; Ezra 9:2, 10-12; 10:10-14; Neh. 10:28-30, 13:3, 27; Hosea 5;7; Mal. 2:11-12).

FOXTROT

1.

The next move in this dance of unexpected turns left Choy completely disoriented.

"Mr. Mason will be here in a few minutes," Tom said curtly, inside a small sparsely equipped office in the administration building of the University of Nevada, Reno. He was the same security guard who had confronted Tait the day before in Lassen Volcanic National Park. "Sit there and prepare for the interview. He doesn't have much time."

Did this mean that the rich guy on the helicopter yesterday was Mason? Choy looked at Wainwright, who sat down, then took a notepad and recorder from his briefcase.

Potential explanations for Mason showing up at the park while they were there?

While coincidence was a remote possibility, it was much more likely to have been a purposeful display designed to send some sort of a message. A display of his power? Proof that he knew where they were at all times? Something else? There must be a tracking device somewhere in the car. Did Mason have access to a satellite?

Choy opened his backpack and pulled out the camera that he had borrowed from Marianne Kempki, a journalism prof from the University of Nevada who Tait had set up a meeting with the evening before.

"So Tom, was that Mr. Mason on the helicopter yesterday?" Wainwright asked, trying to be friendly. "With that woman? She was awfully good looking."

"Thought you said you're a faggot."

Wainwright paused before he spoke, as if carefully considering his words. "You have a problem with that?"

"'You shall not lie with a male as one lies with a female; it is an abomination.'"

"Leviticus condemns lots of things, like eating shrimp or rabbit, crop co-mingling, and wearing linen and wool at the same time," replied Wainwright. "You follow everything in the Old Testament or just the homophobic parts?"

Choy was impressed by how his reticent, almost mousy friend stood up to this giant of homophobic thought.

"The Lord will forgive your sins, but you must repent."

"I see from your tattoos that you've been in prison," said Choy, interrupting the glaring contest. "Did you get the 'AB' inside or after you got out?"

The initials 'AB' were a mark of the Aryan Brotherhood. Tom had the letters tattooed on his right wrist, above which was a spider web, topped with the number 88. The web meant a long sentence and the 88 stood for the eighth letter of the alphabet twice, or Heil Hitler. A few years back Choy had done a feature on a very popular anti-gang speaker from the United States who was setting up a program for at-risk youth in suburban Surrey. He had three similar tattoos and explained their meaning.

Tom said nothing, but kept eye contact with Wainwright, who said: "What did you do time for? Something not condemned in the bible?"

A slight smirk developed on Tom's face, as if he was wiser than his adversaries. Or maybe it was the sort of false bravado necessary to survive in dangerous places.

"You were in the Marines too?" said Wainwright, pointing to his left forearm. "Before prison, I assume. You do anything there that was against the Ten Commandments?"

"You know my favourite song?" asked Tom, his smirk growing into a full smile as he began to sing. "99 journalist scum on the wall

— Take one down, smack him around — 98 journalist scum on the wall."

Choy stared for a moment at this obviously crazy and violent guy and then had a thought. "Have you ever been in Birch Bay, Washington?"

Tom barely reacted.

"Did you know former Vancouver police chief Wong?"

Tom looked Choy in the eye.

Wainwright took out an iPad from his briefcase and, after a few finger movements on the screen, held it up so Tom could see. "This is a good friend, who was beaten to death in prison by a member of the Aryan Brotherhood. What do you think of that?"

Tom looked at the screen, then calmly, quietly and carefully said: "I think he was a bum fucking, faggot nigger."

Wainwright sighed, then turned the screen so Choy could see. The torso and face of a good-looking, shirtless young black man filled the screen. Adam looked tired.

This security guard is indescribably mean.

Mean? That's the only word to pop into his head?

How about despicably unpleasant, uncaring, nasty, unkind, callous, cruel and shameful.

"We are the chosen race, elected by God and are called to come out and be a separated people," said Tom, who sounded like he was repeating words spoken by others. "This includes segregation from all non-white races, who are prohibited in God's natural divine order from ruling over Israel."

"Your grasp of the scriptures is impressively shallow," said Wainwright. "You really think hating Black people and homosexuals is going to get you to heaven?"

"Membership in the church of Jesus Christ is by Divine election," answered Tom. "God foreknew, chose and predestined the

Elect from before the foundation of the world, according to His perfect purpose and sovereign will."

"So it doesn't really matter who you hate or what you do in this world?" said Wainwright.

"You really believe this shit?" said Choy, hoping to deflect some of the bubbling anger away from Adam.

"The Day of Judgment is nigh. Will Thou be amongst the Elect? Or art Thou not of the chosen people and therefore will be damned?"

Choy had never before listened, in person, to someone who spoke so vilely using religious language. Of course he'd heard about people like this but had never met one before. Thank God Vancouver was one of the least religious places in North America.

He couldn't help but smile at that thought.

"You think the Day of Judgment is a joke?" said Tom.

"I don't mean to be rude or question your religious beliefs, but actually yes, I do think your ideas are quite comical," said Choy. "I mean how can you have a 'day of judgment' when the 'elect' are, by definition, already chosen."

"If people like you, who are so full of hate, go to heaven, then count me out anyway," said Wainwright, smiling. "I'm not interested."

Tom squinted a few times, but otherwise did not react. Perhaps the best way to deal with this sort of bully was to make light of him.

"I agree with Adam on that one. Ever since I realized at the age of 13 that the idea of a supreme being was childish and ridiculous, I've thought going to a place full of believers would be the last thing any sane person would want to do for eternity."

Again Tom squinted.

Maybe it was best to change the subject. "Where's your supervisor? What's his name? The guy in the suit yesterday? Is he around somewhere?"

"He is busy filing a police report about the assault your friend committed yesterday and the threats that were made against the well-being of Mr. Mason and Miss Bennett."

"Assault?" said Choy.

"Threats against Mr. Mason?" said Wainwright.

"What are you talking about?" said Choy. "Which friend committed what assault and who made threats?"

"The only assault committed yesterday was your verbal attack on my sexuality, repeated today, I might add," said Wainwright.

"We really don't have a clue what you're talking about. Assault? Threats?"

"Read the police report," said Tom, smirking with self-satisfaction.

"This is bullshit," said Wainwright. "Maybe we should leave."

Tom pointed to the door.

Choy looked at Wainwright. Interviewing Mason was important. To get this close, to go through this much weirdness and not ask at least a few questions …

Just then the door opened and the shorter man from the helicopter entered the room.

"I'm terribly sorry to keep you waiting, but this has been a very busy day," he said. "Tom, you can take a break. But don't go too far."

2.

Two minutes into the interview, after George Mason, who definitely was the rich guy with a helicopter and a high-class call girl from the day before, apologized for the behaviour of his security team, Choy decided he didn't trust anything the man said. He sounded like a used Rolls Royce salesman, too smooth, too smart, too full of himself, too friendly, a salesman who pretended not to be a salesman.

Is it fair to define the essence of someone so quickly?

Better to suspend judgement until you have a sizeable body of evidence. Still, first impressions count for something.

"Yes, what an amazing coincidence that we both show up at Lassen Volcano park at the same time," said Mason, answering another of Wainwright's questions as Choy took photos. "My friend Amanda wanted very much to see Bumpass Hell. I've been promising to take her for some time and the helicopter was available, so at the last minute …"

Choy and Wainwright exchanged glances as the word 'friend' was spoken after a slight pause and with a slightly lower tone than the rest of sentence.

"Of course I don't believe in coincidence," continued Mason. "In my experience everything happens for a reason."

At the moment he said this Mason looked directly into the camera as if he were making a point.

What's he saying? A challenge — I dare you to figure this out. An assertion of dominance — Here's a clue, but you don't have a clue, do you?

Mason was being deliberately enigmatic. 'I don't believe in coincidence.' A broad hint that he planned the meeting for some reason.

"Let's start with some background. I understand you are 71 years old, even though you don't look a day over 45," said Wainwright.

"You're too kind."

"You look like a runner."

"Eight miles, at least four times a week," said Mason, looking down at his body. "Plus the weight room, every day for 45 minutes."

"It shows."

"I feel better than when I was in my thirties."

"I admire your discipline."

Amazing how effective flattery could be. It was the perfect small talk to begin an interview, to get the subject relaxed and willing to open up.

"I can find very little about what you did before starting ZZZ-Fund," Wainwright said, finally getting to a question that the four journalists had discussed at breakfast, "except that you were a 'government security consultant', but I am told you were a mid-level CIA analyst, and an expert in PSYOPs."

"Who told you I was a 'mid-level CIA analyst'?"

From the way he spat out 'mid-level' it was clear he objected to this characterization.

"A friend, actually a former agent whose book I worked on, told me you wrote the manual, literally, on Psychological Operations, so of course I was surprised by his description of your place in the bureaucracy. Perhaps he got that wrong or knew you before you rose higher …"

"You know of course that everyone who works for the company must sign a lifetime non-disclosure agreement?"

"I am painfully aware of that fact, given the book I edited was caught up in a legal battle and ultimately never published."

"So you can appreciate my reluctance to make any comment about whether or not I once worked for the CIA?"

"Yes," said Wainwright. "I didn't mean to put you in an awkward spot. Of course I will describe you as a former security consultant in the magazine article."

"Thank you."

"Off the record?" said Mason and Wainwright nodded. "It was my idea to create the operation that ultimately led to the victory of modern capitalism and the end of communism around the world, so I would hardly describe my position as 'mid-level'."

"Wow," said Wainwright. "Which operation was that?"

"Early 1970 I was assigned to the Chile desk. Two years later I was lead analyst in the most successful operation this country ever mounted in Latin America. Then the Chicago boys and I completely remade their economy, a model that would successfully be exported around the world, including the former Soviet Union, Eastern Europe, Africa …"

"I'm impressed," said Wainwright.

"Your friend was correct about one thing; I did write the manual for the most successful PSYOP ever created, the one that convinced an entire world there was no reasonable alternative to the American way. We won, the Communists lost."

"And that was because of your PSYOP?"

"Well I certainly can't take all the credit," said Mason, who looked and sounded as if he were in fact taking all the credit. "It helps when you're playing for the strongest team, and capitalism has always had better players than communism, but the operation certainly worked exactly the way I predicted and in countries on at least four continents."

"Of course I understand you can't get into details, but I would love to hear all about your operation," said Wainwright. "I'm fascinated by the idea and practice of a PSYOP."

"If you promise not to quote me I'll let you in on a secret."

"Of course."

"It was all really rather simple, like any good PSYOP," said Mason, who seemed to grow larger and larger as Choy took more pictures, although it might have been the unfamiliar zoom lens. "Create the appropriate structure by any means necessary and then strictly control the messaging, repeating the most important ideas everywhere and anywhere, ideally over the course of at least one generation."

"'Create the appropriate structure by any means necessary'?" said Wainwright. "What exactly do you mean by that?"

Choy thought of an old reporter who long ago had given him unsolicited advice about conducting interviews. 'Repeat their words but pretend not to understand. Get them to elaborate. Elaboration is the key to unlocking Pandora's box.'

"To make an omelette you need to break a few eggs," said Mason. "At a certain point in the evolution of societies the game becomes solely about power."

"Power?"

"Getting what you need, what you want, it's all about power. Imposing your will might be a better way to understand it."

"Imposing your will?"

"Politics, the economy, the world, everything works better when the smartest, most able people get their way."

"Power should be in the hands of those most capable of using it?"

"Exactly."

"But how do you decide who is most capable?"

"Competition," said Mason. "Capitalism."

"Capitalism?"

"An economic system that is all about winners and losers. The winners get the power and the losers do what they are told."

"That doesn't sound very democratic."

Choy caught the perfect image to illustrate the essence of the man at the exact moment of Mason's response. He oozed disdainful self-confidence.

"Democracy," the word came out like a schoolyard taunt. Then he smiled. "Thank goodness the framers of our constitution insisted on a republic, not a democracy."

"A republic, not a democracy?" said Wainwright. "A system compatible with the way you say capitalism works?"

"A system dependent on the way capitalism works."

"Dependent?"

"Capitalism sorts out who the winners and losers are, giving the most capable people the power to determine winners and losers in the political arena as well."

"And democracy without capitalism?" asked Wainwright.

"A descent into the worst forms of populist socialism. Ineffective, inefficient, indecisive, invasive, inevitably leading to dictatorship."

"Without capitalism, dictatorship?"

"Exactly right."

"What is your definition of dictatorship?"

"The accumulation of all power in the hands of one individual or his cronies."

"Like Augusto Pinochet, in Chile?"

If looks could kill, Wainwright would have suffered a painful, lingering death.

"No, the man defeated Communism and dictatorship. He rescued capitalism and created the neoliberal system that much of the rest of the world has now copied. He encouraged competition. He was a hero."

Choy thought of Jaime, one of his best friends in elementary school, whose family fled Chile after the coup and whose uncle had been tortured to death. Jaime certainly didn't think Pinochet was a hero.

"So your definition of dictatorship is a lack of competition? But isn't that what big corporations do, buy up their competition?

I have a quote here from you in the *Wall Street Journal*, about three years ago, I believe. 'The security sector is characterized by a lack of pricing power. It requires consolidation. That is our objective.' Aren't you really saying there is too much competition?"

Mason smiled. "Life and business are complicated, full of contradictions. But aren't we getting off topic here?"

"Yes," said Wainwright as he looked back at his notebook. "Ertha. Is she comfortable around a security guard who is an ex-convict, Aryan Brotherhood member and now is into some fringe racist Christian Identity religion?"

Mason said nothing as he stared, smugness oozing from every pore on his frequently spa'd skin.

"You must know Tom's background and his current views. He doesn't seem to hide them."

"Mr. Wainwright, as I said earlier, I understand how upset you are at his behaviour and you have every right to be angry, but I assure you, the religion and politics of my security detail are not matters that require my everyday attention. If you believe Tom's political views are relevant to the story you are working on perhaps you should take up the matter with him or his supervisor Jefferson Davis. I believe his card is here somewhere."

Mason picked up a business card and held it out for Wainwright to take.

"But I was told this interview was for a story you were doing about Ertha Wong."

"Yes, of course, I am sorry," said Wainwright, again looking at his notepad. "When did you first meet her?"

"Please, this charade has gone on long enough," the older man said, reaching some tipping point. "Do you really think I don't know who you are and what you're doing?"

Mason watched as Choy and Wainwright made eye contact.

"Waylon Choy, but you're not Chinese."

"My father got involved in Indian numerology in his hippy youth and the letters of the name added up to a good number."

"I heard you were adopted."

Choy shrugged.

"You're digging into matters that could cause grave offence."

"To whom?" Choy asked.

"To people you do not want to offend."

"You?"

"That's for you to figure out," said Mason. "My concern is Ertha. She's gone through enough trauma recently."

"Your concern for her is very touching," said Wainwright. "Are you as fatherly to all your employees?"

"We plan to announce our engagement, as soon as it seems appropriate, under the circumstances."

The words had an effect like a fastball pitcher's change-up. Choy swung wildly. "Married? You're at least twice her age."

"Yes. One could say love is strange. Or one could contemplate the effect money and power have on some women."

Choy stopped himself from responding. Fortunately or unfortunately, Wainwright was batting behind him. "Does she know about the sort of rental women you take to national parks?"

Mason's laugh was genuine this time. "Oh dear," he said. "I really thought you were better informed than this."

3.

"You're surprised I know you are reporters investigating what you think is a story of corporate malfeasance and perhaps the murder of a former Vancouver police chief?" said Mason. "My business is security and of course I take my own very seriously."

"You believe we are a threat to your security?" said Wainwright.

"Anyone who snoops around asking questions about one of my companies is a potential security threat."

One of his companies? Did that mean Mason only knew about the interview in Seattle but not about Celeste or anything else?

"How much do you think you know about us?" said Wainwright.

"I know this fellow who is not Chinese is also not a photographer," said Mason. "He's a reporter for the *Vancouver Sun* newspaper in Canada. Which, I might add, is a precarious position to be in. Friends in the hedge fund business tell me the owner of the company you work for will soon be bailing from all their media investments. My advice would be to get another job. One as far away from newspapers as you can find."

"Thanks for your concern."

"And you are a freelance editor and writer, mostly of puff pieces in travel magazines, business publications. Which means that despite how good you may be, your economic position is precarious. A few phone calls from a powerful person to other powerful people could easily result in all your sources of income drying up."

The smile continued. The gauntlet had been thrown down.

"That's it?" said Wainwright, as he held up the business card Mason had given him. "That's all this Mr. Davis gave you? How much do you pay your security team? Is it by the inch or by the pound? He gives you the results of a two-minute Google search and some pathetically bad advice about how to intimidate two veteran journalists?"

"I have no desire to intimidate anyone," said Mason, now looking serious. "But I do not like people lying to me or asking for an interview under false pretences."

"I am interviewing you for a feature piece in *Vancouver Magazine* about Ertha, which is exactly what I told your secretary," said Wainwright. "Do we have other interests as well? Yes, of course. As would any good journalists."

"If you want to ask questions about my business or anything else, be a man and do it directly," said Mason fixing his eyes on Wainwright.

The two men stared at each other.

"What do you know about the death of Ertha's father?" said Choy deciding to participate in the interview, now that their cover was blown. "Her sister believes it wasn't suicide."

"That's why you're here?" said Mason. "Celeste has a vivid imagination. I assure you that I had nothing whatsoever to do with the death of Victor Wong. Did you know he was being treated for post-traumatic stress disorder?"

"Yes," said Wainwright. "Ertha told me."

"I hope you can work a mention into your story of how debilitating that can be, especially to soldiers returning from defending our country or to police officers keeping our communities safe. I intend to set up a foundation dedicated to researching both causes and treatment and it will be named the Victor Wong Foundation. It's too bad it took such a tragedy ..."

"Yes," said Wainwright. "Were you two close?"

"I wish I could say we were, but unfortunately he was a difficult man to get to know. Cautious in his relationships, private, a man who focused on his family. I'm sure Ertha told you how close they were, how very difficult this has been for her."

"Yes," said Wainwright.

"Did he approve of your relationship with Ertha?" asked Choy, purposefully aggressive. "The age difference and you being her boss?"

"We never told him about us," answered Mason.

"He never found out or suspected?"

"What are you suggesting? That I had him killed because he disapproved of our relationship?" Mason shook his head.

"Perhaps it was a factor in his suicide?" said Choy. "How was he doing in his position with your company?"

"ZZZFund has consistently been ranked one of the top five in the world, based on return to investors. We have been and are an excellent investment. Victor Wong was an important part of our team."

"He had no reason to be concerned about the fund's or his performance?"

"Victor was a worrier, a stickler for detail, a perfectionist. It made him an excellent police chief, but it got in the way of him ever feeling satisfied with his performance."

Choy considered asking a question based on information from the files but decided not to. The interviewee could learn as much about the interviewer as the other way around and, as Donicelli pointed out, Mason likely agreed to the interview because it was a way for him to figure out exactly what some annoying journalists knew. No point in making it easy for him. Instead Choy decided to change direction. "Can you understand why we might be suspicious?" he said. "The behaviour of your security team yesterday? The revelation that we have been reported to the police for assault, when in fact it was your security guards who were trying to intimidate us."

"You must understand the very real dangers and opportunities of the milieu in which I and my fund operate," said Mason, looking at Choy.

"Dangers and opportunities?" repeated Wainwright in the form of a question.

"Dangers that require an aggressive security team," said Mason. "A fund that has grown quickly, to over $4 billion, attracts detractors, malcontents, con artists and outright thieves."

"Malcontents?"

"We are very selective about who we allow to invest in our fund. One must be nominated by a current associate and then my personal approval is also required. Too much growth too quickly is an interesting problem to confront, but we must limit the capital we accept to that which we can profitably employ if we are to maintain the excellent rates of return we have so far managed to generate. The screening is necessary but it does breed disappointment."

"And some of those who suffer disappointment make threats?" said Wainwright.

"Unfortunately yes. As the fund achieves ever greater levels of success there seems to be a corresponding increase in declarations of intent to cause me harm."

"You mentioned both dangers and opportunities that shaped your security program," said Choy. "What did you mean by opportunities?"

"Well, because of the fund's focus on the security industry, we find it useful, in a marketing sense, to have a proactive team who attract attention. One of the fastest growth areas in the security industry is the personal protection of high net worth individuals."

Of course, thought Choy, as inequality grows, personal protection would be a booming business. The rich get richer but need to get even richer to pay for the protection they need because of getting richer. "Your proactive team of security is 'useful in a marketing sense'. What exactly do you mean by that?"

"I mean there are some very wealthy people who are impressed by the enthusiasm of my security team."

"Impressed by its enthusiasm?" said Choy.

"When my guys come on like the Secret Service on steroids, let's say when I attend an event in San Francisco, among the people who witness this display, are a few who think to themselves 'I'm important enough to have that level of security.' Then the next day they are asking: 'Where can I get a team like that?' And voila, they turn to one of the companies that our fund now owns."

"How much of what your security team did yesterday and today, what you're telling us right now, is part of a PSYOP?" said Wainwright.

Mason smiled.

"'Psychological operations (PSYOP) are planned operations to convey selected information and indicators to audiences to influence their emotions, motives, objective reasoning, and ultimately the behaviour of governments, organizations, groups, and individuals'," said Wainwright, looking at Choy. "Is that what your security team filing a police report claiming we committed an assault and threatened you is all about?"

"A journalist is someone who knows a little about everything and not a lot about anything," said Mason, sounding like he too was quoting someone.

"I don't see what advantage you'd get from making a false accusation to the police," said Choy.

Mason looked at Wainwright, as if daring him to answer.

"A way of hassling us if we get too close to the truth," said Wainwright. "An obstacle in our path that we must go around. A diversion. A way of dismissing whatever we find because of our demonstrated animosity to rich people in general and Mr. Mason in particular."

"But he has no proof, no witnesses, nothing. The police would laugh at him."

"He has friends in law enforcement who would love to do him a favour."

Choy quickly grasped the implications of Adam's words. "So he can make things up and yet people will take him seriously?"

"'The conscious and intelligent manipulation of habits and opinions', to quote the founder of modern propaganda," said Wainwright. "'Information is just another battlefield on which wars are fought'."

"But where's the morality?" said Choy.

"There's no morality in war or business," said Mason, in a tone that suggested only incredibly stupid people did not understand this. "Only success or failure."

"You're saying the key to your business success was what you learned working for the CIA conducting PSYOPs?" said Choy.

"I never said I worked for the CIA. He did," said Mason, sharing a smirk/smile with Wainwright. "And I will deny it, if you ever write that I did."

"Debating the morality of a PSYOP is the same as debating the morality of a machine gun. It's a weapon; it works; that's all that matters," said Wainwright.

"And if you believe business is war ..." said Choy."

"Exactly," said Wainwright.

"Everyone can be manipulated?" asked Choy.

"Everyone is manipulated," said Mason.

"Including you?" said Choy.

"The winning strategy isn't to avoid manipulation," said Mason. "It's to understand it and think three or four steps ahead."

"Give me an example," said Choy.

Mason looked as if he were deciding something. "Okay. I made sure Tom told you about our filing of a police report. Why? Because I knew how you would respond."

"Because you wanted us to respond," said Wainwright.

"Of course," said Mason.

"Why?" said Choy.

"Because I know how cops think," said Mason.

"The more vigorously someone denies doing the nasty deed the more likely they are to think he is guilty," said Wainwright.

Mason nodded.

"But I still don't see what you get out of the cops thinking we're guilty," said Choy. "They're not going to press charges without independent witnesses."

"The point is steps ahead," said Wainwright.

"The point is to get inside the cops' heads," said Mason. "Plant a seed that will grow into an idea they will think is their own. That is always the most effective way of manipulating a person or a population."

Choy looked to Wainwright and then to Mason.

"You still don't get it, do you?" said the man who thought he was the smartest person in the room.

Choy shook his head.

"Let's say I or my company is guilty of some crime, which we're not, but for the sake of illustration ... You write a story with these wild allegations. When the police are sent to investigate they are going to find reports about assault and accusations of threats, then your vigorous denials. What do you think they will make of that?"

"It will plant a seed of doubt," said Wainwright.

"Exactly," said Mason. "Maybe it's all a shakedown. Maybe you simply don't like successful, rich people."

"Gives your lawyer something to work with," said Wainwright. "Or at least gives the police another line of enquiry that may buy you enough time to fly off in your private jet to whatever country you've paid off enough officials to help you hide."

Mason smiled triumphantly. He stood up.

Was that it? Was this all they would get out of the interview? Choy decided to ask one more stupid question. "Isn't this all just a complicated way of saying that when you worked in government you learned how to be very sneaky and no one should trust you?"

"No one should trust anyone," replied Mason. "That's especially true of reporters trying to get at the truth. Whatever that is."

Wainwright smiled and Mason smiled back.

"One last question, about Ertha," said Wainwright. "What kind of businesswoman is she?"

"She's a brilliant engineer, a fantastic businesswoman and one of the brightest marketing managers I've ever had the pleasure to work with."

"Thank you," said Wainwright. "I believe we have what we need."

Well at least the dance had become faster, thought Choy, from a slow foxtrot to a foxtrot. They were getting closer to figuring out what was going on, but many twists and turns were yet to be performed.

Judgment

Dear WaylonChoy@yahoo.com,

Politically correct blindness prevents you from seeing The Truth. The chosen seedline making up the "Christian Nations" (Gen. 35:11; Isa. 62:2; Acts 11:26) of the earth stands far superior to all other peoples in their call as God's servant race (Isa. 41:8, 44:21; Luke 1:54). Only these descendants of the 12 tribes of Israel scattered abroad (James 1:1; Deut. 4:27; Jer. 31:10; John 11:52) have carried God's Word, the Bible, throughout the world (Gen. 28:14; Isa. 43:10-12, 59:21), have used His Laws in the establishment of their civil governments and are the "Christians" opposed by the Satanic Anti-Christ forces of this world who do not recognize the true and living God (John 5:23, 8:19, 16:2-3).

JIVE

1.

"Mason all but admitted he was guilty," said Wainwright, downing his cocktail in one gulp.

"And I'm positive that security guard was involved in killing Chief Wong," said Choy. "The look on his face …"

"The look on his face?" said Tait.

"Mason told us how he would get away with it when he was finally found out," said Wainwright.

"Get away with what?" said Donicelli.

"Never said," said Wainwright.

"Said he was guilty but not of what?" said Donicelli. "What does that mean?"

"The interview was part of a PSYOP," said Wainwright.

"A psychological operation," said Choy. "He's toying with us. He's full of himself, convinced of his invincibility."

"I got the feeling he was trying to lead us in a certain direction," said Wainwright.

"You mean help us?" asked Tait.

Wainwright shrugged.

"Lead us in what direction?" said Donicelli.

"I don't know," said Wainwright. "The security guard, maybe. He gave me the card of his supervisor. Why did he do that?"

"Security as a whole — the cops, military and CIA — that was the direction he was steering us," said Choy.

"He's definitely former CIA and worked in psychological operations," Wainwright said. "Which means he's probably planned out in very fine detail whatever scam he is pulling, including ways to cover his tracks. Whatever he has going on will be full of 'false flags' and 'plausible deniability' and who the hell knows what else."

"I don't see why you are so excited," said Tait. "You got nothing except confirmation something fishy is going on and we knew that already."

"We knew it, but we didn't know it," said Choy.

"We learned who we are up against," said Wainwright. "And now we know he knows about us, there's no point in worrying about exposing our investigation."

"His weakness is how smart he thinks he is," said Choy. "We didn't know that."

"He threw down the gauntlet," said Wainwright.

"You think you played Mason, but what if he was really playing you?" said Donicelli. "What if the interview, the confrontation at Bumpass Hell, meeting the twin sister at the drone company, the cabin blowing up were all part of his 'psychological operation'?"

"To what end?" said Wainwright.

Donicelli shrugged.

"To get inside our heads, plant seeds of doubt, have us chase off in all directions," said Choy.

Wainwright shrugged.

"We need to interview disgruntled former employees, pissed off investors," said Donicelli.

"Now you're talking like a real reporter," said Tait.

"We need to systematically go over everything in those boxes," said Wainwright.

"Maybe there's names of people we can talk to," said Donicelli.

"Did you get the feeling Mason knew about the boxes?" Choy said to Wainwright, who shook his head. "Me neither."

"So he doesn't know about the locker or that we were at the cabin?" said Donicelli.

"I think he knows about Celeste calling me," said Choy.

"He could know about that, but not about the locker or the

boxes," said Tait. "He could think the files were all destroyed in the explosion."

"He must think that," said Donicelli.

"Or he would have sent those goons after the files," said Wainwright. "He probably has a legal right to the papers. They did belong to the company."

"So the fact he hasn't sent cops or the goons proves he doesn't know what we have," said Donicelli.

"Or that there's nothing important in the files," said Choy.

"Adam is right," said Tait. "We need to carefully go over those files right away. Build on what we already know."

"So we're staying in Reno?" said Donicelli. "I vote for moving to the biggest suite we can find, spread out everything and continue looking through the files for as long as it takes to find what we're looking for. Except for occasional breaks to go play craps and black-jack. We order room service when we're hungry."

"I don't want any waiter coming in the room," said Tait. "Who knows where Mason's tentacles reach in this town."

"Okay, we bring food in," said Donicelli. "I volunteer to drive Waylon's car to pick up Chinese or whatever."

"You wish," said Choy.

"Let's get the hotel suite like DD says, buy a decent quality multi-function laser printer — pretty sure we can get a good one for three hundred or so — scan and print every piece of paper in those boxes so we have back-up copies just in case, then go over everything at least twice, maybe three times," said Tait. "We divide up the work."

"How long is this going to take?" said Wainwright.

"Depends when we find what we're looking for," said Tait. "Maybe we find it after a few hours or maybe a few days."

"Anyone have something better to do?" asked Choy.

Only Wainwright put up his hand. "But I could do a travel piece on Reno, to justify spending more time here."

"Okay?" said Tait. "So we have a plan."

Each of the men nodded assent.

2.

Choy daydreamed as he worked the first two hours on the scanning and printing detail. Tait, who had also drawn one of the first two "shit shifts", had complained that it was a waste of his time as the most experienced investigative reporter, but Choy took advantage of the drudge work to think about where they were at with the investigation. First, he focussed on relaxing, a technique he picked up in theatre class over 25 years earlier at Templeton High School from Mr. Sinclair, who was very much into controlled breathing, clearing your mind, and finding focus. In university and then early in his career at the *Vancouver Sun* Choy had built on what he learned as a drama student to clear his mind and then leave it free to wander. That was with an "a" not an "o". Although it was a wonder how much it could wander. And where it ended up. Fellow reporters over the years had asked him where he found the creative ledes that everyone marvelled at and he had always answered "they just pop into my head" but he never revealed the exercise that enabled the popping.

After all these years he could do it at his desk, even when seemingly engaged in another activity, so long as it was of the boring monotonous sort. It started with consciousness of his breathing, then focusing on various parts of his body, letting each relax, then imagining he was floating in an isolation tank with absolutely no inputs, then allowing his thoughts to disappear by repeating the word "free" over and over, but only inside his head and then, when his mind was completely clear, the magic happened. Ideas, images, phrases, words, feelings — a stream of consciousness — bounced about in his brain like a ball played by the Who's pinball wizard.

Celeste is beautiful. And crazy. Crazy devious or crazy crazy?

The story so far, how would I write it? What would be the lede?

George Mason is an enigma at the centre of a mystery.

Okay, not great.

Celeste.

Something about the files. How would a former police detective organize them?

The explosion. The smell.

Something about the files. File boxes piled one on top of each other to build a chimney-like structure in the centre of the storage room.

Ertha. The same but different. She was definitely not crazy.

Helena. When did he stop having sexual dreams about his ex-wife? Had he stopped? He couldn't remember anymore what she felt like. How could you dream if you couldn't remember?

Celeste on the sand of English Bay, the sun setting behind her. Is she someone I could get to know better?

There's no staples in any of the files. Copies. Former chief Wong made copies so we are making copies of copies.

Sam and Ben, laughing. Tickling.

Security guards jumping down from a helicopter.

Sam and Ben, lying on either side of him, just being there.

There's no staples in any of the files.

The feeling of happiness that thinking of Sam and Ben produced.

There's no staples in any of the files. There are no staples in any of the files.

The realization entered another part of Choy's brain. This was important. "There's no staples in any of the papers in any of the files," he suddenly said out loud to the three other men in the room. "There's no staples in any of it. What does that tell you?"

"None?" said Tait.

"Haven't come across a one. Have you?"

Tait shook his head.

"What does that tell you?" asked Choy.

"That these are all copies of the originals?" said Wainwright.

"No," said Donicelli. "There's at least some originals. Look at this one here, it's got a signature in ink."

"There's also papers with a hole from where the staple was pulled out," said Wainwright.

"It tells you that Wong made copies, just like we're doing now," said Choy. "The first thing you do when making copies is take out all the staples, so you can put them into a paper feed."

"So?" said Donicelli.

"So, where are the copies?" said Choy. "And why did he make them?"

"Same reason we're making copies," said Tait.

"Exactly," said Choy. "We're making them just in case all this somehow disappears. We're making them as a back-up."

"So he was going to put these ones back wherever he got them from?" said Donicelli.

"Maybe," said Choy.

"If Chief Wong also made copies as a back-up ..." said Wainwright.

"Where did he put them?" said Donicelli.

"Maybe they were in the cabin," said Tait.

"How carefully did we look in that storage room?" asked Choy.

"Not very carefully," said Donicelli. "If you remember at the time, there was nothing strange happening. You said we were down in Bellingham to pick up the boxes and that's what we did."

"What was the storage room like?" asked Choy.

"A storage room," said Donicelli. "Bare, unpainted wallboard. A single light."

"With roof tiles, right?" said Choy.

"Roof tiles, right," said Donicelli. "Yes there were."

"Perfect location for hiding the important files, the ones you really want to keep," said Tait. "Just in case you lost possession of these."

"I don't understand," said Wainwright. "Are you saying we don't have the really important files? That Wong kept them somewhere else?"

"Maybe," said Choy. "Or maybe we have a complete set of files, but there's also other copies of the really important ones hidden somewhere else. It could be either, I don't know."

"So, we might be looking at tens of thousands of pieces of paper that have already been culled of their important bits. That's a bummer," said Donicelli.

"The only way of knowing is by continuing to look," said Tait.

"It might be faster if one of us flew back up to Bellingham," said Donicelli.

"You volunteering?" said Tait.

Donicelli shrugged and no one else spoke up. Having one of them fly to Bellingham and take a close look at the storage locker might not be a bad idea. On the other hand, expenses were mounting up and who would pay for it all? Given the severe cost cutting the newspaper was going through it was unlikely to be the company, even if it turned out to be an important story.

"I still have the key," said Choy, mostly thinking out loud.

Of course it was not like he couldn't afford it, he had money in the bank, but if he was going to take a buyout and transition to freelancing or teaching, resource conservation would be important, at least until he had another job or a clear path to a source of income. On the other hand he could always sell his house. With the crazy real estate market in Vancouver, it might be worth $1.8 million. After paying off the mortgage he'd have a million and a half. There were plenty of places where he could buy a nice property for $500,000 and have a million left over to live on, plus the $150,000 buyout. If he did that, all his time could be spent writing whatever the hell he wanted. But he might have to move away from Vancouver and his kids.

"Let's just focus on the job at hand," said Tait. "If we do this right, we should have a pretty good idea soon if there's anything useful here or not."

"Oh, there's useful stuff here alright," said Wainwright. "Look at this."

The file he held up was at least three inches thick.

"Names, addresses and phone numbers of investors, along with the amounts invested, when it was made and their affiliation," said Wainwright.

"Affiliation?" asked Tait.

"It's all mostly police forces, and some branches of the armed forces," said Wainwright, quickly skimming through the file. "Jesus, they seem to be almost all retired. Looks like their life savings — $106,525, $312,000, $97,000, $146,500 — there's thousands of them listed here, from all over the country."

"How recent is the information?" asked Tait.

"Hard to say," said Wainwright, digging into the pile of paper. "Some as recent as six months ago, maybe, and going back to the beginning. It's a contact list for the marketing department."

"Can you imagine how ape shit Mason would be if he knew we had this?" said Donicelli.

"Here's a guy, used to be a Nevada State cop, now lives in Lake Tahoe, with $220,000 invested almost four years ago," said Wainwright. "And he added another $75,000 last year."

"Does it say what his return has been?" asked Tait.

Wainwright shook his head. "No, it's just a contact list."

"But the return must be pretty good if he added to his original investment," said Donicelli. "Those are big sums for cops."

Wainwright nodded. "They sure are."

"Why don't we ask him?" said Tait. "Call up the guy and ask him what his return has been. Ask him if he's happy with his investment."

As soon as the words were spoken Choy had contradictory responses. From a journalistic point of view it was a great idea but considered from a self-preservation angle it was very dangerous.

"We could contact a random sample of investors and see how pleased or displeased they are," said Wainwright. "If there's some hanky-panky going on we'd probably come across it pretty quickly."

"I like that," said Tait.

"Hold on," said Donicelli. "If we did that how long do you think it would take for Mason to find out? Just one phone call to the wrong investor and he could be on to us."

Choy was a little surprised that it was Donicelli who shared his concern. The two "toy department" writers were the ones who immediately thought of their personal safety.

"Do we have some moral or ethical obligation to identify ourselves?" said Wainwright. "Under the circumstances I don't believe we do. "We could simply say we are journalists writing a story for a business publication about investor satisfaction. That wouldn't be an outright lie."

"Under the circumstances, you don't think Mason would figure out in two seconds it was us snooping around," said Choy. "And about another three or four seconds to realize we must have these company files. I mean, how else did we get the names of the investors?"

"And then what does he do?" said Donicelli. "Who does he send after us?"

"Are you scared of him?" said Tait.

"Yes," said Donicelli. "Any sane person would be."

"I am too," said Choy. "I admit it. I have kids and a vintage car I plan to keep driving. If we're right he or somebody else close to the fund has already killed the former Vancouver chief of police. Do you think he'd hesitate to come after us?"

"You can't think like that and be an investigative journalist," said Tait.

"If you're going to be an investigative journalist, I'd say you'd be crazy not to think like that," said Donicelli.

"Guys like him thrive on your fear," said Wainwright. "Bullies win if they scare you so much you live your life in the shadows. Trust me, I know."

"Look, we're having a disagreement about timing, that's all," said Choy. "Timing and doing things as safely as possible. We finally found a file that's useful, but that doesn't mean we have to act on it immediately."

"Oh, there's something to be said for acting immediately," said Wainwright.

"Grab the momentum," said Tait.

"We need to finish going through these files," said Choy. "Maybe there's something else even better that we need to act on as soon as possible. How do you know there's not? Then what about any files that might still be up in Bellingham?"

Donicelli nodded his agreement, but the other two men were not convinced.

"And we've got to protect these files, finish copying and scanning all of them, make sure he can't steal our evidence," said Choy. "That's just basic good journalism, right?"

It was hard to argue with basic good journalism.

"Okay, so we wait until the copying and scanning is done," said Wainwright. "And we continue going through the files until it is, but our next play after that …"

"Subject to what else we may find," said Choy.

"Subject to what else we may find, our next play is to start calling investors," said Wainwright. "Agreed?"

"Agreed," said Tait.

"Okay," said Choy.

"Sure," said Donicelli. "But I'd like to test my luck with a few hundred dollars at the craps tables before I test it with my life. Does that sound reasonable?"

Wainwright smiled. "The macho love of my life is a revealed as a chicken."

"The macho love of your life has a bad feeling about this story," said Donicelli. "And is not afraid to admit he is scared."

"Me too," said Choy.

"After a few more hours of this shit work I could go for a break too, maybe some wrestling with one-armed bandits," said Tait.

"Sounds good," said Choy.

"Blackjack table for me," said Wainwright. "I've always wanted to try it, ever since I edited a book …"

"Christ almighty Adam, is there a subject you haven't edited a book about?" said Tait.

"A few, but I'm working on them," said Wainwright.

All four smiled, as they went back to work.

3.

In the moments between sleep and waking a weird experimental film was playing in Choy's brain. Celeste and Helena had lead roles, but the plot was elusive. Celeste was walking on a beach, at first a bright sunny day, then suddenly rain began to pour and who appeared but his ex-wife, open umbrella in hand, offering to share a small dry space beneath the taut fabric. They were talking but he couldn't hear what they were saying and he couldn't understand why until realizing that their walk was taking them through English Bay crowds during the annual fireworks competition, except that there were no other people at all, just exploding pyrotechnics. Then they sat down so Helena could breastfeed one of the babies, he couldn't make out which one because popcorn from the half-eaten bag in his hands was caught in his teeth and making him uncomfortable. He needed dental floss so badly he was squirming in his seat, unable to concentrate on the movie until Celeste reached out from the screen to hand him a nice long piece of floss that was wrapped around her fingers. Touching his hands she simultaneously unwound the floss from her thumb and forefinger while gently, sexily wrapping it around his. Suddenly they were dancing the jive. But then Helena also escaped the two dimensionality of the silver screen as she grabbed the floss, which caused a struggle to ensue between the two women, except that it wasn't between them anymore, they were trying to strangle him with the dental floss.

And he was awake. Someone was saying his name from the other side of the bedroom door.

"Waylon, Waylon, you awake? Waylon wake up."

"What?" he shouted.

"Do you know where Adam is?" The voice belonged to Donicelli.

"No," Choy answered, as he climbed out of bed, slipped on his pants and opened the door. "What's wrong?"

"I don't know, maybe nothing, but look at this," said Donicelli, holding up a notepad.

The top piece of paper on the pad was empty. Not one hundred percent recovered from his interrupted REM sleep, for a moment Choy thought he was still dreaming.

"I don't get it," Choy said.

"Look carefully," said Donicelli.

"What am I supposed to be looking at?"

Donicelli walked to the desk where he held the pad under a lamp and changed the angle of the light shining on it. "Look."

Choy grabbed the pad and looked carefully at it. There were indentations from someone writing on the sheet above that had been ripped off.

"It's Adam's writing," said Donicelli. "It says 'Harold' and then 'CalNeva casino by the craps tables'."

"So?" Choy shrugged. "What do you think it means?"

"It means I woke up an hour ago and Adam wasn't here and there's still no sign of him. It means he called somebody named Harold and was going to meet him at the CalNeva casino."

"I still don't get it," said Choy.

"Who do you think he called? My money is on one of the investors."

A shot of fear-induced adrenaline completed the waking process. Something bad had happened, Choy could feel it, but there was no point in panicking.

"He's probably out having breakfast with someone," said Choy. "For all we know it's an old friend."

"He didn't mention anyone," said Donicelli.

"Maybe he's interviewing someone who has lots to say. Or maybe he started working on that Reno travel piece. The door to the suite could open at any moment, with Adam walking in."

"Ya, I guess. But I don't have a good feeling," said Donicelli. "I'm worried."

Choy nodded but didn't say anything about his own sense of dread. "Where's Tait?"

"Still sleeping."

"Let's wake him up and see if he knows anything. Adam and he were the last ones working, right?"

"I don't know. I came back from the casino pretty late and no one was here, so I assumed you were all in bed. I crashed on the sofa."

"When I went to bed the two of them were still working," said Choy.

He knocked on the door to the bedroom that Tait had claimed the day before, but then turned around and looked at Donicelli.

"You don't think?"

"What?"

"Adam and Doug?"

Donicelli laughed. "You can't be serious."

"Stranger things have happened."

"No way."

The two men exchanged looks.

"There's no fucking way," repeated Donicelli. "But if there is, I want to be the one who catches them in bed together."

Dominic opened the door, as he smiled at Waylon. They shared a guilty moment of scandalous expectation. But, there was only one person in the king bed and it wasn't Adam. The two men entered the room, their smiles and light conspiratorial tone immediately replaced by seriousness and a hint of panic.

"Doug," said Choy. "Doug, wake up."

"What?" said Tait, sitting up. "What's going on?"

"Do you have any idea where Adam might be?" said Donicelli.

"What time is it?"

"Just after eight," said Choy.

"Adam?" said Donicelli. "You have any idea where he might be? He's not here and he didn't leave a note. And ..."

"We're worried," said Choy.

Tait shook his head and then shrugged. "I don't know. I went to bed and he was still working. He was focused on that spreadsheet, trying to cross-reference some names from a file I found — scores of investors from the gaming industry. Mason and Wong gave a major presentation in Las Vegas about ten months ago— it drew casino employees from all over the state — and, according to the file, it was the most successful meeting ever."

"He was looking for people who worked at casinos here in Reno?" asked Choy.

"That's what it looks like," said Tait. "Adam and I had a conversation about how Mason told you the fund was very picky about who could invest in it and how selling to pit bosses, cocktail waitresses and doormen seemed to contradict that."

"Ten months ago they were selling the fund to retail investors from the gaming industry?" said Donicelli.

Tait nodded. "And it looks like in relatively small amounts. The minimum investment was $25,000."

"That's definitely catching Mason in a lie," said Choy. "He told us there were all kinds of disgruntled investors who were turned away and angry because the fund couldn't use their money. If that was true why would they be out selling to working stiffs?"

"I guess that's what Adam was trying to figure out," said Tait.

"But you don't know who he might have gone out to interview?" said Donicelli.

"He went out in the middle of the night to interview someone?"

"Maybe," said Choy.

"Probably," said Donicelli, holding up the notepad. "Look at this."

Tait took the notepad and looked at it closely. "Where's the Cal-Neva casino?"

"A few blocks away," said Donicelli. "I was there last night. An old, kind of authentic, seedy sort of place. I liked it."

"And we don't know when he left?"

"When did you go to bed?" asked Donicelli.

"One or so," said Tait.

"I got home about 2:30, although it could have been a little later given how much I drank," said Donicelli, thinking about it. "No, I'm pretty sure it was around 2:30. I remember this woman I was chatting up telling me she was going back to her room because it was past two — think maybe she was inviting me — and it couldn't have been more than ten minutes later that I left too. I guess he could have been in his room when I got in, but I don't think so — there were no lights — and I certainly never heard him leave."

"So he most likely left between one and two-thirty and it's just past eight now," said Tait, who thought about this for a few seconds. "He could be meeting a friend, an old lover."

"That's what I said," said Choy, even though he knew it not to be true.

"Or he could have done an interview and then decided to have a drink and met someone at the bar," said Tait. "They could have gone back to this person's room."

"That's possible," said Choy.

Donicelli nodded. "It is possible."

While the three men agreed there were many theoretical possibilities, their body language made clear all felt a similar foreboding.

"But you know what he told me one time?" said Donicelli. "That he couldn't do the whole anonymous gay sex thing."

Tait's look insisted on further explanation.

"For about the tenth time he was hitting on me to 'just try it out' and I, once again, told him I wasn't into having sex with men. He was never obnoxious about it, kind of sweet really, like a little boy asking for candy — that sounds pretty weird. Anyway, I was trying to be firm, but nice and I said something like, 'if you're horny I don't know what the big deal is, gay men can always find someone to fuck' and that's when he told me that even thinking about casual sex made him sick to the stomach. He really was a romantic."

"Is," said Tait. "Is a romantic."

"Ya," said Donicelli. "Is."

That was Choy's hope as well, but he had to sell himself on the undeniable truth that his feelings were sometimes wrong.

"It's definitely too early to call the police," said Donicelli. "They'd laugh at us."

"Way too early," said Tait.

Choy thought about this before saying what was on his mind. "It would normally be too early, but we could come up with a story that made it seem more urgent."

The other two men looked eager for him to continue.

"We could call the police and say he's missed an important meeting and he never misses meetings."

"He is one of the most punctual people I ever met," said Donicelli.

"So what if it gives us an excuse to call the police?" said Tait. "They still won't do anything about it until he's been missing for three days. That's the rule everywhere. And it's probably even longer in a place like Reno."

"True," said Donicelli.

"But the point wouldn't be for the police to do anything right away," said Choy. "All I want is to call the police and give them a description and tell them where we are, just in case … you know … in case something bad has happened. A car could have hit him as he crossed a street and who would the cops have tried to call? He lives alone. He told me he doesn't have any family."

"He has family but they disowned him," said Donicelli. "Right wing fundamentalist Christians back in Iowa."

"The point of calling would be so that the police had our contact information, just in case anything has happened," said Choy. "I mean his name is not even on the hotel registration here."

"A very important point," said Tait. "If something has happened."

"Okay," said Donicelli. "You want me to do it? I can probably describe him best."

"That would be great," said Choy. "You call and I'll go get some coffee and muffins from Starbucks. Then we can finish looking through these files while we wait for Adam to come back."

"Ya," said Tait. "Grande with cream, no sugar and a fruit scone, instead of a muffin."

"Grande with lots of cream and lots of sugar," said Donicelli. "And a bran muffin."

"What about Adam?" said Tait. "What does he like in his coffee?

"Just black, I think," said Donicelli. "And whatever is the least sweet thing they sell. Or, do they have something like a breakfast sandwich? He really likes those. I remember he would go to Tim Horton's a lot when he lived in Vancouver."

"Okay, I'll see," said Choy. "I'll be back in ten minutes."

Donicelli lifted up the receiver on the hotel phone as Choy grabbed his car keys and wallet.

He opened the door as Donicelli was saying, "Can you connect me with the local police, non-emergency number." The door closed and Choy walked down the hallway, his bad feeling about Adam growing. At about the same time he entered the elevator the thought "I'm buying coffee for a dead man" entered his consciousness and he couldn't shake it.

Judgment

Dear WaylonChoy@yahoo.com,

The sinner who does not repent shall never hear the Word of God or receive His blessings. Instead he shall burn in hell.

Do you understand that men and women should conduct themselves according to the role of their gender in the traditional Christian sense that God intended. Homosexuality is an abomination before God and should be punished by death (Lev. 18:22, 20:13; Rom. 1:24-28, 32; I Cor. 6:9).

You were warned.

PASO DOBLE

1.

Since returning home after Adam Wainwright's death Choy was frequently in a bad mood and was taking it out on his children.

"Would it be possible for you to spend at least a few hours each day not plugged in?" he said to his daughter Samantha. "Give your ears and brain a rest."

Her response was a defiant but not too angry glare.

"You know what happens when your mind is stimulated all the time?" he continued. "You never develop an imagination."

Her eyes rolled.

"That's bullshit, Dad," she said.

"Bullshit," said Ben, as he unplugged the earphones from his X-Box. "You told us to call you on your bullshit and we're calling you."

"Oh, so you both can hear me now."

The truth was he had been in a funk the past three days. When bad things happen to parents, they inevitably take it out on their kids. They may try not to, but they do.

"I've got a very good imagination," said Sam. "Mr. Spock said I was the best writer in all the Grade 8 English classes."

"Mr. Spock? What kind of name is that for a teacher?" said Choy, trying his best to change his tone. "Does he have pointy ears?"

"No, but he does say 'live long and prosper' a lot," said Ben, obviously proud of his cleverness.

"How would you know?" said Sam, poking her brother. "You're still in el-em-en-tary school."

Ben plugged the earphones back into his Xbox.

"El-em-en-tary school," she repeated. "El-em-en-tary school."

"Leave your brother alone. "There's nothing wrong with being in elementary school. Seems to me it wasn't very long ago that you were also going to Hastings El-em-en-tary."

"He's such a geek," said Sam.

"What's wrong with that?" said her father. "I was a geek."

"Ya, but you had a cool name," she answered. "Waylon. Did you ever thank Grandma and Grandpa for naming you that? My friends and I voted on which of our parents had the coolest name and you won, Waylon."

"What's wrong with Benjamin?" said Choy.

"Nothing if you want to be like the least cool guy in high school," she said. "You know that a 'Ben' is American slang for a hundred dollar bill?"

"Where did you learn that?"

She shrugged.

"It's drug slang," said Ben, able to hear his sister again. "'Two Bens an ounce for the good stuff.' That's where she heard it."

Choy stared at his daughter, giving her the 'is this true, concerned father look' but was not too troubled. He assumed at least some of Sam's friends had already experimented with marijuana and she would as well soon enough, if she had not done so already. When he attended the same East Van high school three decades earlier, the grass was certainly as green and maybe even more plentiful than today. Parents who try to prevent their kids from doing stuff they did at the same age were ridiculous. How could he get all worked about pot when it was more or less legal — cannabis dispensaries on almost every corner — in Vancouver? And both the Liberals and NDP were promising to legalize it completely if elected in October. Not that he enjoyed the thought of his little girl smoking up. But there were lots of things he knew Samantha would eventually do that he didn't enjoy thinking about. If you're going to be a parent you better get used to it.

Sam made faces at her "little bother", a description she had come up with at the age of four. He made a face back at her, to which she responded with a mimed punch to the face. In return he pretended to be scared.

Despite the reason he had to return so abruptly from the States back to Vancouver it was fun to hang out with his kids. Took his mind off all the bad things happening, — Adam, the way Celeste reacted to his news, his car, the Reno police, the vanishing profession of journalism — all stuff that was more or less out of his control. Felt good for the past three days to be in charge, in so far as you can ever really be in charge of a 13- and 11-year old. They'd taken the bus to Stanley Park and Jericho Beach, after spending the mornings reading, listening to music and making picnic lunches. Today a bike ride around False Creek and a visit to Science World were on the agenda. Not having a vehicle had turned out pretty well, despite his and the kids' misgivings about returning to a carless life. The truth was his neighbourhood had pretty good public transit and a bike ride downtown only took 15 or 20 minutes.

The house phone rang and Samantha immediately pounced on it. "Hello."

She'd already started the teenager phone thing — her record so far was just under two hours on one conversation — even though, or maybe because, her parents had so far refused to get her a cellphone. The words "all my friends have one", spoken in a particularly guilt-inducing 13-year-old pleading whine immediately came to mind.

"It's the police for Mr. Waylon Choy," said Sam. "And they have a Mandarin translator available, if that is necessary."

Police? Reno? Why would they offer a translator? I spent enough hours with those asshole detectives that my file must make clear I speak English.

"Hello."

"Is this Mr. Waylon Choy?" a woman's voice asked.

"Yes."

"You're the owner of a 1965 AMC Ambassador 990 convertible?"

"Yes."

"This is the Las Vegas Police Department forensics unit."

Las Vegas?

"The Reno Police Department sent your vehicle to us in order to run some tests that they are not equipped to perform," the woman said.

"My car is in Las Vegas?"

"Yes. That's why I'm calling. I understand you are a resident of Canada. Is that correct?"

"Yes," he said, stopping himself from adding "a pretty good assumption given you called me at a Canadian phone number." His experience so far with American police had made him sensitive to saying anything they could construe as "sass" or sarcasm.

"We will be finished with the tests later today and I'm calling to ask if we should ship the vehicle back to Reno or if you would prefer to pick it up here?"

"In Las Vegas?"

"Yes."

"I could pick it up in Las Vegas?"

"After about noon tomorrow."

"Or you could ship it back to Reno and I could pick it up there?"

"Yes."

"Do I need to make up my mind right now? Could I consult with my friends and call you back?"

"Yes," she said and then the tone of her voice changed. "Mr. Choy?"

"Yes?"

"I just want you to know not all Nevada police are ..."

There was a silence on the other end of the line.

"I understand," said Choy, trying to make it easier for her.

"My name is Joy Lee and I can be reached at 702-828-3111. Ask for Forensics, Trace Evidence Unit."

"Thank you."

"I wouldn't trust sending the vehicle back up there, if I were you," Ms. Lee said. "There's already been some damage. A shame on such a beautiful vehicle."

He was afraid of this.

"Did you do the restoration yourself?"

"Yes."

"I thought so."

"What sort of damage?" he had to ask.

"Well, there's been some scratching of the paint. Nothing too serious."

"And?"

"I tried to start it and it wouldn't, just before I called. So I could let you know. The mechanic took a quick look and said something about all the belts being slashed."

"Is that all?"

"He didn't mention anything else."

New belts and little scratched paint wouldn't be so bad.

"I am sorry."

"Thank you."

"I shouldn't be telling you this, but there are a few officers in our department, more than a few actually, who seem very angry with you and your friends and this car. If I were you I'd come and get the vehicle as soon as possible and get it out of Nevada."

"I appreciate the heads up." Why was she telling him this? "Can I ask you one more thing? Why are they mad at me and my friends and my car?"

After a few moments, she answered. "Well, it is a murder case."

"Our friend was murdered and instead of looking for the killer they confiscate my car and treat us like criminals."

Choy took the short silence before she spoke again as an indication of concern.

"At first I thought it might be racism, you know how it goes?"

Once again assumptions were being made because of his name. At least this time he seemed to benefiting.

"But then I heard a few of the detectives talking. I believe it has something to do with investments in a fund. Zee Zee Zee or something like that. They were saying your snooping around could put their investment at risk."

"That's what the detectives said?"

"I really shouldn't be telling you this. But you're ..."

He thought she was about to say "Chinese" but she didn't.

"Everyone should have the right to due process, I really believe that. Even if you've done something wrong."

"I know every criminal says this, but we have done nothing wrong. In fact we're trying to uncover some wrongdoing, in which at least one former police officer was the victim. And, I'm beginning to believe more and more, that those detectives who you heard talking are also potential victims, even if they don't know it yet."

"You could tell me about it, if you came here to pick up the car. Over coffee or whatever."

"Yes, I'd like that," Choy said, and actually meant it.

"Maybe I could help. If there's something I could do that wouldn't jeopardize my job. Not that it would be a bad thing to get out of Las Vegas. This place is really getting to me, you know? I'm from San Francisco, Oakland actually. I have relatives in Vancouver and the way things are going down here — Donald Trump and all— maybe I'll check it out. You know anyone looking for an experienced forensic scientist? I have a PhD from Berkeley."

"I don't actually look Chinese," Choy blurted out. "Despite my name."

There was an awkward silence.

"I mean I am Chinese, or at least my great-great-great-great-great grandfather was, but people tell me I don't look it. My daughter however …" Samantha definitely looked a little Chinese.

"You're married?"

"Divorced. Joint custody."

"So would you like to have coffee? If you come to Las Vegas? You really should, quickly."

"Yes," he said and then realized his affirmative answer could be taken as assent to numerous questions. "I would like to have coffee, if I come to Las Vegas and I will call you back within the hour. I need to talk to my friends. Okay?"

"Yes. I look forward to hearing back from you, Mr. Choy."

"Thank you Ms. Lee. Talk to you soon."

"Good-bye."

"Good-bye."

2.

"The pigs shipped your car to Las Vegas?" That was Donicelli's reaction.

"The bastards! They did it to intimidate us," said Tait.

The truth was Mason had done an excellent job of intimidation. In fact, if someone was writing a how-to book on the subject, his actions could serve as a case study. Murdering Celeste's father, blowing up the cabin, killing Wainwright, having the police treat his friends as suspects instead of potential victims to be, and then the cherry on top of the intimidation cake: impounding the car by claiming it might contain evidence related to a murder investigation and then shipping it off, damaged, to Las Vegas. This was bullying at its brilliant best.

The question that Choy wrestled with was not "is Mason trying to intimidate us?" but rather "what should we do?" in response. The obvious and easiest answer was to back off. It wasn't their job, they weren't police investigators, he had kids who needed their father; these were all good reasons to forget about it.

But letting a bad guy get away with killing a friend, that's not right.

Then there were the journalistic principles. Journalists uncover the truth. Journalists stand up to the powerful and bad people. Journalists aren't easily intimidated.

Give voice to those who can't tell their own story — that's what I'm supposed to do.

That's what real journalists do.

The thought made him smile. His newfound enthusiasm for the fourth estate seemed too much like a deathbed conversion. The truth was he had always been cynical about such things. He had viewed being a reporter as a good job, nothing more. People treated you with respect when you told them you worked for the *Vancouver*

Sun — politicians, businessmen, the guy in the street, everyone. The truth was he had never taken journalistic principles all that seriously before, so why now when the profession was abandoning its practitioners? Was a dying craft worth dying for?

While Tait and Donicelli agreed to accompany him to Las Vegas to pick up the car they hadn't come to a consensus about what to do once they were there. Should they drive straight back home, getting out of Nevada as quickly as possible, like Ms. Lee suggested? Should they drive back through Reno, stop to visit the detectives assigned to Wainwright's case and pick up the boxes of files they had stored at the hotel? Should they continue chasing the story that Wainwright died pursuing?

If they decided they owed it to Adam to take up the chase, they were recommitting to journalism, something none of them was necessarily prepared to do. Dominic had become a flack and enjoyed it, was making good money from it; he could be putting it all in jeopardy. It would be understandable if he decided to bail. Even Doug had settled into a nice quiet gig as a college instructor and despite his theoretical commitment to journalism, he was in his late fifties, not exactly an age when people typically begin to battle the rich and powerful. Deciding to wash his hands of this entire matter would make sense. As for himself, why would Waylon Choy want to risk his life?

He tried to ask himself that in a manner that suggested the question itself was the answer. Why **would** anyone want to risk his life? Why would **anyone** want to risk his life? But weirdly enough, as he rode with his kids on the seawall around False Creek all he could think about was journalism. Despite the fact he had never dreamed of being a journalist and only incidentally defined himself as one during many years working in the *Vancouver Sun* newsroom — it was just a good job, a transition, something that paid well before he figured out what he really wanted to do — at some point he had become committed to the craft.

What did that commitment mean? He had some vague ideas. The buzzword answers were obvious. But what did it really mean to him? Like any good father facing a dilemma he decided to talk about it with his children.

Their first destination was a favourite seafood place, Go Fish, on the seawall near Granville Island. While normally the long summer line-ups were a reason to avoid the "shack" beside the public fishermen's wharf, today the 20-minute wait to order lunch and then another 10 to collect their food offered the perfect opportunity to seek the wisdom of youth. Or at least the thoughts of two people who would be most affected if he were to suffer the same fate as Wainwright.

"Does it bother you guys that I'm going to Las Vegas tomorrow?" he asked as they locked their bikes to a post near the public dock.

Samantha shrugged. She was at an age when not caring about anything her father did was "cool" but really more of an aspiration than a reality.

"We were going back to Mom's place anyway," said Ben. "So no big deal."

"Do you understand why I'm going?"

"To get the car," said Ben.

"Emily Dickinson says we have the coolest car of anybody she knows," said Sam.

"I still can't believe you have a friend named Emily Dickinson."

"I'll be able to drive it when I turn 16, right?" said Sam. "Once I get my licence."

It was her father's turn to shrug. "That's a long way off," he said, hoping it was true, but understanding it wasn't.

"Don't let her drive it until I have my licence, so I have a chance to try it at least once," said Ben. "My prediction is she wrecks it the first time you let her take it out alone."

Sam punched her brother hard on his shoulder.

"She and her friends want to drive it up Mount Seymour and smoke dope," Ben said, wincing, but trying to pretend the punch didn't hurt. "I heard them talking."

She hit him again.

"My advice would be not to do that because in another few years he's going to be a lot bigger than you and the puncher inevitably becomes the punchee."

His kids glared at each other as they got in line behind an American couple with New England accents.

So far the family conversation was distinctly unsatisfying, having strayed far from the topic he wanted to discuss.

"We're not just going to Las Vegas to pick up the car," said Choy. "We're probably going to pursue that important story I told you about. The one we were working on when Adam was found dead in the river."

"Your journalist gay friend from Portland?" asked Sam.

"The one you think was murdered?" asked Ben.

"Yes."

"Will that be dangerous?" he said.

"Maybe. We don't really know."

"So why do it?"

"Because he's working on a story," said Sam. "And if he stopped just because some bad guy was trying to scare him, what kind of journalist would he be?"

Sometimes your kids pleasantly surprise you. This time it was by proving Sam had heard and understood important things he said.

"Journalists don't catch bad guys," said Ben. "Cops do."

"You're right, most of the time," said Choy. "But if cops don't know about something or are ignoring it for some reason and a reporter finds out, that's a pretty good story, don't you think?"

"There's lots of good stories, you don't have to chase them all."

"But this one concerns a friend of mine and if I don't pursue it, probably no one else will. Somebody could get away with a lot of very bad stuff, including murder."

"Why don't you just tell the police all you know?"

"Because some of the police are helping the bad guys, right?" said Sam.

Choy nodded.

"The American police," said Ben. "Not the ones in Vancouver."

"As far as we know. The point is all the crimes we think may have been committed happened in the United States and that means only American police can look into them."

His son looked upset. If past behaviour predicted the future, Ben would refuse to talk about what was bothering him and go off by himself when they returned home to play violent video games. Since he almost certainly got the not-talking-about-it thing from his father, it was necessary for Choy to avoid doing the same.

"I'm scared about what might happen if we continue working on the story, but sometimes it's important not to let fear stop you."

"Sometimes being scared stops you from doing stupid things," said Ben. "Remember that's what you said when I told you about those older boys who wanted me to steal a bottle of whiskey."

"I do and it's true. Sometimes."

"Sometimes being scared is just one more obstacle to overcome," said Sam.

Despite the corny women's talk show sound of this, it too was true. "You're both right, that's why it's so hard for me to decide. And why I wanted to talk about it with you."

The people in front of them in the line passed a menu back. Choy glanced at it and then handed it to Ben. "Fish and chips?" he asked his son.

"Fish tacos," said Sam, who always ordered the same thing.

"It's all good," said Choy to the couple ahead of him, who were looking at the menu as if it was their first time. "Scallops are my favourite, but they often don't have them anymore — global warming has raised the temperature of the water around Vancouver Island where most of them used to grow."

"One piece halibut and chips," Ben said to his father, before passing the menu to the people behind him.

"So what do you guys think?" Choy finally said to his kids. "Should we keep working on the story or not?"

Ben shook his head but did not speak.

"'When powerful people tell lies the job of a good journalist is to call them on it', that's what you told us," said Sam. "Remember in Grade 6 when you came to my class?"

It was both gratifying and terrifying to hear your child quote you.

"Your job is to tell the truth and 'speak for those who cannot speak for themselves'. If your friend is dead he can't very well speak for himself. I mean if a journalist can't confront the people who killed a friend, how will he confront Donald Trump, if he becomes president?"

One vote for journalism.

"I know sometimes you have to do things that scare you," Ben finally said after listening to his big sister. "But is this stupid story more important to you than us?"

"That's not fair," said Sam.

"Would you want a father who let bullies win?"

Ben shook his head. "But if the choice I had was between no father at all and having one that let bullies win …"

How could you argue with logic like that?

"Ben," said his sister, her voice actually sounding soothing. "Dad's got to do what is important to him. We all do."

"Look, if the newspaper asked me to go to Syria to cover the civil war, I'd say no, because that would be too dangerous and there would be no principle involved except making a name for myself as a journalist. And if I did go, you'd have every right to feel like I chose my career over you. But if I put myself in danger to defend a friend, or an important principle, that's not the same thing. That's doing what is right, that's being a good example."

"Like if he went into a burning house to save a family and he got killed," said Sam. "Would you be mad at him or proud of him?"

"Probably both. I'd be proud but mad and sad."

His father nodded. That made sense. That would be good, he thought. I could die content knowing that. Instead of saying anything he put his arm around his son's shoulder as they stepped up the stairs to the order counter.

Choy had a chance to become a real journalist. One that makes a difference, one that confronts power. Something he had never done before. Something he had to do if he wanted to face himself in the mirror every morning.

And his kids would be fine. They would understand. That's all a parent can realistically hope for.

3.

Joy Lee came quickly to the reception counter of the Las Vegas Metropolitan Police Department's Forensics Laboratory after the three men, each carrying a bag, asked for her.

"Mr. Choy?" she said looking from one man to the next.

"Him," Donicelli said, pointing at Choy.

"I'm Joy Lee," said the mid-30s bookish sort of woman, offering her hand. "We spoke on the telephone."

"Yes. Good to meet you."

As the uniformed woman at the reception desk stared, Choy turned directly towards her, put his right hand up to his face and said: "Plastic surgery. Terrible accident when I was a child. Damn Caucasian doctor made me look like this."

The woman looked embarrassed and turned away. Lee smiled, ever so slightly, as she led the three men out the front door. "Please follow me, your car is in the compound out back."

As they walked to the back of the one story warehouse-like building Choy found himself smiling at this woman he just met. He liked her. Her smiled suggested she liked him.

As she opened the door to the compound, Lee looked back at the main building as if someone might be watching. "I've called the Automobile Association like you asked and they will tow the vehicle to a garage about a mile away. It's where I take my car and the mechanic says you can borrow some tools if all you need is to put on new belts. I told him you were a friend. I'll give you a lift there."

Choy smiled. "Thanks," he said. "You're very kind."

"You're very funny," said Lee. "That remark about plastic surgery. Susie is such a busybody."

"I get the question about my name a lot and …"

"What can we do to repay you?" said Donicelli to Lee, interrupting Choy. "Can we buy you lunch? Somewhere near the garage?"

"That would be nice," she said, looking at Choy.

She was not beautiful like Celeste, but good-looking nonetheless, with a librarian sort of sexiness that he had always found attractive. And she had a sense of humour.

Thirty minutes later the four of them were sitting around a table at a northern Chinese restaurant a few blocks from the garage.

"It was awfully nice of Pete to insist on installing the belts and taking a look at the engine himself," said Choy.

"Like he said, it's not every day he gets to work on such a beautiful car," said Lee.

"How is this restaurant?" said Donicelli, again interrupting the connection between her and Choy. "What should we order?"

"It's not the Bay Area, but it's pretty good," Lee said. "Best noodles in Las Vegas."

"You order, we'll eat and I'll pay," said Donicelli, who sat across from her, while Choy and Tait were on either side. "You're the first representative of U.S. law enforcement who has treated us with any dignity and respect."

She ignored Donicelli and continued to look at Choy. "Yes, well, as I told Mr. Choy ..."

"Waylon."

"As I told Waylon, everyone deserves due process."

"What exactly did you overhear about ZZZFund?" Tait said, taking his turn to interrupt.

She looked at Tait and then back at Choy. "I'm not sure ..."

"It was two detectives talking?"

She nodded but looked uncomfortable.

The waitress came to take their order. As the men deferred to her, Lee was able to buy a little time to think about her answer.

"Look," said Tait, who was the only one of the three men who had experience writing about crime, "I've talked to hundreds of cops and I know you're never comfortable ratting out your colleagues, especially to a reporter …"

"I don't really consider myself a cop," she said. "I'm a forensic expert. I like to think of myself as a scientist whose job it is to help catch bad guys."

"You're made uncomfortable by questions about your colleagues," said Choy, who definitely felt a connection with this woman. "That's perfectly understandable."

Weird how sometimes I instantly feel comfortable with people.

She nodded.

"Please don't worry, we're not working on a story that in any way reflects badly on the police," Choy continued. "In fact, our investigation started with a plea from the daughter of Vancouver's former police chief to look into her father's supposed suicide. She thinks he was murdered and if he was it might have something to do with ZZZFund."

"Vancouver's first and only Chinese-Canadian police chief," said Donicelli.

Lee seemed interested in this. "Are you friends with his daughter?"

"They weren't before, but they are now," said Donicelli.

Lee stared at Donicelli for a moment before looking back at Choy.

"She called me because of my name. She thought a Chinese reporter might be best."

Lee nodded as if she understood.

"Since we've been working on the story the former chief's cabin has blown up; we've discovered company files that strongly suggest irregularities in the financial structure of ZZZFund and another friend who was working on the story with us turns up dead in a river in downtown Reno," said Choy.

Tait looked annoyed, as if he thought this woman couldn't be trusted, but Choy relied on his instincts about her. It was the right tactic to give Lee the facts and let her decide whose side she should be on.

"And your beautiful car is shipped down here," she said, "even though …" She thought better of what she was about to say.

"Even though?" repeated Choy, looking into her eyes. He knew it was unscientific, irrational and perhaps even ridiculous, but felt she was honest and reliable. He liked her and knew she felt the same about him.

"It's just that the paperwork the Reno detectives sent was so vague, a 'fishing expedition' one could say and it immediately raised a red flag when I read it."

"What do you mean?" said Tait.

"It's a murder case but their only specific request was to look for illegal substances."

"Drugs?" said Donicelli.

She nodded.

"Indicating the detectives were more interested in finding something they could hassle us with than figuring out who committed the murder?" said Tait.

She nodded again. "Well, at least that's what crossed my mind. I phoned the requesting detective to confront him with my suspicion and he was evasive. But it was abundantly clear that neither you nor your car were really suspected of involvement in the death. In fact, all he cared to discuss was how there was no rush to return the vehicle. And then when I searched our criminal databases for information about Waylon, there was none. All I could find was you were a reporter for the *Vancouver Sun*, and then when I heard the two detectives talking about this ZZZFund, it seemed very strange."

"What exactly did they say?" asked Tait.

"I only heard bits and pieces, but my impression was they thought whoever owned the car was doing something that was putting their investment at risk."

"That's how Mason gets the cops to do his dirty work," said Tait. "So many of them have invested in his fund."

"It's in the tens of thousands across the country and even in Canada," said Choy.

"Anytime someone starts looking into the fund, he lets the word out," continued Tait.

"He tells the cops their investments are at risk," said Donicelli.

"And voila," said Tait. "Something bad happens to anyone poking his notebook into company business."

"Do you think the police murdered your friend?" asked Lee.

"No," said Choy, shaking his head as he regained eye contact.

"Probably not," said Tait.

"Or this former Vancouver police chief?" she continued.

"We have absolutely no reason to suspect that," said Tait.

"The guy who runs this fund is former CIA and he has a security detail that includes at least one ex-Marine who joined the Aryan Brotherhood in prison," said Donicelli.

"And our friend Adam had a few confrontations with him," said Choy. "This AB guy is seriously homophobic and Adam is, was, overtly gay."

"I'm sorry," said Lee, then added uncomfortably, "I have a cousin who is gay."

"But the Reno detectives weren't interested in hearing anything about it," said Donicelli. "They just asked us stupid questions about our sexuality because Adam must have been killed by some jealous gay lover."

"They never requested any blood or body fluid work ups," she said.

"This billionaire, Mason, doesn't like reporters, or anyone else looking into ZZZFund," said Tait. "We think the former Vancouver police chief discovered something and all of a sudden he 'commits suicide'. We start looking into it and within a few days one of us is killed by what the Reno police claim is an angry, conflicted homosexual. But we don't buy it."

"I understand your suspicion," said Lee. "But …"

In Choy's experience a "but" followed by hesitation was usually a sign that the speaker was about to disagree with the thesis being presented.

"Isn't it possible that your friend did try to pick up a man who reacted violently? It does happen. And the rest is not in any way related to the murder?"

"It's possible," said Tait.

"But extremely improbable," added Donicelli. "And then the other improbabilities …"

"All we're saying is that Adam's death should be investigated properly and the same with former Chief Wong's so-called suicide and to do that requires looking into ZZZFund," said Choy. "You said you believe in due process. Doesn't every suspicious death deserve a proper investigation?"

Again she was allowed extra time to think about her answer when the waitress arrived with a large bowl of peppery fish soup and filled the four smaller bowls at the table.

"This is great," said Donicelli, after taking a sip. "The hot contrasted with the sour …"

Lee nodded politely, as she too put spoon to mouth, then looked back into Choy's eyes. "To answer your question, yes. Every suspicious death should receive a thorough investigation, but …"

Another "but" with a pause after it.

"I'm a small cog in a very big machine. I've done all I can."

"And we really appreciate it," said Choy.

"Yes, we do," Tait added. "But saying you have done all you can to help may not be entirely accurate."

She glanced at Tait before quickly locking her eyes onto Choy's once more.

What does she want? She looks 'interested', but am I misreading the signal?

He imagined the two of them dancing the Paso Doble, hands and feet carefully choreographed.

"We wouldn't want you to do anything uncomfortable," he said, doing his best to return the 'interested' look. "But, if we had a relationship, you know, that allowed us to discretely ask you questions — a relationship based on trust and honesty, as well as mutual satisfaction — we could do what was right for our friend and you could live up to your ideal of due process for all."

Tait and Donicelli looked surprised as they joined in staring at Choy.

What did I just say? How has she interpreted my words?

But his nervous uncertainty was immediately overtaken by an impulse to demonstrate that he liked her. He reached across the table and put his hand on her free one.

"I feel you are a good, trustworthy person and I hope you feel the same about me," said Choy. "We just met, but I feel … I want … I hope … to be … your friend."

He half expected to be slapped across the face, but she squeezed his hand.

"This evening?" she said. "You won't leave until morning? For Reno? It's a fascinating drive in the daytime. You can stop in Goldfield. My great-great-great grandfather ran a laundry there over a hundred years ago. It was the biggest city in Nevada and now it's almost a ghost town."

"Yes," said Choy. "We'll leave in the morning. Would you like to do something with me tonight? After the car is ready?"

"I would love for you to give me a ride," she answered. "Down the Strip. It's the perfect car. I always dreamed of living in the 1960s, you know the whole Haight-Ashbury groovy free love Mamas and Papas, Doors kind of scene."

Tait and Donicelli looked at each other.

"I have an uncle who told me stories," she said.

"So, do we have a date?" said Choy.

She nodded.

Judgment

Dear WaylonChoy@yahoo.com,

The sinner was warned. The Bible warned him and I warned you. You will listen now.

God the Son, Yahshua the Messiah (Jesus Christ), became man in order to redeem His people Israel (Luke 1:68) as a kinsman of the flesh (Heb. 2:14-16; Rom. 9:3-5)/ died as the Passover Lamb of God on the Cross of Calvary finishing His perfect atoning sacrifice for the remission of our sins (Matt. 26:28); He arose from the grave on the third day (I Cor. 15.4) triumphing over death; and ascended into Heaven where He is now reigning at the right hand of God (Mark 16:19). Yahshua will return to earth in like manner as He departed (Acts 1;11), to take the Throne of David (Isa. 9;7; Luke 1;32) and establish His everlasting Kingdom (Dan. 2:44; Luke 1:33; Rev. 11:15). Every knee shall bow and every tongue shall confess that He is King of kings and Lord of lords (Phil. 2:10-11; I Tim. 6:14-15). The race traitors, the sodomites and the devil people shall all be struck down by the righteous.

RUMBA

1.

Choy was feeling good at Caesar's buffet breakfast as his buddies quizzed him about the night before. "I like her a lot," he said. "We had fun."

Donicelli's silly smile suggested what he understood 'fun' to mean.

"She seems nice," said Tait. "Will she help us?"

"I'm not making friends with her so she'll help us."

"We know that."

Choy was happy with Joy. Everything was simple with her; they were comfortable with each other but at the same time he felt a quickening of his heartbeat when she was near. A few hours after they met he already felt close to her in a way he hadn't with anyone but Helena and his children. Joy was the first person he ever told the truth about why he restored his car. How, six years earlier, when he was sitting on the couch watching an episode of the *Big Bang Theory* with Helena, she told him about an affair with another lawyer and it wasn't her first. How he had been feeling so utterly content and comfortable with his life and then his wife told him how miserable she had been with hers and that was why she had fallen in love with someone else. "Our life is boring," she said. "You're boring." And he realized it was true. Being content and comfortable had led him to a boring existence. He realized his marriage was falling apart and he didn't like the person he had become, so he decided to change. He told Joy how he had never even worked on a car before taking up the challenge of a restoration; how everything mechanical had been foreign to him. How the challenge had been internal, to prove he could overcome his fears and do anything he wanted. And how his next goal was to become a ballroom dancer, something that was even further from his comfort zone than rebuilding an old car. Then, after that, learn how to become a hockey goalie or maybe a boxer to overcome his fear of physical confrontation.

"Still, do you think she might help us?"

Choy shrugged, his consciousness returning to the present. "Maybe. It depends on what we ask. It's not like we have carte blanche just because the two of us get along."

"She does have access to databases?"

"Yes."

"Could she at least see if there's anything useful about Mason," said Tait. "Not necessarily give us anything but maybe point us in a certain direction?"

"I was going to surprise you guys with this later," said Choy, pulling a few pieces of paper out of his computer backpack. "From Joy. Mason's house in San Francisco is also for sale — $14.7 million. But he has another place right here in Vegas. No state income tax in Nevada."

"She gave you the address?" asked Tait.

"Yes, and that of an office in Reno that supposedly employs over a hundred people."

"Another security company?"

"No, a phone room, set up about nine months ago."

"A phone room? For what?" said Tait.

"Financial services."

Tait and Choy shared a knowing look.

"I'm lost," said Donicelli. "What's the significance of a phone room for financial services?"

"You know what a boiler room is?" said Tait.

"I know it was the name of a movie with Giovanni Ribisi and Ben Afleck back around the turn of the millennium. About high pressure stockbrokers or something."

"If you had worked at the *Sun* 40 years ago you'd know exactly what they are," said Tait. "Back in the heyday of the Vancouver Stock Exchange the city was a world centre of shady stock promotion. Even 25 years ago we had a reporter whose sole beat was stock scams."

"Mason is involved in shady stock promotion?" asked Donicelli.

"Joy thinks his entire hedge fund could be a Ponzi scheme," said Choy. "She has a brother who is a forensic accountant working for the New York State attorney general. And she almost became an accountant herself."

"A Ponzi scheme?" said Tait, thinking about it. "That would explain those lists of new investors when Mason claimed the fund was closed except to insiders."

"It would."

"Ponzi?" said Donicelli. "That's like Bernie Madoff?"

"Exactly," said Tait. "A pyramid scheme where the first people to buy in make big returns, which attracts more investors, but there's little real investment going on, usually only a few for show. Instead, the new investors' money is used to keep the big returns flowing to the original investors."

"But most people don't want to sell; instead they want to keep buying because it seems like such a good investment," said Donicelli.

"Until the whole thing collapses," said Choy. "Usually turns out most of the money is being skimmed off to buy mansions, private jets and million dollar art."

"That's what you think Mason is doing?" said Donicelli.

"He's selling his houses because he knows the end is coming soon," said Tait.

"It's a good theory," said Choy. "I made a copy of the memory stick with all the scanned files on it and gave it to Joy. She's already sent it to her brother."

"You sure we can trust her? And her brother?" said Tait.

"I'm sure."

"They're both in law enforcement and Mason is pretty tied in with cops," said Tait. "You don't think it would have been safer to get a better handle on this angle of inquiry before potentially showing our hand to the other side?"

Choy shook his head. He was certain Joy could be trusted. "She gave me something else." Again he reached into his bag and this time pulled out a small pile of papers. "The autopsy report on Adam."

He placed them on the table. His tablemates looked but remained motionless.

"He was tortured to death. A round cylindrical metallic object about five centimetres in diameter perforated his large intestine; he was hit repeatedly on the chest, back, arms, legs and head with the same metallic object. But he was still alive when dumped into the river, so official cause of death was drowning," said Choy.

Donicelli's head shook gently. He was crying.

"They say it was 'likely a crime of passion.'"

"What the hell does that mean?" said Tait.

"Apparently there's been at least four other vaguely similar murders in the past two years in the western United States," said Choy. "They suspect a gay serial killer."

"Bullshit," said Donicelli.

"Yes," said Choy. "Bullshit."

"Jesus Christ," said Donicelli. "So the Reno cops will do nothing. Just hand it over to some FBI task force that will not really investigate. Add the details to its database, that's it. Did the murder even make the local news?"

"I looked on the *Gazette-Journal* website," said Tait. "An item about an unidentified male body found in the Truckee River and then another identifying him as a 45-year-old visitor from Portland.

Both stories ended with the standard, 'Persons with any information are asked to call police.'"

"We've got to do something," said Donicelli.

"We should visit the *Gazette Journal* newsroom," said Tait. "Maybe a reporter there would be interested in what we have so far."

"At a small Gannett newspaper?" responded Donicelli with hopelessness in his voice. "The *USA Today* network? A dozen reporters, paid a little above minimum wage, who spend all their time covering local sports, store openings and rewriting press releases. You think they have someone who is even remotely capable of investigative reporting?"

"You never know," said Choy. "There may be someone who is just dying for the opportunity."

Not until the words were in the public domain did he realize what he had said.

"Was that an intentionally clever sarcastic remark in very poor taste, or a callously shallow slip of the tongue?" said Donicelli.

Choy felt blood rushing to his face like electricity to brake lights. "I ... "

He hated being embarrassed.

"I know we're all upset at what happened to Adam and scared that these people could go after us," said Tait. "But we can't just back off. We owe it to Adam to keep digging."

Donicelli nodded.

"Maybe you're right that the *Gazette Journal* is useless, but we could talk to Marianne Kempki at the university," said Tait. "Remember she won a Pulitzer Prize for her work on exposing right wing militia groups and she told us her graduate level intensive course in investigative journalism is starting this week."

"Get her students to help look into ZZZFund and Adam's murder?" said Choy, eagerly hopping on board Tait's train of thought.

"A school at a university that is receiving a huge endowment from Mason is going to investigate ZZZFund?" said Donicelli. "And even if the school was prepared to defy that conflict of interest do you really think, after what happened to Adam, it would want to put its students in jeopardy?"

"If nothing else, Kempki might have some contacts," said Choy.

"That's it? That's the best we have?" said Donicelli. "Adam is dead, an iron rod shoved up his ass, dumped alive in a river and our plan is talking to a journalism prof?"

"You have a better plan?" asked Tait.

Donicelli looked down at his plate.

"What if the three of us just show up at Mason's door," said Choy. "What is the one thing that someone running a Ponzi scheme fears most?"

"Exposure," answered Tait. "We threaten to expose him?"

"And we end up like Adam," said Donicelli.

"Not threaten to expose him," said Choy. "Say we've already done it. We visit Mason to ask for comment on a story we say is already written. Convince him he is about to be exposed and see what he does. Tell him we have the files and the New York State attorney-general's office has gone over them, which is almost true."

"You're saying he'll run?" said Donicelli. "Rather than order his goons to kill us?"

"If he's about to be exposed," said Choy, "he'd have no reason to kill us, but every reason to run."

"If he's guilty of running a Ponzi scheme, running would be the logical response," said Tait.

"He more or less told Adam and I that's what he'd do," said Choy.

"It might work," said Tait. "Assuming we're right about the Ponzi scheme. Assuming we're right that Adam's death was related to our investigation of ZZZFund. What if we're wrong?"

"If we're wrong, what's the downside?" said Choy. "If he's not a murderer and not a scam artist, but a legitimate businessman, then what? We have a half-a-billionaire laugh at us, and we look like fools. I'm sure that wouldn't be a first for any of us."

They were ready to rumba.

2.

Mason's house was surprisingly modest, a working class family rancher with a single-car garage and a small yard in an older neighbourhood east of the Strip.

"Not exactly what you'd expect from a Bernie Madoff wannabe," said Tait.

"Not a Bill Gates mansion, that's for sure," said Donicelli.

"Nothing like his other places," said Choy.

The three men walked to the front door and Choy pressed the doorbell. They stepped away, on alert for any sign of the security detail. After about ten seconds the door was opened by Mason himself, wearing a pink housecoat and holding a mug of coffee in his right hand.

The scene was so unexpected, so absurd, that Choy couldn't help but smile.

"Mr. Choy, to what do I owe this unexpected pleasure?"

The three men stared, rendered silent by this unforeseen comedy.

"I am George Mason," he said, offering his hand to Donicelli.

"Dominic Donicelli." The silly grin on his face may have looked friendly, but Choy could tell it was DD's way of trying to contain his laughter.

Mason held out his hand to Tait.

"Doug Tait, investigative reporter and journalism professor."

"I must be a sight," said Mason, as he looked down at his housecoat and then up at Donicelli. "It belongs to Ertha."

The three men continued to stare.

"How did you get this address?" said Mason, suddenly serious.

"We're journalists," said Donicelli, attempting to look authoritative. "We have our ways."

"Mr. Mason, we would like to ask you some questions," Choy said, finally getting back on track. "We would like to get your response to certain allegations, information we've gathered."

"Of course," he said, remaining polite and even friendly. "Why don't you come in and have some coffee? I'm afraid I can't offer you milk or sugar, because I prefer to keep those poisons out of my house, but I do have honey or maple syrup as sweeteners."

Choy looked at Tait and then Donicelli before they followed their host into his house.

Is this a trap? Are there security guards inside who will tie us up?

They followed tentatively as he led them through a sparsely furnished living room into a decent-sized kitchen that was dominated by a large, round, maple table, 20-year-old appliances and fake-wood-Formica-covered countertops.

"Where is Mr. Wainwright?" Mason said. "I was hoping to hear from him about when we can expect that story about Ertha."

The three men stopped in their tracks and looked at each other. He hadn't heard? Why would he pretend to have not heard? This "confrontation" was unfolding in an unexpected fashion. How to respond?

Mason was at the sink. "Three coffees?" He continued pouring water into the coffee pot, his back towards them. "I could also make tea." He turned to see if anyone preferred the other beverage. He froze when he saw their discomfort.

"I'm sorry, did I … is there something wrong?" Mason said, looking confused.

"You haven't heard?" said Choy.

"Heard?"

"About Adam … Wainwright?"

"What?"

"He was murdered," said Tait. "The night after he talked to you. In Reno."

"Beaten, tortured really," added Donicelli. "And then thrown in the Truckee where he drowned."

Mason's look of shock seemed genuine.

"The Reno police didn't contact you?" said Choy. "We told them about the story he was working on and about the confrontations with your security guard."

Mason shook his head. "I've heard nothing. This is horrible. I'm so sorry."

The man was delivering an Oscar worthy performance. Or telling the truth.

"I flew down here a few hours after the interview …" he said, as if he were thinking about something. "I prefer this house to the others, quiet, no staff … not many people know about this property … Have the police caught whoever did it?"

"They haven't been looking," said Donicelli.

"They seem convinced he was just a gay tourist killed by another tourist he tried to pick up," said Tait. "Not a priority."

"Or a victim of a gay serial killer, in which case they simply pass along the information to the FBI," said Choy.

"They've been more interested in hassling us than in doing any real police work," said Donicelli. "And we kind of developed the impression this was thanks to you."

"Oh dear," said Mason. "I am afraid you may be right."

Another unforeseen reaction. Choy felt twangs of doubt. Had he misjudged the man?

"Quite a high proportion of our investors have security backgrounds — police, military, intelligence — a fact we pride ourselves on. And I did recently mention to someone quite high up in the Reno police department that there were reporters sniffing around, looking to dig up dirt on the fund. Probably generate some bad publicity, maybe even damage the return, in the short run."

"How long ago was this?" asked Choy.

"The day before our interview," answered Mason. "My chief of security told me …" Again he seemed to stop himself from saying something and instead thought about whatever it was. He shook his head. "I never thought … I apologize."

The three men continued to stare at their suddenly more human nemesis.

"But you don't think … not the police themselves?"

"We have absolutely no evidence to suggest the police were in any way involved in the murder," said Tait. "And I don't think any of us even suspect that."

"Unlike your gay-bashing Nazi wacko religious security guard," said Donicelli. "Him we suspect, and if the Reno cops were at all professional they would have called him in for questioning."

"You are referring to Tom Tennyson?" asked Mason.

"The guy who was in your office when Adam and I waited for you is who we're talking about," said Choy. "The one Adam and I told you about and you said you didn't check into your employee's religious or political beliefs."

"Tennyson. I told him I never wanted to see him again right after our interview," said Mason. "He'd been acting in an extremely unprofessional manner. Uncontrollable rages. I think he is abusing steroids. And now … "

"The guy had two confrontations with Adam," said Choy.

"You have any idea where he is?" asked Tait.

"No. But I may be able to find out. He was owed some back pay, I believe. Let me get my phone and I'll call my assistant."

When Mason left the room, the three reporters looked at each other, each with his own visual indicator of incredulity: Donicelli's hands were spread wide, Tait's jaw dropped and Choy's head pushed back with eyes wide.

"What the fuck!" whispered Donicelli.

"What do we do now?" asked Choy. "Do we confront him with the Ponzi scheme?"

"Not if that shuts him up about Adam's killer," said Donicelli.

"We milk him for all the information we can about this Tom Tennyson and take it to the police," said Tait. "We owe Adam that, right?"

They definitely owed Wainwright that. Although it was strange to think you could "owe" a dead person anything. Kind of like Asian ancestor worship, thought Choy. It makes us feel better to think we will be remembered and honoured when we die, so we remember and honour those who die before us. A comforting logic, even if the dead are dead and cannot, in truth, appreciate our actions. Or give a damn about what they are owed. It's not really about them, but rather about us.

"Alicia, I need the contact information for Tom Tennyson, the security guard who was fired last week," said Mason into his cellphone as he re-entered the kitchen. "And the phone number — better yet you call him and ask him to call me — for the Reno assistant police chief, Damon something or other. As soon as possible, thanks."

He put the phone on the counter and shook his head.

"I feel so darned bad about this."

How could you not like a guy who said, "so darned bad" and was wearing a pink housecoat? It wasn't the first time Choy had gone into an interview thinking he hated someone, but it turned out the interviewee was actually a nice guy. Happened with celebrities a lot. They could have a public persona that made you think they were absolutely obnoxiously disgusting and then you find out they are not like that at all. Or the other way around, famous people you thought you liked but who turn out to be complete pricks. He'd had that happen a few times as well.

What was weird about this guy was how he seemed so much nicer from one interview to the next. He did have an explanation — firing someone could certainly bring out the worst in a person — but, given the circumstances, it would be appropriate to suspend judgement. Give the guy the benefit of the doubt but keep a close eye and a mind open to the possibility that he's a brilliant actor only playing at being a nice guy.

"I really should do something else to make amends, as much as possible in these unfortunate circumstances. What if I offer a reward? A hundred thousand dollars for information leading to the arrest and conviction of Mr. Wainwright's murderer, that might spur the police into action. What do you think?"

"I think that would be a great idea," said Donicelli.

"Very generous of you," said Tait.

Choy merely nodded. Rich people giving money to influence events or make people think well of them had always made him uncomfortable. It seemed so undemocratic, so unequal — pathetic really — like all those "public" buildings named after rich guys who did nothing more than donate money. It seemed such a lesser accomplishment than that of someone honoured for his work. It was all about ego, not about doing a good deed, about demonstrating power rather than trying to make the world a better place, about paying for sins instead of being saintly. If he were advising rich people on how to truly be generous and helpful he'd tell them to pay for the building but insist it be named after someone else; a cancer clinic should bear the name of a selfless cancer researcher; a hospital wing the name of a nurse who quietly cared for thousands of patients over the decades. That would be charity worthy of respect.

"Now, who wants coffee and who wants tea?" said Mason.

3.

It was kind of cool to hang out at Mason's kitchen table shooting the breeze with a rich guy wearing a pink housecoat. He listened attentively and nodded in all the right places as they spoke about the tragedy of Adam Wainwright. He seemed appropriately outraged when they told him the story of Choy's car being sent by the Reno police to Las Vegas. He joined in the wailing as they talked about the death of North American newspapers. They were four buddies, just chilling, enjoying each other's company.

"People think it is easy being rich, but it's not," Mason said, more or less out of the blue. "Not that I'm complaining but having been in the 99 percent for most of my life, it is my opinion that being middle class comfortable is much simpler, much healthier, and a hell of a lot more fun, than being wealthy."

He took a big sip of his black coffee.

"Don't get me wrong, it is not my intention to romanticize poverty — being poor is no fun at all."

He looked at his guests, individually. "Is this a subject that bores you?"

All three indicated their interest and stressed that they were not merely being polite. Choy certainly was intrigued.

"Please let me know if I am. You see, that is one of the downsides of being rich and famous. People listen attentively to whatever you say, but you can never be entirely sure what is actually going on in their heads. I long for the good old days as a simple department head when it was painfully obvious that I was being a bore — yawning, coughing, falling asleep — oh how I miss honesty and plain dealing."

While listening to the woes of a half-a-billionaire was bizarrely entertaining in itself, what was truly beguiling about Mason's performance were his words. They actually made sense. Choy understood and even felt empathy. It would be a drag to think people were only pretending to be interested in what you had to say, or only pretending to be your friend because of your money and power. And what about your children? Did billionaires worry that even their kids only loved them because of their cash? He thought of Ben and Sam and how their love, his love, was unconditional. He had no doubts about that at all; in fact this was the first time he had considered the possibility of someone doubting the love of his children. The very idea was unsettling.

"Now, it could be because of the people I've been spending time with these last few years, I grant you that," continued Mason. "The police and military, 25 watt bulbs illuminating as well as they can in a room filled with bright sunshine. And the "intelligence community" — hell it's only called that because they hang out with soldiers and cops. There's a reason why all three groups focus so much on the chain of command, their only hope for survival is that a couple of links near the top actually have enough brains to find their way to the other end of the bell curve."

He smiled at his cleverness.

"We have no choice but to insist they blindly follow orders — having such people think for themselves would be dangerous for everyone. So maybe it's not my money that makes people act like sheep around me, perhaps my problem is that I'm hanging out with the flock."

"Money and power do change the people around you," said Donicelli. "I've seen it."

"Don't get me wrong, there are perks that come along with the money," Mason continued.

"We saw one of them last week," said Donicelli. "She was gorgeous."

"I'll bet she listened to your every word," added Tait.

Mason smiled. "You boys are fun. No bullshit."

"Oh, I hate to disappoint you, but they're full of bullshit," said Choy.

For a moment Mason was confused, but then began to laugh. "That's a good one."

"We're journalists," said Tait. "How could we not be full of it?"

As Mason's laughter ceased to be genuine Donicelli interjected, "So why do you hang out with the sheep? I mean, if you don't like them and think they're 'baaaaing' yes men?"

For a moment it seemed the darker side of Mason was about to reappear, but instead he let loose another burst of laughter. "You got me," he said. "I admit it, I'm a wolf who chooses the company of sheep instead of his own kind. But who can blame me? The hunting is so much easier inside the flock than out. Putting on the fleece and blending in means that rancher who is the proud owner of a DSR 50 sniper rifle is not out there scoping for me. I get to sleep peacefully at night in my $300,000 rancher instead of howling at the moon in a $5 million mansion across town. I mean what's the worst a sheep is going to do to you? 'Baaaaa' you to death?"

He let out another burst of laughter. Tait and Donicelli smiled, then chuckled along with him for a few moments, but Choy was too mesmerized by the man's over-the-edge performance to do anything but stare.

"Seriously though," said Mason as he looked at Choy. "This is the point I was trying to make last week to your friend Wainwright when he made me look like some simpleton Ayn Rand spouting politician. I am not. Yes, I was part of the 'intelligence community' that I just disparaged and I stand by every word of my analysis. But I was one of those on the far right side of the bell curve and I can assure you I have considered the core and nuances of every political philosophy known to humankind — it was my job for 20 years — so please do not underestimate the subtlety of my world view or my drive to join the ranks of the world's elite."

Choy got the feeling that the man was about to say something important.

"Most people are sheep," continued Mason. "That's a plain and simple observable fact. While Karl Marx and Adam Smith and Frederich von Hayek all came up with elaborate theories to explain why some people become rich and others don't, the straightforward, obvious truth is that most people are sheep and the few who figure this out can easily take advantage of the 'baaaaing' majority. Turns out it is actually rather easy to become wealthy. Turns out all it takes is … well I'm sure you fellows know exactly what it takes because after all you are experienced journalists."

He smiled again, but neither Tait nor Donicelli joined in. Instead they both looked at Choy, who was wondering if Mason had been spiking his coffee with whiskey.

"You don't find that funny? I admit to having a chip on my shoulder, a bee in my bonnet, something to prove when beginning this journey to join the world's wealthiest zero point zero one per cent. And you want to know why? This may surprise you, although it's a classic tale really. I was laid off, made redundant, fired and told I wasn't needed anymore, because my speciality was communism and that no longer threatened our capitalist system. The Reds were dead. I killed them. History had ended. Everyone knew capitalism was victorious, so why the hell did they need a specialist in anti-communist PSYOP? Clearly they didn't. Fighting Muslims was what got the funding; they were the problem. Everyone said so and when I went to a couple of the very wealthy individuals who I had often liaised with during my over 30 years at the company even they refused to argue the case for continuing my employment. You know what one of them told me? 'You were a soldier in the victorious army fighting communism, but that war is over son, and you need to get on with your life.' And then he offered me a job as his chief of security. That's what he thought of me, nothing more than a soldier, a servant, his son and I vowed right then I was going to accumulate more money and more power than he ever had. So I did."

This was a story he had kept bottled up but once shaken it fizzed out like a can of Coke dropped and kicked down a long crowded corridor.

"I proved I could do it, but so what? In the end that's the revelation I had, so what! I proved worthy. I gained entrance to the hallowed halls of extreme wealth but once in there and after spending some time hanging out in the 'hood what did I learn? That my new homeys were just as much sheep as my old crew. Smarter sheep, but still awfully damn 'baaaaaaing' and interested in only one damn thing."

He paused for effect.

"And it's not what you think."

Another silence as he made eye contact one by one with his audience.

"'Do people respect me? I mean really respect me.' That's it. That's all they talk about with each other. Their employees, their government, their country, their friends, their family, 'do they really respect **me**?' Or some pathetic variation on the same theme. It turns out the more money you get the more you worry about what people think about you. You feel compelled to impress: So you pay for a 40-room mansion complete with bowling alley, indoor swimming pool and an entertainment room with a bigger big screen television than the ones in Madison Square Garden; You give some university $40 million to name a building and an entire program after you; You buy a Jackson Pollock canvas for $80 million that looks suspiciously similar to a drop sheet used by your Uncle Harry the housepainter; You attend boring galas to raise funds for one-legged transvestites who suffer from depression. This is what the rich and famous do. And yes, despite this reality, many of them do think of themselves as John Galt, a great individual who has risen far above the collectivist hordes. They fund politicians spouting this juvenile 'I'm rich because I'm smarter than you' transparently self-serving justification for a sclerotic ruling class that impresses all those sheep who really, really want to impress their betters by being the best sheep money can buy. Pretty pitiful, right? And then I realize this is me. I'm that sheep from deep within the flock who desperately wanted to be a leader so he fought his way to the front of the flock, only to realize there is no front, the flock moves this way and that not because of leaders, but because that's what sheep do. We're all sheep — rich, poor, middle class — and our most primal desire is to simply be part of the flock. And that's why we care what other people think, that's why we try to impress."

As he looked at his audience like a Shakespeare character finishing his soliloquy, his cellphone rang.

"Alicia, talk to me," he said, immediately back to being the boss. He listened for a moment before continuing. "Great, email me that address and phone number and I'll forward it to the boys here."

The switch from one personality to another was so abrupt that Choy marvelled at his skill, although he wasn't entirely certain it was a talent to envy. Personality disorder might be a better diagnosis.

"Martin Luther Damon, right," continued Mason talking to his phone. "I knew there was a Damon somewhere. He is? Okay, great. Well then, we should end our conversation. Thank you. We'll talk later."

As he used his thumb to press the end button on the screen, Mason looked up at his company. "Good news, deputy chief Martin

Luther Damon is calling me any moment. I'll tell him about the reward and I'll make sure he and those Reno detectives you dealt with previously see you first thing tomorrow. Nine a.m.? I'm certain they will listen much more carefully this time."

"Great," said Donicelli.

"We really appreciate your help," said Tait.

"Do you all have cellphones?" asked Mason. "Write the numbers on this paper so I can contact you. And here is my private card, with all my contact information."

"Great," said Tait, as he wrote his number on the piece of paper then handed it to Donicelli.

"Is there anything else I can help you with? I really should get back to work."

"There is one more thing," said Choy, looking at his friends and then back to Mason. "Did you know former police chief Wong had concerns about the financial affairs of ZZZFund?"

"Yes," said Mason, after a short silent stare.

"He contacted you about those concerns?"

"Yes. And I will tell you the same thing I told him. Come to a complete understanding of who you are up against before deciding whether or not to proceed."

What did that mean?

"Friendly advice, from someone who likes you," said Mason, opening the front door of his house to let them out.

Judgment

Dear WaylonChoy@yahoo.com,

The evil should fear the wrath of YHVH God. Are you filled with dread? The ultimate destiny of all history will be the establishment of the Kingdom of God upon this earth (Psalm 37:9, 11, 22; Isa. 11:9; Matt. 5:5, 6:10; Rev. 21:2-3) with Yahshua our Messiah (Jesus Christ) reigning as King of kings over the house of Jacob forever, of this kingdom and dominion there shall be no end (Luke 1:32-33; Dan. 2:44, 7:14; Zech. 14:9). When our Savior returns to restore righteous government on the earth, there will be a day of reckoning when the kingdoms of this world become His (Rev. 11:15; Isa. 9:6-7) and all evil shall be destroyed (Isa. 13:9; Mal. 4:3; Matt. 13:30, 41-42; II Thes. 2:8). His elect Saints will be raised immortal at His return (I Cor. 15:52-53; I Thes. 4:16; Rev. 20:6) to rule and reign with Him as kings and priests (Rom. 8:17; II Tim. 2:12; Rev. 5:10; Exodus 19:6; Dan. 7:18, 27).

SAMBA

1.

"What do you think he meant?" said Donicelli.

"A threat?" said Tait.

"All that friendliness and then a threat?"

"'Come to a complete understanding of who you are up against before deciding whether or not to proceed'," said Choy. "Maybe it was a warning that there's a bigger picture we are unaware of."

"A kind of 'head's up'?" said Donicelli. "That makes more sense."

"A warning of what bigger picture?" said Tait. "Who? The cops? The Aryan Brotherhood? If he was trying to help why didn't he just come out and tell us what the hell we need to know?"

"What if his house is bugged?" said Donicelli.

"By whom?" said Tait.

"By whoever it is he's trying to warn us about."

"Mason is not the bad guy?" said Tait. "But a victim? Some sort of corporate hostage taking?"

"Just a thought," said Donicelli.

"A far-fetched one."

Maybe, but Choy always tried to remain open to wild possibilities. Reality had a way of trumping imagination as far as strangeness was concerned. And he too felt that Mason was trying to point them somewhere. A distraction perhaps, but not necessarily.

"You sure there's no tracking device or microphones in the car?" Tait said to Choy, who was sitting in the back seat for the first time.

"I hand built this thing and I didn't see anything suspicious," said Choy. "Unless they put something on it while we were in Mason's house."

All three men fell silent.

Donicelli's persistence in asking to drive had finally worn him down, so Choy agreed to give up the wheel as they headed north on Highway 95 out of Las Vegas. The car seemed to be working well — Joy's mechanic had done a good job —his 287 cubic inch AMC V8 matched with a Twin Stick overdrive transmission simply purred. But the sound was definitely less of a thrill than when his foot was on the pedal.

Even though the temperature was 104, the Slurpee he had bought just before leaving town had lost all of its slush within 20 minutes, and someone else controlled the fate of his most prized possession, the wind and the view from the rear bench seat were wonderful. While not as comfortable as the buckets in the front he had done an excellent job with the upholstery, even if he said so himself. It was even nicer not to hear Doug and DD bickering.

He didn't trust Mason, but also had doubts he was The Bad Guy. Maybe there was some bigger picture. And the way to discover it was through investigating the details. That's how journalism always worked.

Is Joy the one? She's really nice. I enjoy her company. But am I ready?

He'd gotten used to being alone, filling his time working on the car, but now that it was done … Joy said she liked dancing.

Something we could do together.

That was important. What else? Honesty. The truth was he hadn't been a very good husband to Helene. He was boring and too comfortable and a coward and too focused on work and on the kids. He never considered her needs. And the car — he told himself that he was restoring it to prove he could change, to do something new, but that was for him not Helena. She hated the car and how he spent all his spare time working on it.

If I'm going to have a successful relationship with Joy … Don't get ahead of yourself.

Who killed Adam? They had a suspect and might make progress in catching him if the promised help of the Reno police actually materialized. On the other hand, this murder wasn't really part of the story they had started working on. It was more of a distraction from the death of Chief Wong and on that front they had made very little progress, other than Mason acknowledging Wong had had concerns over finances, which they had known already from the files. If Wong had been murdered this was the likely motive for someone to have killed him. Maybe he had found out that ZZZFund was in fact a Ponzi scheme and someone staged a suicide to prevent him from spilling the beans.

"You don't think he came across as a nice, regular guy?" he could hear Donicelli say. "Sure, one with lots of money, but … "

" … [C]lever, I'll give you that," Tait was responding.

"Spill the beans." Where the hell did that saying come from? Tait or Donicelli would know the answer. Derivation of expressions was their sort of speciality, another meaningless subject they could endlessly debate.

He liked them both, even if sometimes they were annoying. Each in his own unique way was a good journalist, but together they were like his maternal grandparents who enjoyed bickering more than anything else in the world.

Was Mason steering them towards some other bigger picture? If so, why? And what bigger picture? A PSYOP? What had Mason told Adam? The point was always planning a few steps ahead. What was Mason planning?

They didn't have enough evidence yet to prove the ZZZFund was a Ponzi scheme. He needed to call Joy and get her to call her brother to see what he had found. Someone needed to fly back to Bellingham to check if there were more files in that storage locker. Someone needed to visit that boiler room operation in Reno. Someone should start calling investors. Kempki's students could do some of this work, if they were interested. Did Adam write something on the list of investors just before he left the hotel on the way to being murdered? They didn't have time to look before the police chased them out of town five days ago. Looking for that list would be a priority as soon as they got to the hotel. The police would want to see that list tomorrow morning.

What exactly should they tell the police? Given Mason's admitted close relationship to the Reno department, they could hardly be entirely truthful. But how could they avoid "spilling all the beans" about their investigation? The cops would ask, "what were you doing in Reno?" and "what was Mr. Wainwright doing before he went out?" and answers to both meant giving up details of their investigation. "Where did he get the list of investors?" "Why are you investigating Mr. Mason and his fund?" "You didn't tell the police in Birch Bay about being in the cabin shortly before the explosion?"

Nothing good can come from talking to the police.

They had been set up. Again.

Mason has outsmarted us. Manoeuvred us into a choice between police help in finding our friend's murderer or keeping the details of our investigation into Mason secret.

The cellphone in his pants pocket began to vibrate. He looked at the number on the screen: 775. He didn't recognize the area code. Certainly not his kids or anyone else from back home. Not Mason, that was 702. He let it go to message. It was problematic to use a cell in a moving convertible with the top down anyway. The other side usually just heard garbled noise because of the wind.

As the phone stopped vibrating Choy noticed a sign on the road ahead. "Report Drunk Drivers, Call …" The number began with 775. Definitely a Nevada number. The state must be split between Las Vegas and the rest. It had to be the Reno deputy police chief or the detectives they had spoken to before. What should they say?

He leaned forward close to Donicelli's ear. "Dominic, could you pull over at the next place we can get something cold to drink?"

He nodded.

"We need to talk. I just thought of something extremely important."

It was another hour before they pulled into Goldfield, which was hardly a place you could "pull into" because it was hardly a place at all: A couple of substantial old buildings from the early twentieth century when it was the largest city in Nevada but which now towered over a highway, an occasional old house, a few newer mobile homes, rutted dirt roads and some rusting remnants of an industrial past, a store, a gas station, a diner and fields of barren high mountain desert pockmarked by collapsed mine entrances.

While the place did not have many amenities it obviously had a working cell tower because as the car slowed along the few blocks of what must have once been downtown Choy was finally able to listen to the message left an hour earlier. It was the Reno deputy police chief, asking him to return the call.

"So what do we do?" asked Choy after he finished outlining their dilemma in the diner where all three men felt safe from listening devices. "We have to talk to the police for Adam's sake, but we risk losing any element of surprise we might have regarding what we do or don't know. The cops will ask for it all."

"Not to mention being arrested for obstruction of justice," said Donicelli.

"You still think Mason was trying to help?" Tait said to Dominic.

"I said he came across as authentic, an ordinary guy. Not that he was trying to help."

"Give him credit for cleverness," said Choy. "We went to his house to scare him and what does he do? Completely takes control of the agenda with his 'oh what a terrible thing happened to your friend' and 'I'll offer a reward' and 'being rich sure is tough'" — all of which we completely swallowed. Three experienced reporters."

Each of them stared in embarrassed silence at the table in front of them as they waited for the waitress to bring their food and for someone to come up with a plan.

"I've got to phone this deputy chief back and tell him something," Choy said minutes later.

"Do you?" said Tait, after another short silence. "Who is to say your car didn't break down somewhere in the desert with no cell coverage or you shut the phone off because of the outrageous bills Canadian cell phone companies charge for U.S. roaming? Or we wanted to consult a lawyer before we talk to the Reno police because of how we were treated last time?"

"Stall a meeting with the cops?" asked Donicelli.

"That's just the first step," said Tait. "Kempki has emailed me. She's talked to her students from the graduate investigative journalism seminar. They all want to help. Some of them are experienced working journalists, taking summer courses towards a graduate degree. She says we have to be careful, but no one is too worried about danger. She says there are steps we can take. Don't know what that means."

"Going over the files, calling investors, that can all be done from campus," said Choy. "And if the students help with any interviews, we make sure no one is ever alone and there's always a cell phone with 911 on speed dial."

"We avoid the cops for a few days and put the full course press on the story," said Tait. "Who knows what we dig up?"

"That's how long we give this?" said Choy.

"What about Adam?" said Donicelli.

"What about him? He's dead."

Donicelli's reaction to these words caused Tait to look guilty and restate his reaction. "I'm sorry. I don't mean to be unkind. But, we can't talk to the police yet. We don't know which side they're on. That's part of what we're investigating."

"Every day we wait, the killer could be farther away," said Donicelli.

"I have a feeling the killer is not very far away and is certainly not on the run," said Choy. "And if he did run, he'd be so far away by now … and that's not on us, that's on the fucking Reno police."

"The point is, we owe it to Adam to find his killer."

"How is it going to help the murder investigation if the Reno cops find out everything we know about Mason and ZZZFund?" said Choy.

"Truth is Adam doesn't care," said Tait, "but if he could, what do you think he'd want us to do? Continue working on the story, would be my guess."

"All of us want to nail the bastard who killed Adam," said Choy. "What's up for debate is the best way of going about it. I like Doug's plan. Let's go see Marianne as soon as we get in this afternoon. For now I say fuck the police."

Donicelli nodded. "Okay, I agree, for now fuck the police."

"Fuck the police," repeated Tait.

The three men smiled and raised their glasses of water to each other.

"If nothing else comes of all this this it will be a great case study for your journalism ethics course," said Donicelli.

Tait nodded. "Maybe it will. 'Police and journalists, allies or adversaries?'"

"It is complicated," said Choy.

"'A Complicated Relationship: Cops and Journalists, Allies or Adversaries' — not a bad title for a journalism textbook."

"And you can charge each J-school student $120 a copy," Donicelli said, smiling. "You should go for it."

"Fuck off DD," said Tait, also smiling.

It felt good to lift the feeling of being trapped. Once again, they had a plan to uncover the truth. And they could tell each other to fuck off with a smile, like journalists everywhere did.

2.

Marianne Kempki was a 64-year-old, second-wave feminist, former reporter with the *Rocky Mountain News* in Denver who left the paper two years before it shut down and five years after winning a Pulitzer Prize for a series of stories on right wing militias that had been sympathetic to Timothy McVey, the Oklahoma City bomber who killed 168 people and wounded over 600.

"Of course we're still interested," she said after the three men outlined everything they had discovered so far, including the two deaths. "I talked about the possible dangers, but no one is too worried."

"You understand that Mason has promised millions of dollars to your university and the administration will freak out as soon as they get wind of you helping us," said Tait, as he helped clean up the remnants of Mexican takeout.

"We're planning on retiring in six months anyway," said Kempki's partner Lucy Parsons, a poet who taught in the Gender Studies program. "So what's the worst they can do? Give us an opening to sue the bastards as our going-away present?"

Clearly not someone close to the administration of her university. Choy liked Lucy, a "woman of colour" who when introduced had said: "Choy? You sure as hell don't look like any Choy I met in Oakland," and then after he explained his background asked him to talk to her class on Gender, Race and Class. "I'm always looking for ways to challenge stereotypes," she explained. "If you tell them your great-great-great-great-great grandfather was Chinese and you dance the samba it will blow their minds."

"Of course this is summer semester," said Tait. "Most of the administration will be on vacation so it will take weeks before they hear anything and if we don't have what we need by then, it won't make a damn bit of difference if they shut the whole investigation down."

"This will be a real opportunity for the class to experience investigative journalism as a team sport," said Kempki.

"I have another 12 days to decide if I'm going to take a buyout or not — move on to something else or stay in the business," said Choy.

"Well I don't know how bad things are in Canada, but it's terrible down here," said Kempki. "Papers are closing, jobs are disappearing, wages and benefits falling."

"At least you guys have more rich people and foundations that fund start-ups which are trying to find new models," said Donicelli.

"Just what we need, journalism more directly in the hands of rich people," said Parsons, who was pouring coffee for anyone who wanted it.

"But we do need to find new forms of funding," said Tait. "The advertising-driven model is most definitely dying."

"How about rich people-free, corporate-free journalism?" said Parsons.

"So long as it still pays well, I'm all for it," said Choy.

"You should try hanging out with young people to get their take on all us old fogies addicted to corporate money," said Parsons.

"Lucy's always been more radical than me," said Kempki. "She joined the Black Panthers when she was 14."

"What do your students think about the future of journalism?" Choy asked Kempki. "I mean why do they want to get master's degrees in a dying craft?"

"To get a teaching job," said Donicelli, smiling at Choy.

"Why don't you ask them yourself tomorrow," Kempki said.

"Why would anyone want a gender studies or an English or a history degree?" said Parsons. "Kids want to learn about stuff that interests them. They want to think about how the world works and how to change it. Why does it have to be anything more complicated than that?"

"Journalism was never taught like other liberal studies programs," said Tait. "It always had an element of hands-on craft about it. Preparing for a job. Almost like going to school to prepare for an apprenticeship. The program I teach in is still very hands-on."

"That's why the Reynolds school hired me ten years ago," said Kempki. "Bring in a real live journalist."

"One with a Pulitzer Prize," said Parson. "What they really wanted was a professor who attracted students. Academia is schizophrenic about real world experience, especially in the liberal arts. On the one hand you get your degrees by analyzing what someone else does, but on the other hand bring in an actual doer and that's who gets all the attention and attracts students."

"All my students aspire to be working journalists," said Kempki.

"Isn't that sad, given the state of the industry?" said Donicelli.

"He owns his own PR and marketing firm," Choy said to Parsons.

"It's called Cultural Hegemony," said Donicelli, smiling proudly.

"In reference to Gramsci?" asked Parsons.

Donicelli nodded. "I'm subverting the system from within. Building a counter culture."

"Really?" said Parsons.

Tait and Choy shook their heads and rolled their eyes.

"And the company is successful?"

"I'm the only guy still hiring," said Donicelli.

"Sad, but true," said Tait.

"Speaking as a non-journalist and an unabashed idealist, the one thing really attractive about journalism is this vision of a reporter as the seeker of truth, willing to afflict the comfortable and comfort the afflicted," said Parsons. "Why would anyone aspire to a job where you get paid to write or say whatever a client wants?"

"Because working people need jobs," said Donicelli.

"But they don't need to dream?" asked Parsons. "Aspire to accomplish something great? Help make the world a better place?"

"You can live a very comfortable life without any of those," said Donicelli. "But try living without a job."

"That's an illusion the system is selling," said Parsons. "And the result is depression, consumerism, alcoholism, drug addiction, born-again Christians, Republican politicians and Donald Trump."

Tait and Choy smiled.

"The best journalists, the best novelists, the best poets, all want to make the world a better place. It's what gives us passion."

"All us second-best, working-class journalists just want a job to pay our bills," said Donicelli.

"It's hard to hold on to that passion for an entire career," said Kempki.

"Especially if you stay at one job," said Tait. "That's what's so refreshing about teaching and hanging around with young people, you get that passion back."

"Exactly," said Kempki. "My experience too."

"Not that I agree with Dominic, but being a professional journalist does mean doing it for money, which means a job, and that means every day, even when you don't feel like it," said Choy. "Even when there's absolutely no passion whatsoever."

"So, maybe journalism would be better if there were fewer 'professional' journalists just going through the motions and more 'amateurs' with passion," said Parsons.

"Except that's what's happening now with all these blogs and I see no evidence whatsoever that journalism is improving," said Tait. "Sure, getting paid, being a professional has downsides, but on balance society gains from having people whose job it is to report on what governments and corporations are doing."

"Except that isn't really what most journalists do," said Parsons. "They avoid stories that offend the rich and powerful. Money buys journalists and all the news rich people want. And why do you think being a 'professional' is necessarily such a good thing? When women get paid to do it they're called whores and prostitutes."

"Oh come on," said Tait. "You're talking apples and oranges."

Choy smiled at his friend's indignation. Journalists could be pretty damn self-righteous when their profession was attacked.

"Am I?" responded Parsons. "Which is more critical to human survival, sex or journalism? Sex, quite obviously. But when you're paid for that …"

She was amusing and thought provoking. Choy could understand why young women would love attending her classes.

"Do you even ask your students to think about who has the money and what power it gives them?" Parsons said looking at Tait and then back at Kempki.

"That's why there has to be a Chinese wall between the newsroom and the sales department," said Tait.

Everyone immediately looked at Choy. "Why are you all looking at me? He's the one who used the racist term."

"It's not racist," Tait immediately replied. "Its derivation is the Great Wall of China. How is that racist?"

"Whether a term is racist or not has nothing to do with its derivation, but rather its intent or effect," said Parsons. "And the argument that you can have an organization which derives most of its money from advertising not be ultimately controlled by the buyers of that advertising is either naïve or a wilful distortion of how the system really works."

"See, she agrees with me," said Donicelli, beaming. "Money buys a flack, but it also buys your so-called professional journalist. We're all part of the same system."

Kempki looked at DD and then at Parsons in mock horror.

"I'm not saying the system is perfect," Tait said, "and I'm not naïve but trying to maintain that wall is the best we can do."

"I'm pretty sure we can do better than that," said Parsons.

"The professor agrees with me and says you are full of bullshit."

"You're missing her point," Choy said to Donicelli.

"No I'm not," he answered, looking at Parsons. "You agree that advertising, PR and journalism are part of a single system that convinces people what to believe, how to act and the necessity of doing more or less what the rich and powerful want them to do?"

"Of course. How could anyone disagree?" said Parsons, shrugging. Donicelli smiled.

"But you use this analysis to justify your working within the system," said Choy "while she uses it to delegitimize the system itself."

"Exactly," said Parsons, turning to Choy. "Thank you."

Choy sensed an ongoing source of irritation in an old lesbian couple. In his experience it was impossible to find two people who saw eye to eye on everything. That was why Joy seemed, well, such a joy. So far they seemed to be exactly on the same page.

Choy was getting tired; the day had been long and tomorrow promised to be even longer. "Much as I've enjoyed the conversation, we should call it a night," he said. "It's getting late."

Tait nodded. Their hosts did not disagree.

"What time are we meeting tomorrow?" asked Tait.

"How about 8:30?" said Kempki. "At the school. If you pull up in front of our building at 8:35 I'll get the class to come out and help carry the files in."

"That would be perfect," said Choy. "We'll see you then."

3.

The 11 students in Kempki's graduate seminar were enthusiastic and demonstrated no fear at all despite the two people who had been killed while investigating the matters they were about to look into.

"If journalists were too scared to investigate murder or fraud or crooked cops what would be the point of journalism?" one young woman said.

"You can't go to the police because they might be involved," said another. "So, if we don't help, who will?"

Hard to argue with that logic.

After two hours going over what had been learned so far, the rest of the morning was spent organizing a plan to move forward and dividing into teams to carry it out. One would look at Wainwright's death, another would be responsible for completing the examination of the files, and the third would be in charge of taking a broader look at ZZZFund, primarily by contacting investors and pretending to conduct a customer satisfaction survey. Choy was assigned to the murder, Tait to the files and Donicelli to the investor contact committee. Kempki and one student would coordinate and assemble an up-to-date visual representation of hypotheses, leads, information gathered and possible links among it all.

Three students volunteered for the murder committee, despite Choy's caution that it had the most potential to be dangerous. After a quick meeting during which the four of them went over the autopsy report, the contact list that Wainwright had been going over just before he was killed and the confrontation he had with Tom Tennyson, they decided to split into two teams, one to check out the CalNeva Casino to see if anyone remembered Wainwright and the other — Choy and Melissa Fung — to look at the area where his body was found.

Fung was in her mid-twenties, a bundle of energy who was less than five feet tall and a former gymnast, apparently a nationally ranked one from the age of 12 to 21, but who had given up the sport and embraced journalism with the same commitment and enthusiasm that had been required of a dreaming-of-the-Olympics athlete.

"I know exactly where we should go next," Fung said after the spot on the Truckee River bank where the body had been discovered revealed no clues. "There's a homeless shelter a few blocks away and I'll bet lots of them hang out by the river. Maybe somebody saw something."

The shelter was a newish building across the street from a baseball stadium. As they approached it a steady stream of mostly younger and middle-aged men, but a few women, headed away from the building.

"Hi," said Choy to the first guy they approached. "My name is Waylon and I'm looking for someone who might have seen something six nights ago down by the river when a friend of mine was killed. Have you heard anything?"

The man shook his head and walked on.

The two journalists split up to speak with as many people as possible. About 15 minutes later, when Choy had entered the building, Fung and a woman of indeterminate age approached him.

"Mr. Choy, this is Faith, she can take us to someone who might have seen something," said Fung.

"Malcolm," said Faith. "He only talks to me, so nobody else knows nothing. Malcolm told me yesterday he saw this really big white guy dragging a smaller white guy with tape wrapped all round him and he was hitting him with a piece of pipe like from when they put natural gas into houses."

Choy and Fung made eye contact. According to the coroner, there was adhesive residue all over Adam's head and hands. And a piece of pipe used in natural gas connections would fit with the report as well.

"Did Malcolm say anything else?" asked Choy.

Faith shook her head. "He doesn't talk much. He only likes me because sometimes I bring him milk and sandwiches. He likes milk and sandwiches, especially egg, but he'll eat any of them except ham. Won't eat no pig at all."

"Do you know if he talked to the police about what he saw?" asked Choy.

"Malcolm don't talk to no police," said Faith. "And I ain't heard nothing about no police asking about this. They're too busy chasing us away."

"Well, let's buy Malcolm a big carton of milk and some sandwiches and you take us to him, okay? Can we buy you something as well?" said Choy.

"I'll take 20 dollars," said Faith, "but don't be giving it to me here cause someone will see. Guys will be coming after me for money and there'll be no end of misery. I'll have to spend the next week with Malcolm cause everybody is scared of him."

On the eight or so block walk Faith told them her life story, which involved growing up in the coal mining region of Kentucky and an abusive husband who got a job at a gold mine in Nevada. The guy beat her up one too many times so she tried to make it on her own working as a cleaner at a Reno hotel but white people couldn't compete with the Mexicans or maybe she got fired because of her drinking and so she'd been living on the street off and on for three years or maybe more. It was dangerous being a woman on the streets so she had to make male friends who would protect her and Malcolm was one of those. He was black and big and people said he could crush your throat with one hand but he had always been kind to her.

"He'll be down by those bushes," said Faith after they crossed a pedestrian bridge onto an island in the river in the middle of downtown Reno. "You won't see him if he don't want you to. I best go talk first. Give me that hamburger and when I wave you hold up the carton of chocolate milk and the other sandwiches."

Malcolm was indeed, as advertised, probably six-foot six and very powerfully built; even though life on the street had clearly taken a toll, he was definitely someone most people would steer clear of. Yet when he spoke he sounded like a child.

Choy immediately understood why this man kept to himself and imagined various life stories for him, but his reporter instinct told him that the truth was more heart wrenching than anything he could dream up. It would be worth gaining Malcolm's confidence in order to learn about his life, but one step at a time. Today he needed to hear about Adam's last minutes.

"Please, tell us exactly what you saw and heard," said Choy.

"The one who died was your friend?"

"Yes and when he died we were working on a story about a very bad man," said Choy. "We were trying to warn other people about what that bad man is doing, but the police seem to be protecting him."

Malcolm nodded. "I've got to hide from the police too. They make me go to that shelter where people try to beat me up and steal my stuff."

"We understand," said Fung.

"You're small," said Malcolm.

"I am," said Fung, "compared to you."

She smiled up at him and he smiled back.

"But I can jump very high and I can do this," she said, doing a complete 360 degree flip from a standing position on the grass.

Malcolm's smile grew larger. "Do that again," he said.

So she did, three times and then ran about ten feet before twirling herself in the air and landing square on her feet.

"She's great, isn't she," said Choy. "But we really need your help now Malcolm. We need you to tell us what you saw and heard the night our friend was killed. Okay?"

He turned and pointed across the island to the bridge that Choy and Fung had crossed a few minutes earlier.

"I think they came from that way and first there was another man, I could hear them talking but I was hiding in the bushes so I didn't see."

"But you did see them, eventually?" asked Choy.

"When they got close and I could look from my hiding spot there was two white men, one as big as me and the other with black tape all round his head and his hands. The big man was dragging the smaller man into the bushes and then he pulled his pants off ..."

Malcolm looked around nervously.

"He did some very bad stuff with that pipe."

"We know," said Choy.

"And then he started hitting him everywhere, until there was no more moaning and then he took off all the tape and dragged the body down there," said Malcolm, pointing.

"Our friend was still alive," said Choy. "He died from drowning."

"I don't know about that," said Malcolm.

"Where did the big man put all the tape?" asked Fung.

"He rolled it up in a ball and threw it in the river after the body started floating away."

"Then what did he do?" asked Choy.

"He walked back across the same bridge there."

"And that's it, that's all you saw?"

Malcolm shrugged.

"You saw something else?" asked Fung. "What else did you see?"

"I was scared."

"I'd have been very scared," said Fung.

"But you're tiny," said Malcolm. "And I'm big."

"Still, I'd have been scared if I were you, seeing something like that."

Malcolm nodded. "People shouldn't do things like that. It's not right."

"It's terribly wrong," said Fung.

"I know that," said Malcolm.

"Did you follow him?" asked Fung.

Malcolm shook his head. "No, I was too scared."

"But you did see something else?"

He nodded. "The next day."

"What did you see?"

"I saw him again looking around the bushes where he did it. He was with another man."

"That's all?"

"Saw them getting into a van."

'What kind of van?" asked Choy.

"Did the van have any writing on it?" asked Fung.

"I don't read so well," said Malcolm, who looked ashamed.

Choy winced as he heard this. So close, but …

"That's okay," said Fung. "Don't worry about it."

"Was there anything unusual about the van?"

"It had a picture on it."

"A picture of what?"

"A hole in the ground with wood around it."

"A hole in the ground with wood around it?" repeated Choy.

"Yes sir."

"A mine?" said Fung. "The entrance to a mine?"

Malcolm looked confused. "I don't know what that is."

"A hole in the ground with wood around it. It has to be the entrance to a mine," said Fung. "There's mine tours in Virginia City. I've seen them advertised."

"A van that advertises a Virginia City mine tour?"

"What else could it be?"

Choy shrugged. "It's worth checking out. How far to Virginia City?"

"I've never been there, but I don't think it's very far. I've read one of those 'what to do in Reno' mini magazines and it said less than 45 minutes away from town."

"So we could drive up there, take a look around and still be back here before dark?"

"I think so."

"Malcolm, are there any other people who sleep on this island?" asked Choy.

"Sometimes Faith, but she wasn't here that night."

"Nobody else?"

"Some new fellas sometimes, but they don't know where to hide and the police they come around every night and chase them away."

"Thanks Malcolm," said Choy. "Would it be okay if we came back later and brought you something else? We want to see what the island looks like at night."

"Chocolate milk is nice."

"Okay, we'll bring you another carton of chocolate milk."

"See you later Malcolm," said Fung.

"Mam, could you do that jumping thing again? Please."

Fung smiled. "Sure." She quickly ran about ten feet to gather momentum and performed a series of aerial twists and turns. Malcolm was smiling. Faith was smiling.

"We'll see you guys later this evening," said Choy.

Judgment

Dear WaylonChoy@yahoo.com,

Do you have any chance of being saved? The Word of YHVH God says no. Salvation is by grace through faith, not of works (Eph. 2:8-9). Eternal life is the gift of God through the redemption that is in our Savior Yahshua (Jesus Christ) (Rom. 6:23) who will reward every man according to his works (Rev. 22:12). Membership in the church of Yahshua our Messiah (Jesus Christ) is by Divine election (John 6:44, 65, 15:16; Acts 2:39, 13:48; Rom. 9:11, 11:7; II Thes. 2:13). God foreknew, chose and predestined the Elect from before the foundation of the world (Psalm 139:16; Jer. 1:5; Matt. 25:34; Rom. 8:28-30; Eph. 1:4-5; II Tim. 1:9; Rev. 13:8) according to His perfect purpose and sovereign will (Rom. 9:19-23). Only the called children of God can come to the Savior to hear His words and believe; those who are not of God, cannot hear his voice (John 8:47, 10:26-27).

CHA CHA CHA

1.

The drive from Reno to Virginia City was mostly up, a gain in elevation of a few thousand feet on a highway crowded with various sorts of "recreational" vehicles — a euphemism for large, rectangular, gas-guzzling temporary dwellings mounted on a truck or van wheelbase.

"Why did a successful gymnast decide she wanted to be a journalist?" asked Choy during a lull in the conversation about who or what they might find at their destination.

"I get asked that a lot," she answered. "Why do people find it strange that a gymnast wants to be a journalist?"

"I don't know. Maybe because one seems so athletic and the other so not physical."

"I was four years old when I started gymnastics and it's like people want to define my life by choices my mother made."

"Did you like gymnastics?"

"You might as well ask me if I liked breathing or not."

"But you quit. You can't quit breathing."

"Younger, better girls were making the national team and I realized there would never be an Olympics for me and my scholarship was coming to an end so I had to pick something for graduate school or get a job."

"But why journalism?"

"I don't know. I always liked writing. There's a lot of waiting around at competitions and I filled notebooks with poems and short stories to keep out bad thoughts. Got pretty good at it, won a few prizes."

"There's lots of graduate level creative writing programs."

"My mother … Let's just say there's a lot of pressure in a Chinese family to be practical, find a job."

"That's ironic given the state of journalism."

"Newspapers, TV newscasts were something my mother had experienced so she knew there must be jobs. But novels or poetry?"

"Well you certainly won't be the first journalist who wants to write novels. Every decent sized newspaper has at least a few of them. But jobs are disappearing, especially the ones that pay well."

"Newspapers still pay you to write while you learn the discipline of doing it every day. That's what I'm after. I don't really care about the money."

"Good for you, but trust me, you will."

"You all say that."

"Who is 'you'?"

"Older working journalists," she answered.

So that's what I am now, an 'older working journalist.'

"Don't let us beat the idealism out of you."

"I won't," she said as traffic slowed near Virginia City.

While the town was small, less than 20 square blocks, tourists crowded the wooden sidewalks on the main drag and clogged the side streets with their vehicles.

Because of the traffic it took almost an hour to find what they were looking for, but when they did it was obviously the right spot to start their enquiries. On the south end of town a few blocks off the main road there was a heavily timbered entrance to an old mine, with a small mill beside it, and a jammed parking lot. A line of tourists snaked from the mill into the mine entrance. If someone had taken a photo or drawn a picture of the mine entrance and placed it on the side of a van for promotional purposes, it would be exactly what Malcolm had described.

After finding a parking spot and attracting a crowd of elderly men who wanted to talk about a car they remembered from their youth, Choy and Fung finally made their way to the mill, which was now a museum and the place to buy tickets for the mine tour. They entered a gift shop, at the back of which was the ticket counter and entrance to the museum. They spent a few minutes checking out what they could while looking at rather tacky trinkets and T-shirts, then went to the ticket counter, behind which were a fortyish woman and a very large man with a bushy beard that made it difficult to determine his age.

"Excuse me," said Choy. "Could one of you help settle a little disagreement my niece and I are having?"

The man stood still as a statue, but the woman smiled.

"I've been visiting Reno where Melissa here goes to university and we saw a van on the street, with a picture of a mine on it, that made us think of driving up here to Virginia City and she says it must be this place, but I am not so sure."

"Your niece has better eyes than you," said the woman. "We have a van that has a picture of the mine entrance on both sides of it and we send it into Reno most every day during the summer to pick up people who want to do the tour."

Choy made like he was disappointed, but then thought of something. "Would you know if you are the only mine tour that has a van with a picture of a mine entrance on it?"

"We're the only one around these parts, I can say that with some authority," said the woman. "I can't speak for the entire world."

"No, of course not. Thank you."

"Are you and your niece planning to take the tour?"

"Yes," said Fung enthusiastically.

"Then that will be thirty dollars," said the woman.

Fung looked at her "uncle' then back to the woman.

"Yes, of course," said Choy, pulling his wallet from his back pocket, while attempting to make eye contact with Fung.

"Thank you Uncle Waylon," she said as he paid for tickets.

"We could have just watched what's going on from the parking lot," whispered Choy as they entered the museum.

"I have a feeling. I don't know why but I think we need to go into that mine."

Choy nodded even though his plan had been to stake out the place and wait for the van. While he was a believer in following hunches, he also suffered from claustrophobia and the thought of being inside a mine with dirt walls closing around him induced a feeling of panic that required consciously monitored breathing to control. He could insist she go into the mine alone, but what if her hunch was right and there was something or someone important inside? He couldn't very well let a journalism student go into a dangerous situation by herself. Besides, the sign said the mine tour consisted of 400 yards of level shaft, so how bad could it be?

A few minutes later they went out the back of the mill building and got in line to enter the mine. Then, when they were within a half dozen spots from the front of the line and Choy's panic level was rising in direct correlation to their proximity to the mine's entrance, Fung tapped his shoulder. As he turned, she pointed to the van pulling up to a parking spot beside the mill. Malcolm had indeed seen a picture of the mine entrance on the side of a vehicle and here it was. More incredible still, they watched as Tom Tennyson climbed out of the front passenger seat and one of the other members of Mason's security detail climbed out of the driver's side.

"That's him," whispered Choy to Fung, but then quickly turned away. "We can't let him see me. You watch what he's doing."

It was very difficult for a person under five feet tall to see over the line of people behind them to the mill building.

"There's eight, ten people getting out of the van," she said, looking to the side of the couple behind them. "They're taking tourists into the museum."

As people were exiting the mine, newcomers were being allowed in. Choy could see a group of a half dozen people coming from the darkness of the shaft and about to enter sunlight, which meant it was about to be their turn to enter. Partly because it was true and partly because he wanted to keep an eye on Tennyson, Choy told the couple behind them in the line: "Please go ahead. I'm feeling a little bout of panic from my claustrophobia and I need to get myself together before I go in. Please go ahead."

He made a show of taking deep breaths as the people behind them in the line entered and Fung kept close watch on the mill building. Eight more people passed them before Tennyson came out the back door of the museum, leading a group of tourists.

"There he is," she said as quietly as she could. "And he's coming this way. We've got to enter now."

Just as she said that, a couple returned to the sunlight so Choy and Fung quickly headed in the other direction. Ten feet in, with only the light from outside at their backs, their irises were trying to adjust to the darkness ahead of them.

"Welcome to the Champer's Mine," came a booming voice from somewhere in the darkness. "First opened in 1861, this mine produced about $80 million in silver over its 80 years of operation — the equivalent of more than a billion dollars today."

Choy and Fung moved towards the voice and quickly entered a space where the shaft widened and twenty or so people surrounded a man with a bushy beard who was lit by a half dozen candles on the floor around him. While keeping a close eye on the mine entrance, Choy scoured his surroundings for somewhere they could hide, as the panic from claustrophobia duelled for domination with the panic from being caught by a murderer. He ran his hands over the warm damp walls to check for spaces hidden in the shadows. Finally, about ten feet behind the nearest tourist, he came across a tiny space, probably an old storage area that might be big enough for them not to be seen and yet give them a view of the bigger room. He grabbed Fung's arm and pulled her towards him as he crawled into the hiding spot.

As the guide was blowing out candles to demonstrate how dark the working space for nineteenth century miners had been, Choy tried his best to control a growing feeling that the walls were closing in on him. Breathe. In and out. In and out. Slowly. As the last candle was blown out the room disappeared into nothingness for a few seconds, but then shapes and shadows did become visible again, until suddenly a switch was thrown and a dimly lit corridor on the other side of the room appeared.

"Okay ladies, gentlemen and children, follow me down this corridor please and pick up your safety lantern."

As the guide said this, they saw Tennyson and his fellow security guard appear from the entrance shaft, each carrying a bright safety lantern to guide their way. Pushing themselves deep into their hiding space they watched as the two huge men waited for the tourists and guide to disappear down the lit mine shaft and then shone their light onto a boarded up section of wall nearby. The guy whose name they didn't know pulled at a board and a section of the wall opened and the two men disappeared, shutting the door behind them. Fung immediately sprang to her feet, crossing the room to the door and motioned for Choy to follow.

He hesitated. This was definitely not part of his plan and he was getting a bad feeling. But he followed anyway. Perhaps it was courage, but more likely he simply didn't know what else to do. He couldn't let her go off on her own.

In a moment they were on the other side of the door, desperately trying not to make any sound that might give them away. Fortunately the two men were walking quickly and were already fifty feet ahead of them, their bright lights easily visible. Fung and Choy followed carefully, staying close to the walls of the shaft, just in case either of the men turned and shone a light in their direction. A few seconds later the light disappeared and the shaft plunged into almost complete darkness. Choy froze, incapacitated by an anxiety that overwhelmed all his senses.

Fortunately, Fung flicked a lighter that produced a flame bright enough to guide their way. She was about 20 feet ahead of him before he could move again, but he quickly caught up because she had to walk carefully to keep the flame burning.

When they reached the shaft that branched off to the right, Fung looked carefully around the corner before extinguishing the flame on her lighter and motioning for Choy to quickly follow. She was fast, quiet and embarrassingly hard to keep up with, but he did his best and they were soon again only about fifty feet behind the two men, whose conversation echoed back through the tunnel.

"Did you talk to any of those geeks working in the computer room?" one of them asked.

"No fucking way," said the other. "They're all kiss-ass liberals who think they're smarter than everyone else."

"Why are they even here?"

"Working on some hush hush project for the Trump campaign. The geeks are some of the best programmers in the country."

"Is it true that the Reverend actually met Donald Trump?"

"That's what he told me. Shook his hand."

As their voices echoed back along the tunnel, Choy stubbed his toe on a loose rock and he almost swore out loud. The men ahead stopped talking and Choy pressed himself against the strangely warm wall of the shaft. He looked ahead and Fung had done the same. The silence was full of a menace that grew as one of the men cast the beam of his lantern towards them.

"Just a rock fall."

A voice that in other circumstances may have caused fright, instead was a relief. After a few second they were talking again.

"I tell you we don't have anything to worry about. Our guys on the force say no one is looking at anything anymore."

"I got a message from the Reverend. Mason is washing his hands of me. He told the Reverend the police were going to reopen the investigation. Those reporters are about to tell the cops about my confrontation with the little faggot, which makes me suspect No. 1."

"So what? There's no evidence. They'll meet with the reporters, listen to what they have to say and then the file will get buried a second time. The worst that happens is you get interviewed. There's nothing to worry about from the cops, our friends will make sure of that."

The two men stopped and once again opened a door that was in the middle of shoring at the entrance to another shaft. Again the tunnel fell dark; again Choy felt a wave of claustrophobic panic; again Fung rescued him with her lighter. He was about to tell her that they should retreat back to the mine entrance and return later, when once again he found himself following her.

This time the door led to a small room with a ladder up through the ceiling. Once more Choy had a bad feeling about following. Once more he dismissed it as a symptom of his claustrophobia combined with a more general fear for his life and climbed up the ladder behind Fung. As he did so he had an even worse feeling about ignoring his bad feeling.

The ladder led to another room that on one end had a steep passageway to another door, which in turn led to a basement with walls made of stone, the foundation of an old building above. There were two very narrow openings to the outside that let in slim beams of light revealing a disused storage area full of dust-covered boxes, various old tools and stairs that presumably led to the main floor above.

They listened carefully but could hear nothing.

"They must have gone upstairs," whispered Fung.

"I can't hear them moving," said Choy, following Fung towards the stairs.

She stepped very carefully on the first stair and it creaked loudly. Choy put his index finger over his mouth to indicate the need for less noise.

At that moment the door they had just come through on the other side of the basement opened and Tennyson stepped through it.

"Well what do you know, it's the fake chink and a real chink," he said, pointing a rather large handgun in their direction.

2.

Using his gun as a pointer, Tennyson directed them back out of the basement into the tunnel system below. In the room with a ladder into its ceiling there was another door, behind which was a long passageway that opened into a brightly lit, cooler large space with a high ceiling. The room had couches, tables and looked like the recreational area of a high tech company. On one of the couches sat the man who had driven the van and accompanied Tennyson into the mine.

"Johnny, I was right, it is the reporter I told you about, the one with the Chink name but isn't Chinese," said Tennyson. "He's got a real slant eyes with him."

Rather than worry about the gun pointed at him, Choy was filled with offence at the racist language. It was like Fung was his daughter and some protective parental instinct kicked in.

"Hey, there's no call for racist bullshit."

The words came out and then he immediately realized how inappropriate they might be, given the man a few feet away with his finger on a trigger, an Aryan Brotherhood tattoo on his hand and who had killed his friend the week before.

"Oh fuck," he said, more or less under his breath.

Fung smiled.

Smiled.

"What's so funny?" Johnny said to Fung.

"Slant eyes? You think I'm in kindergarten and you're going to hurt my feelings? I'm scared of the gun, but not your pathetic insults."

Tennyson took a few menacing steps towards her.

"Tom! You know the drill. We don't do anything until checking with the boss. You're already up shit creek without a paddle. You want a hole kicked in the bottom of your canoe as well?"

Tennyson stopped, but did not look pleased.

"Chain of command. Follow it."

Tennyson muttered as he turned away. Choy realized he had been holding his breath and let it go. The man who murdered Adam opened a door across from them and went inside a room with at least one wall covered with computer screens.

Johnny came closer to the sofa where Choy and Fung were seated. "Everything out of your pockets please," he said, then pointed at Fung's bag. "And I'll need that." He picked up the purse/backpack, placed it on a table about ten feet away and then returned to the sofa with his hand out. Choy passed him his keys, wallet and some change, all of which Johnny also put on the table, then returned to Fung, who shook her head.

"No cell phones?" said Johnny. "Either of you?"

Fung shook her head and glanced at Choy, who shrugged. He often took the phone out of his pocket when driving. He must have left it in the car. But where was hers?

"Stand up please," he said to Fung, then patted her down, careful not to touch her breasts or between her legs. Choy also stood up, his pat down more thorough. "Sit. If you behave yourselves, I won't bind your hands or tape your mouths."

As he went through Fung's purse and Choy's wallet they looked around the room.

"How far underground are we?" Fung asked.

"Far enough that no one would hear you scream."

"I thought it would be cold in a mine but it's warm in the tunnels," said Fung.

"Geothermal vents. If you'd gone on the tour like you were supposed to, you'd have learned that miners had to strip to almost nothing back in the day, because of all the heat rising up from under this mountain."

"That's like the same geothermal companies use to generate electricity?" asked Fung. "I've got an uncle into that. He owns a company with a project up in Oregon."

Johnny finished looking at their possessions and then sat staring.

"So is it? The same sort of geothermal?"

"Yes."

"In my uncle's project they bring up superheated water from deep in the earth to run a turbine." She was one of those people who talked when nervous. "Once you pay for the piping and turbine and all that stuff the electricity is pretty much free."

"Exactly what we have here. Powers the entire town now, as well."

Useful information. Rooms full of computers, their own power supply and working on a hush-hush project for the Trump campaign. If we get out of here
...

To counter the realization that they may not get out, Choy again focused on his breathing.

"My uncle says geothermal, along with solar and wind could completely replace coal, if the government really got behind it."

"Everything the government touches gets fucked up. We did this all ourselves."

"It's another ZZZFund investment?" asked Choy, realizing that, under the circumstances, talking was better than thinking.

"Beyond my pay grade. What I know is we turn on the switch and everything works. A few kinks in the first three months, but it's been great now for the last half year."

"So what's the big project for the Trump campaign?" asked Choy. "All the computers?"

Johnny gave Choy an angry look.

"You've got surveillance cameras, don't you?" said Fung. "That's how you found us."

He nodded.

Tennyson re-entered the room, a sour look on his face.

"You get reamed out again, didn't you?"

"He wants to talk to you."

Johnny smirked as he stood up and headed into the control centre. Tennyson took a seat at the table and stared at Fung.

"If it was up to me ..." Tennyson spoke the words as if they were a threat, then began to quietly sing. "99 journalist scum on the wall — Take one down, smack him around — 98 journalist scum on the wall."

"If it was up to you, what?" asked Fung."

"In a few years you'll all be gone anyways."

"Gone?"

Tennyson continued his display of anger.

"You got something against Chinese people just like you hate gays?" said Choy.

"Rejects, defects and the decadent," he said, quietly angry.

"What?"

"You'll all be cleaned up. This will be a white Christian country again."

"Cleaned up? Like Adam Wainwright?"

"He was warned."

Is that an admission of guilt?

"All the scum will be scrubbed away and the true America will be revealed."

"All shiny and white?" Choy said sarcastically, pushing his luck with a homophobic, racist, steroids-crazed killer. But he had to say something. Racism was so ignorant, so ridiculous, so twentieth century.

"The niggers will have their opportunity to go back to Africa, the chinks to China, the ragheads to India, everyone's got their place," he replied.

"But not the white trash back to Europe?"

"If any of the inferior races choose to stay they will be ruled by us."

"What does that mean? You're going to bring back slavery?"

"The inferior races will bow down before us, as God has ordained."

"The way you made Adam Wainwright bow down before you?"

Tennyson's face went blank for a moment but he recovered quickly.

"This country is falling apart. We will pick up the pieces when it does and rebuild it the way God planned. We have the power, the will and the plan."

"That's what this place is all about?" said Fung.

"Some sort of right wing, racist conspiracy command centre?" said Choy.

As Tennyson smiled, the door to the other room opened and Mason's head of security from that day at Bumpass Hell came out. "We have one of the largest server farms in North America run by electricity we generate ourselves. And this is just one of many command and control centres that the Committee of One Thousand is building across the country. Like my slow-witted brother here said, when this country falls apart we will be the last defence against the Muslim hordes."

"Committee of one thousand? Never heard of it."

"That's the point, Mr. Choy."

"I saw you before at Lassen Volcano National Park."

"Please excuse my bad manners. I am Colonel Jefferson Davis," he said, holding his hand out for Choy to shake. He then looked at Fung. "And you are?

"Melissa Fung."

They also shook hands, each smiling politely.

"She's a journalism student at the University of Nevada in Reno," said Choy, whose bad feeling barometer was soaring to unprecedented levels. "Her entire class is working on this story and if anything happens to us, there will be cops and journalists crawling all over this place."

"Yes, there will be. That's why we must make your deaths look like you were snooping around the mine, went off the designated path and suffered a horrible accident."

Tennyson grinned.

Johnny came out of the open door wearing food handler gloves and carrying a small bag. He pulled another pair of gloves from the bag and gave them to Tennyson. Then he approached Choy. "Hands behind your back."

"Loosely," said Davis as Choy's hands were bound with plastic cuffs. "We don't want any marks."

"You too," said Johnny to Fung.

"Put everything of hers back in the bag," said Davis to Tennyson, "and put his stuff back in his pockets."

Choy felt like head butting the smirk right off the guy's face as Tennyson put the wallet, keys and change back in his pants' pockets, but the man was so tall that at best he could have reached his chin.

"You know where we're taking them?" Davis asked Tennyson.

"The steam room," said Johnny and Tennyson smiled.

Choy looked at Fung. She seemed surprisingly calm. His hands were trembling.

"You got the lanterns?" said Davis to Johnny.

"Two for them and three for us," he replied.

With Johnny in front pulling and Tennyson behind pushing, the two journalists were led back into the system of old mine shafts.

"It's too bad about your car," said Davis. "I would have liked that for myself, and I would have lovingly cared for it, but our cover story requires it be discovered later. Which reminds me Johnny, as soon as we are done with this please go out and remove the antennae from his car."

Donicelli was right. There had been a tracking device.

As they walked through a maze of tunnels that seemed to take them deeper into the earth, Choy tried to keep a mental map of the turns they made, rather than think about dying. But it was impossible not to let his thoughts stray.

'The steam room.' What does that mean?

It was hard to judge time in this environment, but it seemed no more than ten minutes until they reached the spot. It was another large opening that had once been used as a storeroom. At the far end, the room narrowed while still maintaining a high ceiling until it came to a vertical shaft that bisected the space from below. There was a three-foot wide, very slippery 20-foot long wooden bridge that Johnny and Tennyson carefully took them across.

"Put her purse and the lanterns on the floor and take their cuffs off," said Davis, as he waited on the other side. "Tom, please return to this side."

As Tom re-crossed the bridge, Johnny pulled a crowbar from his bag and walked onto the bridge where he turned back to Choy, then knelt down. He easily pried the first 2X6 plank from its supports and let it fall, crashing off the shaft walls below. Then another and another. When all but a few crossbeams of the bridge had been removed, Johnny carefully retreated the rest of the way to the other side, knelt down again, and began loosening the connections where the 2X10 supports were anchored. The wood creaked and then began to shatter as Johnny stood up. While he used his crowbar to push at one side of the bridge's support, Tennyson used his boot on the other. There was a very loud creak before the end of the bridge collapsed, smashing what was left of the crossbeams and supports against the tunnel that dropped into darkness below. Choy and Fung stood watching.

"We are Christians and not cruel," said Davis in a voice easily loud enough to be heard over the menacing gurgling sound that emanated from the vertical shaft between them. "Your deaths will be quick and relatively painless."

He looked at his cellphone screen and then continued.

"In approximately one hour and forty-three minutes you will be cooked by a blast from our very own steam vent that we call New Faithful. Like its namesake in Yellowstone Park it erupts regularly each day, shooting high-pressure steam from deep within the earth through a crack at the bottom of this shaft that opened about one month ago. You best say your prayers and ask the Lord's forgiveness."

Choy almost spoke, but what was there to say?

"Tomorrow or the day after the police will find your car and come to the mine. Our surveillance footage will reveal you entering, but quickly leaving the designated tour area to sneak off on your own. Of course our cameras only operate in the tourist parts of the mine, so the other shafts will be searched. Eventually they will find your bodies and assume you got lost, somehow ended up there when the bridge collapsed behind you. It will be considered a mysterious tragedy."

Cooked like a lobster, this is how I'm going to die?

"Judgment Day will soon be coming for us all." He smiled again as they turned to leave.

3.

Choy and Fung quickly explored their space at the dead-end side of the horizontal shaft. The tunnel ended about 30 feet from the vertical shaft that must have been blasted out to follow a seam of silver-rich rock that had changed direction.

Cut off from any way out.

His claustrophobia had disappeared, overwhelmed by the thought of an inevitable, impending painful death. Instead Choy was frozen, although also overheated and sweaty. As they grew more familiar with their surroundings it became apparent that heat was constantly rising from the vertical shaft in front of them. The walls were damp and almost glistening from the discharge of steam.

A hellish place to die. The depth of Hades.

Actually that thought was amusing in a big picture, post-personal, biblical sort of way.

You're supposed to go to hell after you die, but here I am.

He would never correctly perform the Cha Cha Cha's triple step that so far had defied his mastery. As he sat on the ground watching Fung sniff about like a bunny looking for food, he smiled.

That dance is the least of my problems.

"Mr. Choy?"

He was trying to contemplate the best way to spend the last hour of his life, but a debilitating numbness was enveloping his consciousness.

"I think I can make that jump," she said, looking up at the ceiling of the vertical shaft separating them from a chance at escape. "Do you see that?"

She shone her lantern at the remains of a metal pulley system that was about half way across the divide and six or seven feet above the level of their shaft's floor.

"If I can catch that and spin off I'm pretty sure I can make it to the other side."

The mere thought of such a manoeuvre caused the butterflies inside Choy to scatter in flight, but at least it was an alternative to accepting a bleak and deadly fate.

"You don't know if the anchor is secure."

"It looks secure."

"After weeks of being blasted by steam every day?"

"The bridge was still there."

"Barely."

"What other option do we have?"

None that spring to mind.

"If I can make it to the other side, I saw some long planks. I can put one across and you could walk over it."

Or I can quietly suffer from heat and claustrophobia as I consider death by acrophobia.

"I can do it. I know I can. I've got to visualize it first."

Choy watched as she stared at the pulley, then turned and walked to the back of the room to look at the route her feet would run along. No words of encouragement suggested themselves.

She paced the route a half dozen times, then handed Choy her lantern. "You put one beam of light on that pulley and one beam of light on my path, okay?"

It was one of the rare times he'd ever been speechless. If this was the end of her life, and minutes later his, something suitably profound was necessary, but he drew a blank.

It was awkward to point one light up to the pulley and the other back to Fung while watching her prepare. As he was thinking how ridiculous it was to have a sore neck at a moment like this she began to run. She reached full speed amazingly quickly and leapt towards the pulley. She grabbed it, did a complete 360-degree spin and then flung herself to the other side, landing with about two inches of solid ground between her and the chasm of death.

Holy shit! She did it.

As hope flooded back into his consciousness he found some rather banal words to express the emotion he felt.

"Olympic gold," he shouted. "Better than winning the Stanley Cup, the World Series, the World Cup. That was amazing!"

"Throw me a lantern," she said, all business.

"You think that's a good idea? It could fall and break."

"Maybe you're right. You light my way from over there. We've got to get out of here fast."

Choy certainly agreed with that. He was feeling positive again thanks to one giant leap from a small member of humankind. Amazing how the absence of a future made even thinking seem pointless, but a faint glimmer of personal possibility allowed imagination to became functional again.

With two lanterns lighting her way Fung quickly found a very long 2X10 plank.

"Oh my god, it's heavy. It feels petrified."

"It probably is."

"I don't know if I'm strong enough to do this."

Choy's slender thread of personal possibility was about to break again. If she couldn't do this and quickly, there was no hope.

She should run. She should get out and tell our story.

That was the best he could hope for. Tell his children that his last words were: "I love you."

Then he saw her begin to drag the plank across the 50 or so feet from its current location.

Maybe.

She moved it a few feet and then dropped it, exhausted. It was too heavy.

"Can you point the light over there," she said with her hand out. As he followed her direction, she said: "Rope, a new rope. Someone was climbing in here."

A few moments later she came running to the edge of the vertical shaft with a large coil of climbing rope over her shoulder. "I've got an idea. Keep the light ahead of me." She dropped the rope, went back to where she had just come from and then returned holding a long thin pole. She knotted the rope onto one end of the pole and then grabbed the other end.

She was putting the rope through the pulley.

Does she think I can use the rope and pulley to swing to the other side?

An overwhelming sense of hopelessness returned, along with his acrophobia.

As she placed the knotted end of the pole over the top pulley of what must have once been a block and tackle, she pushed her end of the stick so that it and the rope flew to his side of the chasm. Just as Choy was about to say he was incapable of swinging across the black hole, Fung grabbed the other end of the rope and ran back to the big plank. As she tied it around the end of the heavy board, Choy finally understood her plan. They would use the rope and pulley to help her drag the plank in place. Brilliant.

The girl figured it out.

He had never been good at solving engineering problems, especially ones that required creative thinking in three-dimensional space. His mind was good at lots of things — even his mathematical skills were better than most journalists — but not at three-dimensional puzzles.

It took only a few minutes, using the labour power of two with the help of a pulley to move the board in place.

As Choy grabbed the board to anchor it firmly, he felt a gooey slime that must have developed from repeated steam baths.

Walking this plank over that empty space ... walking the plank. Breathe. Focus. In. Out.

Once again this tiny brilliant young woman came to his rescue.

"Wrap the end of the rope around your chest and tie it off," she said, "so I can help with your balance. And you may want to take your shoes off, because that plank is very slippery."

The crossing, even with shoes tied around his neck and holding her purse, plus two lanterns, proved easy and quick.

When he reached the other side he hugged and then kissed her full on the lips, a hero's kiss.

"We've got to get going, now!"

"Can you remember the way?" Choy asked, as he put his shoes back on. "I tried to pay attention to the route but I don't know ... I'm not very good at spatial reasoning or remembering."

"Follow me."

And so he did. She was hard to keep up with and he felt a little embarrassed that a five-foot gymnast was rescuing him, but he had always tried to recognize his limitations. It was Mr. Bodski, his Grade 11 math teacher, who said something he never forgot. "True brilliance includes recognizing your own limitations." Not that he was truly brilliant, or even aspired to such status, but the words seemed to capture an important truth. His choice was to accept his limitations or to assert some macho sense of "the man must lead." He had learned over the years, mostly from his daughter, that girls can be leaders too and good ones.

The one time Fung seemed unsure of which way to turn, he thought left, but she walked a few steps to the right and said: "This way, you can smell that aftershave from Johnny down here."

While it might have been hard to trust that a girl had a better sense of spatial direction, it was easy to accept she had a much stronger olfactory system, so they went right. And she was right.

"When we open this door," she said after stopping in front of a hoarding, "we need to shut off the lanterns. It's the shaft that leads to the first hidden door in the assembly chamber where we left the tour. Almost certainly they have surveillance cameras there, so we've got to go through it in the dark. And quickly."

"Can you hold my hand?" Choy asked and immediately felt embarrassed. Still, he was reassured when she intertwined her fingers with his and then shut off her lantern.

Once again his trust in her was rewarded as she guided him in less than two minutes into the assembly chamber, only a dozen metres or so from the mine entrance.

"Okay, the final sprint," whispered Choy, kind of hoping some last challenge would come up that he could help this young woman overcome.

Is that sexist of me? Sam would probably think so.

The biggest challenge left turned out to be a gate at the mine entrance, but a simple turn of a knob from the inside opened it.

"We better run," whispered Choy as they looked at the dimly lit, empty — except for the van — yard between them and the mill. "A silent sprint all the way to the car. Okay?"

It wasn't much of a race. Despite her much shorter legs and Choy's not bad shape, she travelled the 200 or so metres in about ten seconds less than him. Not that it mattered, he told himself, because they both made it to the car unscathed and without raising any apparent alarm.

Choy retrieved the key from his pocket, unlocked the driver side, reached over to unlock the passenger door and then ignited the engine he had spent years rebuilding. But they had no time to enjoy the sweet purring sound. They had to go.

Judgment

Dear WaylonChoy@yahoo.com,

I have no fear of you or the politically correct cucks who work for the AntiChrist's one world government. For the Word of YHVH God says: Individual Israelites are destined for judgment (II Cor. 5:10; Heb. 9:27) and must believe on the only begotten son of God, Yahshua the Messiah (Jesus Christ), in whom only there is salvation (Acts 4:12), that they be not condemned (John 3:18; Mark 16:16). Each individual Israelite must repent, putting off the old corrupt man and become a new creature (Eph. 4:22-24; II Cor. 5:17) walking in the newness of life (Rom. 6:4). This spiritual rebirth (John 3:3-6; I Peter 1:23) being necessary for a personal relationship with our Savior. And I have been reborn. Have you?

SWING

1.

Without the tourists and their small apartments on wheels, the trip back to Reno took only 45 minutes. When he found his cellphone on the floor by the gas pedal, Choy briefly considered tossing it away, but it was his personal phone and had cost $700. He did refuse to let Fung use it though. Or even answer the thing as it rang every few minutes. Perhaps the bad guys could track the phone itself, but he decided to keep it turned off until they were somewhere safe.

"I can't believe I lost my cell," said Fung. "I had it at the homeless shelter. It must have fallen out when I was showing off on the island."

They headed straight to the university and the school of journalism building, where despite the late hour, their 'situation' room was packed with everyone from the class, Donicelli, Tait and Parsons.

"Where have you been?" said Kempki as the two missing team members rushed in. "We've been calling you for hours."

"You won't believe what happened to us today," said Fung.

"You won't believe what we learned today," said Tait.

"We found out a few things ourselves, right Melissa?" Choy smiled.

"You go first," said Tait.

Before he could begin, Choy's cellphone buzzed and vibrated in his pant pocket. Looking at the screen, he recognized the Las Vegas number. "It's Mason," he said.

"Answer it," said Donicelli. "And put it on hands-free."

"Over here," said Kempki, motioning to a room that barely fit a small table and three chairs.

"Hello," said Choy as he, Tait, Donicelli and Kempki entered the room. "How are you Mr. Mason? Are you having trouble getting to sleep?"

"Choy?"

"Yes, it's me," he said, pressing the hands-free button so the others could hear.

"Are you okay?"

"I am wonderful, no thanks to the hospitality at your Virginia City facility."

"I just heard about that. Once again I must apologize. I am so sorry."

"Sorry? Sorry that I and a young journalism student are still alive. Sorry your plan to steam cook us wasn't successful. Sorry we found out about the Committee of One Thousand and your right wing, racist, Looney Tunes survivalist command centre underneath the town that is doing some work for Donald Trump's campaign. Sorry we have a witness to the murder of Adam Wainwright. Sorry we discovered the murderer, Tom Tennyson, still works for you despite your claim he was fired. Sorry that you are going down, down, down, you arrogant, thieving, murdering, convinced-you-are-a-demigod bastard."

It felt good to unleash the anger, despite the three other people in the room who looked stunned by what he said.

"I told you there was a bigger picture," said Mason, in a calm, almost soothing voice. "I told you things were not what they seemed."

Choy fought the fury he felt from the faux-friendliness of a man who had just tried to kill him. "Things are exactly like they seem."

"I understand your anger. I understand you think I tried to kill you. I understand you think I am behind some dangerous conspiracy."

"Do you really understand?" said Choy, mimicking Mason's tone as he finally gained control of his emotions. "You say you do, but quite frankly George, I am doubtful. For example, do you really understand the vast amount of evidence we have against you? The company files that prove your financial skulduggery, that demonstrate your motive for killing former Vancouver police chief Wong, your supposed fiancé's father. Do you really understand how a jury will react when a cute little former gymnast testifies that your employees dropped her into the equivalent of a lobster pot then turned on the heat? Or when another jury hears how your security guard brutalized a journalist with a piece of metal pipe? Or when politicians and judges hear about how you and your right-wing police friends perverted the course of justice?"

Choy smiled at his friends as Tait gave him the thumbs-up sign.

After a short silence, Mason said: "Waylon, I need you to listen carefully to what I am about to say. Are you listening?"

"We all are," said Choy, smirking.

Another silence.

"Mr. Donicelli, Mr. Tait and Mr. Choy, you may not want to believe what I am about to tell you, but it is true, nonetheless."

"We're listening."

"You have stumbled into the middle of an investigation."

Kempki put up her hands in the question pose.

"An investigation?" said Choy. "We're well aware of the investigation because we're conducting it."

"A Homeland Security and FBI joint investigation."

The four people in the room looked at each other. Donicelli mouthed the words "holy shit" and Tait shook his head in disbelief.

"I am doing some work on behalf of various federal agencies who have come together ..."

"Bullshit," said Choy. "Convenient, obfuscating bullshit."

" ... [In] a joint investigation into right wing militias and various other groups and individuals who threaten us with terrorist activity every bit as real and dangerous to our rights and freedoms as any foreign Islamist organization."

"I don't believe you," said Choy.

"I can hardly blame you for not accepting my word, but if I were you, I'd check it out. You owe yourselves that. Before you crash a party you may not want to attend, ask Ms. Kempki there to call her contacts in the Bureau."

The three men looked at Kempki. She mouthed the words "how the fuck did he know that" and shook her head in disbelief.

"I don't believe you," repeated Choy.

"That is irrelevant, is it not? Neither a good intelligence officer, nor a competent journalist depends on what their gut tells them. They seek verifiable facts. And I am told you are a good journalist, so …"

"We have verifiable facts that prove what you have done and are doing."

"You may," said Mason. "But to what end? At the request of whom? You need to be checking into the ever elusive, but critical element of any criminal case, motive. And when you do, you will find exactly what I have told you. Verifiable facts."

"You are good," said Choy. "One of the best I have ever encountered. An absolutely brilliant liar."

"I appreciate why you have come to that conclusion and may even be flattered, but certain facts remain … verifiable. You really should accumulate more information before drawing conclusions. I find that often to be a flaw in journalism, or rather amongst journalists. You see a slice of pizza and you say, 'that's pepperoni' but you fail to consider the possibility that the other half of the pie was ham and pineapple."

"What the hell does that mean?"

"It means there is a lot you don't know. For example, were you aware that Ertha's sister Celeste was once her brother Charles?"

The words had a similar effect as the time in Grade 9 he had suited up for rugby and was tackled by a giant Kiwi attending Point Grey Secondary. He was left gasping for air.

"Another verifiable fact you should check out. But I sense we're finished talking, at least until you've had the opportunity to confirm the veracity of what you now believe are mere obfuscations."

Celeste was once a man?

"So good-bye, for now, Waylon. Call me at your earliest convenience."

All that is solid is now air. Where did those words come from?

Choy couldn't remember but he felt their truth.

Celeste was once a man. What did that even mean?

"Wow," said Donicelli. "You think he is telling the truth? Homeland Security ..."

"He's an expert at getting into your head," said Tait.

"Are we up to this?" said Donicelli. "Jack Bauer and all that shit? I don't know."

"Do you really have a contact in the FBI?" Tait asked Kempki.

She nodded. "I could call tomorrow morning, early."

"What time is it?" said Tait.

"Almost midnight," answered Donicelli.

"Are you okay?" Kempki said to Choy.

He looked at her but didn't completely register what had been said. This had been the most unsettling day of his life.

"Celeste was once a man," he said.

A woman I dreamed of swinging across the dance floor with.

2.

Mason is lying. Those two young men who flew to Bellingham found more ZZZFund files in the ceiling. I fell for a woman who was a man.

These three thoughts were the bacon, turkey and tomatoes in his club sandwich of stress that kept him awake for what remained of the night. The darkness of the tunnels, the smell of the rock and steamy damp air, believing he was about to die, the shutting down of hope, the honest simplicity of Malcolm and the realization that his life could be in danger because Mason now knew there was a witness, understanding he was saved by a four-foot eleven gymnast who was there because … in the end he was very, very lucky — these were the toasted bread, butter, lettuce, mayonnaise, salt and pepper that made up the rest of a meal that remained unfinished at 7 a.m. when Choy phoned Celeste.

"Waylon," she/he answered.

"Celeste," he said, but then the words and the very concept of the question he needed to ask escaped him.

"Have you learned the truth?" she asked.

This sent his wayward brain spiralling further down another vertical shaft to hell.

Why am I calling?

"About my father?"

Police Chief Wong.

"We don't have absolute truth yet that he was murdered," Choy heard himself say.

"You mean 'proof'? You don't have absolute proof yet that he was murdered."

"What did I say?"

"You said truth," said Celeste.

"You said truth," said Choy.

His silence was because he was in shock and words seemed inadequate to express what he was feeling. Hers?

"Is something wrong?"

"I almost died yesterday. If it hadn't been for a tiny gymnast who saved my life."

"Is she beautiful?"

"Very beautiful. The most beautiful person in the whole world."

"I see."

"I don't," said Choy. "I thought I did, but now I don't."

"Please tell me what's wrong."

"Did you used to be a man?"

"I have never been a man."

What did she/he mean by that?

"What did my sister tell you?"

"Your sister told me nothing."

"Who told you then?"

"George Mason, who may or may not be the one who killed your father, who may or may not be the one behind the killing of my friend, who may or may not be the one who tried to have me killed, who may or may not be the one behind everything that has happened since I met you."

"He was my father's boss."

"And your sister's. A fact you never told me. And he may or may not be her fiancé as well. Did you know that?"

"I'm sorry," she said.

"For what?"

"For not telling you everything."

"Which everything?"

"Everything."

"Were you born with a penis?"

There, it came out.

"Yes."

So Mason was telling the truth, about at least one thing.

"Is that important to you?" she said, her voice at least still beautiful. "What I was born with?"

Is it?

"There are many things from my childhood I haven't told you about," she said.

This is undoubtedly true, but irrelevant. Or is it?

He could see her point of view, even though he would have preferred not to. He could see that the fact of having been born with a penis was not something a woman would just blurt out on a first date. You'd want to get to know someone better first.

Why am I doing this? I have no reason to be sympathetic. Empathy is a curse!

"Are you angry with me?"

"Yes," he immediately replied, but then realized he wasn't sure. "I don't know, maybe. I'm confused."

"I understand. I've spent most of my life confused."

"I thought it was impossible for identical twins to be born different genders," he said.

"The doctors said it was a hundred million-to-one chance, but I always knew I was the same gender as my sister."

I have every right to be upset. Don't I?

She used to be a he, or at least looked like a he.

A he, not a she!

Or at least somewhere in between. What did it mean that a woman was trapped in a man's body? Or vice versa?

This is what they mean when they talk about non-binary.

Maybe yes-no, on-off data is less useful than we're taught as we grow up. Good-bad, big-little, child-adult, girl-boy — these are all useful categories, to a point, but reality is more nuanced, less black and white and more a palette of vivid and subtly different colours. Maybe it's childlike to insist the world around us must fit into neat, easy-to-define categories.

"Waylon, I am sorry. I used you because we needed someone to look into the death of our father and for that I am truly sorry."

"We?"

"My sister and I."

And Mason? Did all three of them plan this?

"I know it was wrong but I am weak and defenceless and you seemed so strong."

Confusing. For me and her.

"Was it hard? To go through the sex change operations?"

"I never changed my sex. I changed by body."

Her answer made him feel even more sympathy and pity. What was the difference between the two? Pity was less honest — sympathy plus shame. And why should he feel shame? For her? One could argue what she did was brave.

The shame is mine.

He was ashamed he had fantasized about a woman who wasn't … what?

She felt good when I touched her and that makes me feel ashamed. My problem, not hers.

"I'm not mad at you. I was, but I'm not anymore and I'm sorry I was."

"Thank you," she said. "Can you still be my friend?"

"I don't know. Maybe, but I don't know."

"The people who are listening, or may be listening, they already know who you are so we don't need to fool them anymore. Is that right?" said Celeste.

"Yes."

"So we can end our little charade because it's of no more use?"

"Yes."

"Did someone kill my father?"

"Probably, but we don't know for sure. We have accumulated enough evidence to force the police to at least consider the possibility he didn't commit suicide. His files, the ones in Bellingham, strongly suggest that ZZZFund is some sort of financial scam, most likely a Ponzi scheme, and your father was about to take that information to the police, if he hadn't already."

Should I tell her the truth?

"And it may have been the police who killed him. Your father was being honest, but there are some policemen who didn't like that honesty."

"He was a good man."

"Yes."

He didn't mention the additional files that the two students would be delivering soon. There was probably nothing anyone listening could do now, but why take the chance?

"A good man but I caused him so much pain," said Celeste, quietly crying. "I hurt him deeply. He so much wanted a son and I …"

Uncertainty over your gender must be the ultimate painful experience.

"He hated me. The real me. I should have lied, kept up appearances. All sorts of people do."

What can I say?

"If he committed suicide, I know it was because of me," the radio waves bouncing from tower to tower all the way from Vancouver carried her pain as well as her voice. "If he committed suicide I don't know if I can live with myself. This … everything is so hard."

She was sobbing.

He had phoned to express his anger and now all he felt was empathy. Life could be cruel and painful. Worse, the burden was not shared equally, but rather visited upon an unfortunate few.

"Please, I need to know," she said.

"I understand."

"You'll find out for certain?"

"Yes."

"Promise?"

How can I promise something that might not be within my power?

"I promise to do all I can," he said and felt bad because it was not good enough, so he changed the subject. "You told me that first day we met you have a friend who is an expert in electronic surveillance?"

"Yes."

"Do you think this friend might be prepared to help me?"

"Yes."

"Can you ask him or her to contact me?"

"I will."

The silence suggested their conversation was over.

"Thank you and I'm sorry," she added. "The position I put you in. It's not fair. You almost lost your life for me."

For her?

The truth was more complicated than that.

"And now I ask you for more, but I don't have anyone else."

It's my story now. It belongs to me and to all the other journalists working on it.

"You shouldn't blame yourself. You put me on a path to a good story. That's what I do, write stories, sometimes about bad people. To do that requires gathering information, chasing leads, going where the story takes me, even putting myself at risk. I'm a journalist and it's what we do."

Fear, self-doubt, bad guys, a night without sleep were nothing compared to the power of a real journalist chasing a good story.

Bullshit.

Which made him think of something else.

"I need to ask you two questions before I go back to work and it's very important you answer them honestly."

"I understand."

"You need to think about this very carefully before you answer."

"Okay."

"Is there any possibility that your sister could have participated in or known about the murder of your father? That's the first question. And the second is, can I trust her?"

3.

Choy walked the 15 or so blocks from the Hotel Eldorado to the journalism building on the campus of the University of Nevada. He felt safer now that he had confronted Mason with the information from the files. Whoever was behind the murder, or murders, would know their scam was about to be exposed and it was too late to do anything about it, so what would be the point in killing someone else? Their most likely next move was to run.

He called Joy to tell her what happened and it felt good to hear her concern. He also told her about finding the new files and that they would be sending digital copies as soon as possible to her brother.

The room was once again full when Choy entered it about 10 a.m., minutes after Jeremy and Frank returned from Bellingham with a six-inch thick file folder full of papers that Chief Wong had indeed hidden in the ceiling of the storage locker.

"Look what they found, exactly where you said it would be," said Tait. "Jeremy's uncle is an Alaska Airlines pilot, so he can fly for cheap and yesterday him and Frank volunteered to go up there."

"Have you looked through them yet?" asked Choy.

"Copy, scan, send and then read," said Kempki, who grabbed the file folder from Tait's hands. "That's the protocol."

"Why?" Tait asked a student standing beside him.

"Priority No. 1 is to protect our information," said the young woman who Choy thought might be named Kelly.

"Speaking of protection, where's Melissa?" asked Choy.

Kempki pointed to the room where he talked to Mason last night, or actually earlier that morning.

"Can you please accompany me."

She nodded and they headed to the room.

"Melissa?" said Choy.

She turned, smiled and threw her arms around him.

"Thank you," said Choy, as they hugged. "Thank you again for saving my life."

"I feel like we're best friends or that you really are my uncle."

"How did you sleep?"

She shook her head.

"Me neither, not a wink," said Choy. "I'm dead, but we need to do something, you and I, right now. We need to get Malcolm on a bus out of town. Somewhere safe."

"Who is Malcolm?" asked Kempki.

"The witness to Adam Wainwright's murder."

"A street person," said Fung. "Simple and very sweet."

"And if we can find him so can Mason's guys."

"We still don't know if they are Mason's guys or not," said Kempki.

"We need to get Malcolm somewhere safe until we figure out who is trustworthy. Right now I'm scared to even tell the cops about him."

"Will he go?" said Fung. "Seemed very independent and likes living outside."

"He'd go if you were to take him and said there was lots of chocolate milk."

"I was thinking of going to the island anyway to look for my phone," she answered.

"A place where he could stay outside and drink milk," said Kempki. "How about an organic dairy farm?"

Fung and Choy looked at each other and nodded.

The only place better than an organic dairy farm would be a dairy farm in a cacao plantation.

"Chelsea's parents," said Kempki. "Let's go ask her."

As Kempki and Fung left, dizziness overcame Choy and he had to sit down. Normally an excellent sleeper, his body didn't cope well when he didn't. He shut his eyes and the spinning grew worse, so he opened them and tried to focus on a single spot, a plastic anchor in the wall across from him. The image of a playground merry-go-round, with Celeste on one side and Mason on the other, spinning faster and faster so one face then the other appeared, disappeared, appeared, disappeared. He shut his eyes again and this time thought of Ben.

If he were gay, or if he were a woman trapped in a man's body, how would I deal with it?

"Waylon, Waylon, wake up."

It was Tait's voice. "Wake up. Kempki is talking to her FBI source, we've looked through the new papers and we're going to have a meeting."

"I fell asleep? How long?"

"Over an hour."

He needed a lot more.

"There she is, off the phone," said Tait, walking into the bigger room.

Choy followed, struggling to return to a state of at least semi-consciousness.

"You want a coffee?" asked Tait.

He nodded his head.

"Okay, team leaders, a meeting," said Kempki, pointing back to the room Choy had just come out of. "The rest of you, keep at what you're doing. We'll have a general meeting to update everyone as soon as we're done."

Donicelli, Tait and Choy sat as Kempki looked troubled by what she had just learned.

"Tell us," said Donicelli. "I can't stand the suspense."

"My source confirms what Mason told us. Homeland Security, in cooperation with other agencies is currently conducting an operation designed to infiltrate right wing militias and other like-minded groups and ZZZFund is somehow involved."

"What does that mean, involved?" asked Donicelli.

"I asked that very question, but that was all the information my source was able to obtain."

"Did you ask directly if Mason was working for the government?" said Tait.

"Yes, I did, but that was all the information … "

"'Your source was able to obtain'," said Tait.

"I did ask if it was plausible that Mason was working for the government and my source answered, 'it's not implausible'."

"It's not implausible," repeated Tait.

"The fucking bastard is lying," said Choy, with more emotion than was appropriate.

His roommates stared at him for a moment, as if they "understood" his anger, but were embarrassed by it.

"About what exactly?" said Donicelli.

"About everything."

"How can you tell when Mason is lying?" said Donicelli.

"When he opens his mouth," said Tait.

"But that doesn't really help us, does it?" said Kempki. "Telling the truth, always lying, effectively what's the difference?"

"The key to understanding Mason is understanding the world of public relations," said Donicelli. "Psyops-PR, he has spent his entire working life coming up with what to say to sell whatever it is he has been employed to sell. He doesn't even know what the truth is anymore, if he ever did. He's a burned-out flack. For him, everything is a campaign. Everything is for effect. Probably even what he tells his girlfriend in the bedroom."

"Very good DD," said Tait.

"I'm still not sure where that gets us," said Kempki.

The thought of Mason talking to Ertha in the bedroom intrigued Choy.

What did he say? What did she say?

"Let's get back to what we've learned in the past 24 hours," said Kempki. "Where exactly are we at?"

Tait and Donicelli nodded. Choy's thoughts remained elsewhere. He would listen, but only really pay attention if he heard something useful.

"Me first," said Donicelli. "Well, we've talked to 63 investors from the list and all but two of them are extremely happy with how the fund is doing. But here's the thing, we've been asking them some questions about the fund's reporting, are they satisfied with it, and if they have ever contacted the fund to ask a question or arrange cashing out and are they satisfied with that experience, but none of the 61 have had any contact with the fund, except for reading the investment reports."

"So, the basis of their satisfaction with the fund is solely the reports they have received about how well it has been doing?" said Tait.

"Exactly," said Donicelli.

"And the two who were not happy?" asked Kempki.

"Both had contacted the fund to cash out, both were trying to buy property, and both were unhappy about how long it took to get their money."

"Did they eventually get their money?" asked Tait.

"One did, but the other is still waiting."

"Fits the Ponzi pattern exactly," said Tait.

Donicelli nodded.

"Excellent progress," said Kempki, who then looked to Tait.

"Where to begin? Well, we've had less than an hour to go over the new documents, the ones that Chief Wong hid in the ceiling, but what we've seen so far is explosive. There's a stack of printed email correspondence between Wong and Mason about the Committee of One Thousand. Based on a quick scan, it seems that Wong had discovered tens of millions of dollars were being skimmed from the fund to the Committee and confronted Mason about it. There's one email I did read completely that's about Wong being called a 'chink" by someone from the Committee."

"How does Mason respond?" asked Kempki.

"At first he's denying or pooh-poohing everything, but then as Wong cites more and more proof, he starts saying he'll look into it and asks for details and 'I'll get back to you' and then more stalling, near as I can tell."

"So we know for sure that Mason has been covering up for this committee for some time?" said Kempki.

"Absolutely, for months."

"Which certainly would give him a motive for murdering Wong," said Choy.

"Or for someone from the Committee of One Thousand," said Kempki. "And there's other possible explanations. Like, Mason is working for the government, and they are not done their investigation, so that's why he was stalling. Someone else finds out about the emails and kills Wong. Or Wong realizes the hopeless hole he has dug himself into by being involved with the fund and commits suicide."

"What about the rest of the new stuff?" said Donicelli.

"I'm sure there's a lot more details but we need more time," said Tait.

"But the bottom line is we already have both correspondence and documents that show ZZZFund is a Ponzi scheme, set up by some wacko right wing racists spouting religion to fund their activities," said Kempki.

"I don't know if we have proof that the 'wacko right wing racists spouting religion' set up the fund for that purpose or whether at some point they were offered its use," said Tait. "Or took it over."

"Okay, but we do have proof money has been diverted to these groups?"

"Yes."

"It's certainly enough to get the police involved," said Kempki.

"Except that the police are already involved," said Choy. "As members of the Committee of One Thousand, as investors in the fund, and on the job investigating the right wing militias."

"What proof do we have that cops are members of the Committee?" said Donicelli.

"Based on his emails, Chief Wong certainly thought so," said Tait.

"There's a lot of white supremacist groups that target police," said Kempki.

"And Davis, that guy who was in the mine trying to kill me and seemed to be Mason's chief of security back at Bumpass Hell, I'm pretty sure he said something to that effect as well," said Choy. "At a minimum we have to consider the possibility."

"So we don't take this to the police," said Kempki. "Not yet."

"We continue working," said Tait. "Finish going through the files. We should be done by the end of the day."

"Now that we know they know we're investigating, I'd like to go check out that boiler room," said Donicelli. "Is it still operating or has it been shut down? If it's been shut down …"

"They will be disappearing," said Tait.

"Which would be a reason to give what we've got to the cops as soon as possible," said Kempki.

"To cops we can trust," said Choy.

"I'll work on that," said Kempki.

The three of them looked at Choy.

"You look terrible Waylon," said Donicelli.

"Maybe you should sleep," said Tait.

"Maybe I will go back to the hotel for a nap," he answered.

"Good idea."

Judgment

Dear WaylonChoy@yahoo.com,

The sins of the race traitors are greater than the mud people who have no souls that can be saved. You must be baptized in water by immersion according to the Scriptures for all true believers; being buried into the death of Yahshua the Messiah (Jesus Christ) for the remission of our sins and in the likeness of His resurrection being raised up into the newness of life (Rom. 6:3-6). Baptism being ordained of God a testimony to the New Covenant as circumcision was under the Old Covenant (Col 2:11-13). Yahshua the Messiah (Jesus Christ)is our only High Priest (I Tim. 2:5; Heb. 3:1, 6:20, 7:17, 24-25) and head over His body of called-out saints, the Church (Rom. 12:5; I Cor. 12:12, 27; Eph. 1:22-23, 4;12, 5:23, 30; Col. 1:18, 24). His bride, the wife of the Lamb, is the twelve tribes of the children of Israel (Isa. 54:5; Jer. 3:14; Hosea 2:19-20; Rev. 21:9-12). Are you ready to be forgiven?

QUICKSTEP

1.

Fortunately the maid had already cleaned his room, so when Choy returned, sleep came easily and quickly.

His slumber was sound, but he did dream. Jefferson Davis from the mine was in his room, smiling menacingly, but Melissa Fung, the tiny perfect gymnast, called an ambulance to rescue him and the paramedics lifted him onto a stretcher, enabling his escape down the hallway, into an elevator. The bad guys were chasing him, but the paramedics made it out of the building and into an ambulance that sped away, siren on. They drove to an abandoned hospital, except that it wasn't really a hospital and the vehicle wasn't really an ambulance. It was a 1965 AMC Ambassador 990 convertible, painted to look like an ambulance and the building was an old casino with a neon "emergency" sign, just like a hospital.

When Choy woke up he was no longer on his bed in his hotel room. Instead there was a long plush sofa beside him — perhaps he had fallen off — his hands and ankles bound together by tape. As his brain slowly rebooted, bits and pieces of the surroundings came into focus. There was an old "emergency exit" sign sitting on a shelf behind the sofa. There was a line of slot machines as far as he could see in both directions, old ones with no flashing lights, turned off, in a dimly lit room with a high ceiling.

"Hello," he said, weakly at first, then louder. "Hello."

The sound of his voice suggested a large room, a warehouse or maybe an abandoned casino. He'd heard Reno had a few of those. After about the sixth ever-louder "hello" a huge head appeared, hovering above him like the angel of death, with an index finger pressed against his mouth to indicate quiet. It was Tennyson — not the poet, but the thick-necked assassin.

"If it was up to me, I'd put my hands around your throat and squeeze until I watched life disappear from your face," he said. "Please give me trouble so I can justify shutting you up forever."

Seeing Adam's murderer again produced an adrenaline-fueled state of hyper-consciousness.

"Does nobody love you? Is that why you're so full of anger Tom?"

The words were a purposeful incitement, appropriate if you wanted to show no fear to a bully, or had a death wish.

"The Lord fills his servants with a righteous fury," said Tom, as he began to remove the tape from Choy's ankles.

"But why do you hate me?"

"You are the seed of Satan, through Cain, an anti-Christ."

"Me? Why do you say that?"

"Race mixing is the work of the devil."

Choy remembered a crazy email in his junk folder that he had started to read 10 days or so earlier. Was it Tom who sent it?

"Your hands are soaked in the blood of our saviour."

Choy felt himself lifted off the floor, two strong, angry hands pressing hard against his upper arms.

"Walk."

As he walked Choy could see the shadowy outlines of a large room that had chandeliers, mirrors and a circular staircase to somewhere. The only light came from the direction they were headed. Manoeuvring around various bits of casino memorabilia stacked on scattered shelving or lying on the carpeted floor, they came to an opening, surrounded by upended blackjack tables where three tightly focused, bright beams of light came together to form a small circle on the floor.

Tennyson placed him on the illuminated spot. "Wait here. Don't move."

Choy strained to see what was going on. The contrast of brightness shining on him and darkness beyond was disorienting.

"Mr. Choy," came a woman's voice from the darkness, "you don't look Chinese at all."

"There was a mix-up at the hospital where my mother gave birth, but by the time the administration discovered it, I was eight months old and my family decided to keep me."

"Like all journalists in the decadent liberal media, you are full of shit," said the voice. "But at least modestly creative, amusing shit."

"You're doing this voice out of the darkness thing so I can't identify you?"

"Perhaps."

"Well, that's not a good sign," said Choy, even though he did not have a bad feeling about what was about to befall him. "But I'm guessing if you wanted to kill me it would have been easiest to do it quietly in the hotel room."

"That was the original plan, but I was convinced otherwise."

"Good to hear."

"I was convinced you may be more useful alive."

"An opinion I most definitely share."

"A case was made that our self-interests may, for the next while, coincide."

"Well, a heartfelt thank-you to whoever did the convincing."

"Easy stallion, don't get too excited about your continued existence just yet. I may change my mind."

"For some reason it doesn't feel like that," said Choy, amazing himself with a chutzpah he seldom felt. "And that's coming from a man who faced certain death yesterday."

"You're a journalist? With a major Canadian newspaper?"

"For now anyway. I'm considering whether or not to take a buyout. The business just isn't what it used to be."

"What if I could offer you an exclusive interview?"

"With?"

"The leader of the Committee of One Thousand."

"Hardly a well-known group."

"A state of affairs we have preferred, until now."

"Tell me exactly what this committee is."

"The coming together of various religious and political groups in America to form a coalition, an alternative to the corrupt form of politics that currently dominates this once great country."

"What sort of religious and political groups?"

"Christian, states' rights, white nationalists, pro-life, family values, constitutional militias, sovereign citizens …"

"Far right fringe groups?"

"Left or right are labels imposed by the Washington liberal media establishment to control us, but you can call us the alternative right. The people who we wish to attract are those who care deeply about the future of our country."

A coalition of right wing crazies trying to go mainstream? That's a good story. And what is my other choice? Death.

"I'd be very interested in doing such an interview."

"And how would you react if I told you that the method of bringing you here was all part of the security protocol that the leader of the Committee must insist upon?"

"I'd say you were probably lying, but us journalists can live with a little of that if it gets us a good story."

"You are amusing. And more important, not American, with a name that, under the circumstances, might be useful."

What is she saying? Her right-wing racist fruitcakes would like to have a Canadian reporter with a Chinese name interview their leader. Intriguing.

"If you're asking me would I agree not to file a complaint with the police about being kidnapped if it turned out I wasn't really kidnapped, but rather just carefully and creatively brought to an interview site to speak with someone who is concerned about his security, then the answer would be yes," he said.

"I do appreciate your understanding."

"Of course this agreement does not apply to what happened at your mine in Virginia City yesterday," said Choy.

"I have no knowledge of the events you are referring to. And I have no mine in Virginia City."

"Okay. But perhaps you should inform Mr. Tennyson, Mr. Davis and the guy named Johnny that this deal only applies to our interview today."

"People are responsible for their own actions, or their failure to carry out instructions, as the case may be. This is understood by everyone who knows me."

"So long as we are clear," said Choy. "So when and where do you want to do this interview?"

"No better time than now."

"Now?"

"Yes please."

"With my hands taped behind my back? And without the tools of my trade?"

A few seconds later Tennyson appeared out of the darkness, made eye contact for a moment, which Choy interpreted as signalling more anger, and then began removing the tape.

"So, you don't get to kill me," said Choy. "Does that piss you off?"

Tennyson glared as Choy rubbed his hands together to restore his circulation. Johnny appeared, carrying a folding card table that he opened and placed on the floor, just outside the circle of light.

"Here's Johnny!" said Choy, having fun despite the precarity of his position.

Tennyson reappeared to put a familiar backpack on the table and move it into the circle of light.

"I trust you have all the tools that a journalist needs in your backpack?" the voice said.

As Choy looked in the pack to discover his phone, digital recorder, notepads and pens, Johnny reappeared with two chairs that he placed on either side of the table.

"I do believe I am good," said Choy.

"Please sit down and make all the necessary preparations."

Choy placed an open notebook on the table in front of him, checked that the pen had ink, looked at the screen of his phone to make sure it had sufficient power, held the recorder near his ear and played back a snippet of a previous interview.

"Everything is in working order?" she asked.

"Yes, I'm ready," said Choy. "Is the leader of this committee going to join me?"

"I am."

A slender, well-built blonde, wearing highly sexualized clothing appeared from the darkness. She looked familiar. Choy had definitely seen her before. But where? Then he remembered. It was the woman who had stepped off the helicopter in the parking lot to Bumpass Hell. It was the woman they thought was a high-class hooker.

2.

"You're the leader of the Committee of One Thousand?"

"Does that surprise you?"

"Why would it?" said Choy, avoiding the truth. "Am I allowed to take pictures?"

She definitely was the woman Wainwright had said was a high-end prostitute.

Neither Choy, Tait nor Donicelli had challenged the assumption, because of the way she looked. They were blinded by stereotypical male perception, which allowed her to hide in plain sight.

Why had Mason taken her to the park? Maybe she had taken him. Maybe she is the 'bigger picture' that Mason told us about. Maybe Mason had been trying to reveal her and the Committee of One Thousand but we were blinded by sexist assumptions.

He could see why right wing extremists might want someone like this as their spokesperson. She wouldn't seem threatening, at least not in the normal right-wing sort of way, which was the point of the "alternative right". Plus her sex appeal would be useful in messaging to young white men.

"Yes, of course," she responded, standing behind the table and turning, so the light caught her just right, as Choy lifted his cell-phone to get a good angle.

"I'm going to take a few," he said, also standing.

She seemed to sense exactly what would look best each time he moved the camera. He guessed she had done this before. Her poses were vaguely sexual, but serious and studied at the same time.

"That's great," he said.

"You have what you need?"

"Yes," he answered, looking at the pictures on his phone. "You look very good."

"Thank you," she said, with just a tiny hint of flirtation.

"So, where would you like to begin?" she asked, smiling in a way that made Choy uncomfortable.

He could tell she had been coached, like an experienced mainstream politician, to take control of an interview. They all followed the same script. They'd come across as genuinely nice, usually by expressing interest in the interviewer. They'd keep the interview on topic. They were unflappable, in charge and pleasant. The interviewer was simply a conduit for their planned messaging. Given the circumstances, Choy could live with that.

"You're from Vancouver?" she said. "You grew up there?"

Choy nodded and smiled.

"You're very lucky. It's a beautiful city. Clean."

She does have a sexy smile.

"I know Vancouver well. Lived for a few years in the Kootenays. When my father was hiding out."

Her father? Hiding out? Is she signalling that the interview can begin?

"Your father was hiding out?" he said, turning on the recorder.

"Yes. I forgot, I know all about you, but you know absolutely nothing about me. I am Amanda Bennett."

She held out her hand, but Choy looked down at his notepad.

"The daughter of Harrison Bennett."

She said her father's name like it had meaning and, at the moment she said it, looked carefully at Choy as if waiting for a reaction.

The name was familiar. Her father had definitely been in the news. Recognizing his name was a test.

Famous in right wing circles. That's it. Killed in a shootout with the FBI about five years earlier. Some kind of dispute over the use of federal lands.

He'd have to research him later. Kempki would probably have a file. Choy projected his best poker face.

"Were you there when your father was killed?" he asked.

"No," she answered, looking down, as if the memory was painful or embarrassing, then back, deep into his eyes in an attempt to elicit empathy.

Choy sensed he had passed her test.

"Much to my everlasting regret, weeks earlier we had an argument and I ran off to my grandmother's home in Mobile. I think my daddy knew what was coming and initiated that argument to save his little girl. I was very headstrong, so it was quite simple to manipulate me in those days."

How about these days? How easy is it to manipulate you now?

"So tell me what the Committee of One Thousand is and who is behind it?" Choy said, abruptly changing the subject to test her reaction.

Clearly she had planned to talk about her "daddy" some more, but she recovered quickly.

"The Committee of One Thousand is a new direction for politics in this country," she said, a slightly sour look underlying a forced smile. "We are American patriots who have decided to come together to build a force for change and renewal. People who interpret the Constitution to suit their own interests, rather than follow the wisdom of the original framers, have captured the levers of government power. Radical Muslims, terrorists, illegal immigrants bringing with them drugs and violence, are overrunning our land and yet the government does nothing about it. Wall Street bankers suck the blood out of ordinary hard-working middle-class Americans and use their money to control both the Republicans and Democrats. The Committee of One Thousand has been set up to begin the process of building a new political movement, one that insists free men have the right to defend their hard won freedoms, that certain fundamental rights must remain at the state level, one that demands government be part of the solution and not the problem, one that understands what a government for the people and by the people really means, one that is not afraid to crush this country's enemies and reward our friends, one that respects our Christian heritage, honours it and defends it …"

Because there was nothing more boring than a politician giving a speech during an interview he had to interrupt her again.

"So you're building a new right wing political movement? That's the goal? To challenge the Republicans and the Tea Party? They aren't right wing enough for you?"

He smiled and she tried, but the muscles in her cheeks were frozen and looked about to crack. Still, to her credit she again recovered quickly.

"We invite everyone who cares about this great land, its people and its Constitution to join our movement," she said. "We are not about being more right wing or more left wing than anybody. We are about fixing problems and the biggest one we face today is a broken political system."

"Does this committee have a platform, a plan? Do you have a website where people can go check it out?"

"We have open minds, not a set of easy answers. We want to begin a discussion, not tell people what they should believe. We will be holding meetings."

"Who will be holding meetings?"

"The Committee of One Thousand."

"But exactly who is the Committee? Does it have a thousand members and if so, who are they?"

"Unfortunately there are certain government departments gathering lists of people who disagree with government policies and believe in our inherent right to self-defence and a people's militia. We prefer not to make it easy for government spies, so my answer is this: The Committee of One Thousand has gathered together individuals and organizations with a common desire to fix our broken political system."

"But surely if you're going to invite people to meetings, they will want to know who is sending them the invitation?"

"Everyone who receives an invitation will know who is inviting them. But anonymity will be assured to all those who require it."

"So this is some sort of underground movement?" said Choy, being deliberately provocative. "Right wing fringe groups getting together in secret to build a new political party?"

"I would challenge your characterization of us as 'right wing fringe groups' and we will be very public, at the right moment."

"Which words do you object to? Right wing? Fringe? Or groups?"

This interview is becoming fun.

"I suppose 'fringe' is the word I primarily object to."

He was amazed at how patient she was being.

"We are supported by people from all walks of life. I would characterize the 'fringe' as drug dealers, murderers, radical Islamists, or illegal immigrants, not the hard-working ordinary Americans who support our cause."

She is good.

He now understood why right-wing fringe groups would find her attractive.

"What exactly is the nature of the work the computer nerds you employ are doing for Donald Trump's campaign?" he asked, quickly shifting tack to test exactly how good.

"I don't know what you are talking about." The pause before answering and the slight change in pitch suggested she was lying.

"What are your views on feminism?"

She smiled before answering, as if she had been expecting this question. "Feminism is a word that means very different things to different people. It's difficult to have an opinion on such a word."

"Do you believe a woman's place is in the home?"

Again she smiled. "I believe the idea that a woman should do it all, work outside the home, cook, clean, look after the children and be the family's emotional centre, is a cause of the huge increase in both mental illness and social dysfunction. Women have a special role to play in rearing the future generations and right now we're not doing a very good job of that, are we? We're failing our children and the women who raise them. The billions of dollars we spend treating depression is proof of that."

"Are you saying feminism causes depression in women?"

"I'm saying we have a problem that needs to be fixed," Bennett answered. "And it doesn't help to be politically correct and avoid talking about the problem."

She is articulate, pleasant, sincere, gorgeous. And scary.

He asked more questions, bouncing around topics in hopes of getting some juicy quotes and exposing her extreme views but she was genuinely skilled in the arts of deflection and obfuscation.

"So who supports your committee?" Choy said, this time changing the subject to one where he was certain the upper hand belonged to him.

"As I said …"

"No, I mean your funding. Where does it come from and do you have a lot of it?"

"Our funding comes from our members."

Choy sensed hesitation, as if she knew where this line of questioning could lead.

"And we have the resources to do the work we have set out to do."

"Do you accept corporate donations?"

"We only accept donations with no strings attached. The vast majority of our donations are small amounts that overworked, underpaid Americans freely give us."

"So you do accept corporate donations?"

"I have already answered that question."

"Is it true that you have received tens of millions of dollars skimmed off the ZZZFund, in a kind of Ponzi scheme?"

"A Ponzi scheme? What kind of question is that?"

She looked uncomfortable, glancing towards someone in the darkness. "Where are these wild allegations coming from? Do you have any proof?"

"Oh, we have lots of proof," he said, realizing that it was possible Mason had spun her as well as the rest of them. Maybe she believed he was a rich believer who simply donated tens of millions of dollars. "We have fund documents, executive email correspondence, boxes of it, in our hands as well as copies that we have sent to regulators and other interested agencies."

She glared at him menacingly.

Back off or go on the offensive? What the hell!

"We have all the files you thought were destroyed when you blew up former police chief Wong's cabin in Birch Bay. The story is being written as we speak. The murder of Wong made to look like a suicide. The Ponzi scheme. The involvement of senior police and military officials in this Committee of One Thousand."

She continued to stare.

"I suppose I should ask you for comment."

She turned back to someone she thought was in the darkness.

"I'm surprised you are surprised. I wouldn't have thought someone as intelligent as you obviously are, could have been so easily fooled. You did know about the FBI and Homeland Security?"

She stood up and glared into the darkness.

"Mr. Mason? Mr. Mason? Mr. Mason!"

"George?" said Choy, having more fun than he could ever remember having in an interview. "George, are you there?"

He stood up and put his hand on her shoulder.

"He seems to have disappeared. Johnny? Tom?"

He listened for a moment.

"Have they flown the coop as well? Oh my."

She pulled away, her face flush with anger.

"You didn't know George Mason has been cooperating with the FBI and Homeland Security in a sting operation?" Choy said, without thinking through the implications of spilling these particular dried legumes. As soon as the words came out he had an 'oh oh' moment, but then thought 'what the fuck' let's let all the cats out of their bags and see who scratches whom. "I'm sure they have surveillance equipment all over this place right now."

She glared at him for a few moments longer then walked into the darkness.

3.

Choy returned to his chair, thought about what had just happened and then wrote some concluding thoughts about the interview. He felt energized, ready for the Quickstep to begin. His overall impression of her was one of calculation in the service of a very bad cause. George Mason may have just burned her, but the world had not heard the last of Amanda Bennett.

As he was writing, a familiar voice came from the darkness.

"How the hell did you know she wouldn't pull her silver-plated Glock 42 and pump seven rounds into you?" said Mason. "She is a very good marksman. Her daddy taught her well."

"George, you've been here all along?"

Mason entered the light.

"How did you know she wouldn't shoot you?" he repeated. "With the information you provided her at the end of that interview she had nothing to lose."

"Never occurred to me."

"Never occurred to you? I spent four hours convincing her you are more useful alive than dead — I saved your goddamn life — and it never occurred to you that once it was obvious you weren't going to write the story she wanted ..." He mimed pulling a gun from his jacket pocket, aiming it at Choy and pulling the trigger over and over. "You're one lucky son of a bitch, I can tell you that. She would have enjoyed doing it herself."

"I'm Canadian. Stuff like that just doesn't happen where I come from."

"Bullshit. Vancouver has some of the nastiest drug dealers in the world."

"Not the crowd I normally write about," said Choy, realizing his naivety.

Think before opening my mouth.

"I'll give you credit for one good piece of deflection. Telling her Homeland Security had surveillance equipment here. That's probably what saved you."

"I thought it was true."

"An overestimation of the capabilities of our government. Perhaps on TV they can do it, but in real life the clowns are running the circus."

"Maybe you're the one who should be scared of Amanda Bennett. Now that she knows who you're working for."

"I work for no one but myself," said Mason, anger back in his voice.

"Now you're saying you don't work for the FBI?"

"Never said I did."

"You said you were working with the FBI and Homeland Security."

"With, not for."

Choy smiled smugly while turning his hands upward in a mocking gesture of 'what is that supposed to mean?'

"You don't know when to shut-up," said Mason. "You're a gossip. You have an uncontrollable desire to tell stories. In my business we call people like you useful idiots."

"In my business we call them journalists. Except this time I wasn't all that useful. This time I said something you would rather she didn't hear. So, now she's out there with her silver-plated Glock looking for you."

"I can handle Amanda Bennett."

"Oh and I bet you do."

Mason smiled. "That comment illustrates precisely your lack of understanding."

"What are you talking about?"

"Amanda Bennett. The way you underestimate her."

"What's to underestimate?"

"Exactly. She fooled you and your reporter friends. You took a quick glance and made assumptions."

"She dresses like a hooker."

"She does. And her use of sexuality disables your ability to see who she really is. Did you know her Daddy taught her this? Now, I'm not defending the methods he used, but you can hardly argue with the result. That woman is better at using sex to manipulate people than anyone I've ever encountered. And in my business I've encountered the best."

"But you can handle her?"

"I do not underestimate her. I understand her, see her for what she really is and she respects that. She certainly doesn't respect how you ogle her tits."

The accusation hit home. He had glanced at her breasts. He had reacted like the pathetic patrons of strip clubs who paid money to see what no woman was prepared to show them for free. He had dismissed her as a gorgeous bimbo.

"She certainly doesn't respect how you assume she has no brain. She's going to be a very powerful politician, maybe even president."

"Oh come on. She's a fascist nut bar."

"Eva Peron, Silvio Berlusconi, Adolph Hitler, Donald Trump — masters of spin who never overestimated the intelligence of their supporters."

"And you're predicting she's in their category?"

"There's some very powerful and wealthy people who think she is the one."

"The one?" said Choy. "Like in the Matrix?"

"They say she's exactly what the alt-right needs — a woman who can appeal to young men and undermines the femi-socialism that dominates too much of women's politics today. Someone the real right can trust but who will appeal to those more moderate. A real alternative to the dying Republican Party."

Femi-socialism? A term I never heard before.

"She has what it takes — charisma, cunning, a willingness to use power in all its forms, the desire, the drive — do not underestimate her."

Maybe he's right.

He looked down at his notes. Maybe this idea of underestimating a woman because of her looks was the right angle for his story.

A lede describing her sexuality.

He would write about her long legs, perfectly shaped bum accented by that tight skirt, see-through blouse and bra, but then suddenly switch gears to reveal the subject of the description is in fact a dangerous right wing populist politician.

Would that be sexist? Or would it be sexist not to?

"Under the right set of circumstances, with sufficient resources, I could see her doing great things," Mason continued. "She's a thoroughbred many bettors are putting their money on."

Maybe this is exactly the kind of lede Mason is now spinning me towards. Maybe this whole thing is a two-part act concocted to manipulate me. Maybe Bennett is still out there in the darkness, listening and watching.

"That's why you skimmed off millions of dollars from ZZZ-Fund and gave it to her?" he said, going on the offensive to retake control of the conversation.

Mason frowned.

"Everything I told her is true. We have the documents, the emails between you and former Vancouver Police Chief Wong. There's no way you can deny knowing what was going on."

Mason harrumphed.

"What do you think is going to happen to all the support and cooperation you have received from the law enforcement community when they find you ripped them off?"

"Please spare me your wild conjecture."

"Is she still out there watching?"

"Your grasp on reality is slipping."

"Are you playing both sides? That what's happening? More than two sides? Playing all sides, that's what you do. The right wing nut bars, the cops who bought into your investment fund, Homeland Security, Tom Tennyson, Amanda Bennett, Ertha, Celeste, me, you're spinning us all. But to what end?"

Mason held up his hand in the "stop" motion. "How do you know you're going to make it out of this place alive?" he said, with an ominously calm tone, then waited a few second before continuing. "A few seconds ago, that was your assumption, but now that I've brought up the subject, you are no longer certain. Why is that?"

"I'm certain you're going to tell me."

"The power of suggestion. It's a simple but effective technique that has been employed for centuries by kings, tyrants, democratic governments, magicians, parents and people in all walks of life to deflect attention. Your two-year old is crying because you don't have the time to take him to the park, so what do you do? Pull a popsicle from the freezer. Taxes are up and the standard of living is going down, so what does a government do? Fight a war. Find a really bad enemy to take people's minds off what's happening to them."

"Isn't that called distraction?"

"Distraction is the result, but the means is a suggestion."

"What is your point?"

"The point is all your documents and emails are much less meaningful than you believe. Your 'proof' of something you claim I've done may have multiple interpretations when examined more carefully. And no one may even care because something more important will come up to distract their attention."

Choy stared at his nemesis. "You are an arrogant bastard."

"Kinder words have seldom been spoken," said Mason, distracted by his cellphone, which he pulled out and looked at. "Much as I'd love to stay and chat, the time has come when I must bid you adieu."

He took a few steps into the darkness but turned back. "There is one last thing. While you make wild accusations about my working for Homeland Security, you fail to look at people much closer to you. For example, that tiny so-called gymnast who saved your life who you know as Melissa Fung, is really an FBI agent and guess who made sure she went with you and why?"

Mason gave him one last triumphant smile before walking into the darkness.

"When you're finished with your notes and are ready to leave, follow the emergency exit sign," he said from the darkness. "Or you can wait for the FBI. They will be here in 45 minutes."

Judgment

Dear WaylonChoy@yahoo.com,

Do you understand that sin is the transgression of God's Law (I John 3:4; Rom. 3:31, 7:7) and that all have sinned (Rom. 3;23). Only through knowledge of God's Law as given in His Commandments, Statutes and Judgments, can we define and know what sin is. We are to keep and teach the laws of God (Matt. 5:17-19) on both a personal and national basis. God gave Israel His Laws for their own good (Deut. 5:33). Theocracy being the only perfect form of government, and God's divine Law for governing a nation being far superior to man's laws, we are not to add to or diminish from His commandments (Deut. 4:1-2). All present world problems are a result of disobedience to the Laws of God, which if kept will bring blessings and if disregarded will bring cursings (Deut. 28). The curse has been placed upon you.

MAMBO

1.

"Becoming a police agent is the worst thing any journalist can do," said Tait. "You must know that."

"I'm not a police agent," said Kempki. "I was cooperating with the FBI. I had no choice. And it happened to save Waylon's life."

"'I had no choice'. You, of all people."

"Oh come on, are you really going to sit there and say you never did a favour for a cop, in return for something? Because I don't know any journalist who ever did a crime story who could claim that."

"Trading information, sure," said Tait. "I'll show you mine if you show me yours — you have to be careful, but that's not out of bounds. Permitting a cop to pretend to be a journalist, that is. And you know it."

"She was pretending to be a journalism student. And, I repeat, there was no choice. If I didn't agree, they were going to bring you all in for questioning and your whole investigation would have been blown."

"Every time a cop or government agent uses the cover of journalism to do their work, journalists are put at risk. Our credibility is damaged, all of us become suspect and I know this is part of the curriculum you teach, so how the hell could you have done it!"

"It was a choice between two evils and I chose the lesser one," Kempki answered. "It's called life in the real world and it's a lesson these students need to learn. Sometimes to get a story you go out on a limb. Weigh the pros and cons, decide how important the story is. There's no formula to make the decision for you."

Choy, Donicelli and Parsons were content to listen as the five of them sat in Kempki's office.

"There are lines you don't cross," said Tait.

"Cops and spies and other very bad people pretend to be journalists every day."

"Something no one should encourage, let alone enable. In fact, our only ethical choice is to condemn such practices any time we become aware of them. Did you share any of our information with the FBI?"

Kempki glared at him and said: "There are lines you don't ever cross."

"And that's where your line is drawn?" said Tait. "It's okay for a cop to pretend to be a journalist, but not to share the results of your investigation with him?"

"Look, nine times out of 10 I agree with you, but sometimes the end does justify the means," said Kempki. "After the first time you contacted me, a 'friend' from the FBI shows up saying Homeland Security has a two year-long operation going on, gathering intelligence on some very dangerous right wing militias, but three journalists from Canada have stepped into the middle of it and their lives are at risk. They also tell me that various police and military officers are suspected of involvement with these bad guys, so they have to be extremely careful. 'Do I want to jeopardize their operation?' I say no. 'Do I want to help save these journalists' lives?' I say yes. Of course when they first bring up having an FBI agent pretend to be a student I say no, but then when my actual options are laid out, this is the one that makes the most sense. Oh, and I have like 12 hours to make up my mind and can't talk to anyone else about it."

She looked at her partner, Parsons.

"It wasn't an easy choice, but it was the right one," said Kempki.

"Maybe you guys should have this debate in front of the class," said Parsons.

"Who do you think they'd side with?" asked Tait.

"Good question," said Kempki, looking at each of the other people in the room.

"I agree with you," Donicelli said to Kempki. "I think you made the right call."

"I agree with Doug," said Parsons.

Everyone looked at Choy, as if asking him to break the tie vote. "Well, in theory I lean towards Doug, but in actual practice I'm glad Marianne made the decision she did, so I guess I'd have to abstain."

"I would like to have this debate in front of the class," said Tait.

"Should we invite Melissa Fung?" said Choy. "Or whatever her name is? I'll bet she'd be interested."

"To find out exactly how much more we know now," said Tait.

"I really liked her," said Choy.

"Anybody saving my life would be my favourite person in the world," said Donicelli.

"She didn't seem like a cop," said Choy.

"Way too short," said Donicelli.

"Definitely doesn't look like a cop," said Choy. "No one would suspect her."

"With all this arguing going on, we haven't really talked about what happened," Kempki said. "How are you Waylon? You've been through a lot. Captured by bad guys who threaten to kill you, two days in a row, and drugged. I'll bet there's not many journalists who could claim that."

"Except for the drugged part," said Parsons. "Although that would usually be self-administered."

The remark earned a chorus of smiles.

How do I feel? Funny. Unsettled. Different. Alive.

"I'm okay," he said. "Weird. Like all my senses are heightened. Like I'm some sort of super hero. Journo-Man. Then five seconds later it's like I'm about to burst out crying."

"What do you want?" said Parsons. "Rest? We could find you somewhere safe."

Choy shook his head. He felt like phoning Joy, but knew she was at work.

"I need to do something. Take my mind off what happened — I keep rolling around in my brain that I came so close to never seeing my kids again."

Everyone was staring.

"Can we change the subject?" he said. "Please."

They were still staring.

"Can you guys talk about where we're at with the story? I need to focus on work, that's what I want to do."

"That's a great idea," said Kempki. "A report from each committee head. Let's do it."

She looked flustered, rather than in charge.

"I'll go first," said Donicelli, trying to overcome the awkward moment. "We went to the boiler room and it has indeed been shut down, which of course means the entire operation is disappearing. People scattering."

"Which strongly suggests we need to write the story and have it published as soon as we can," said Kempki. "Agreed?"

Everyone nodded, including Choy, despite the numerous questions that remained unanswered.

Kempki looked at Tait.

"Well, we heard back from Joy's brother in New York after we sent him the last bunch of files. He's very excited. Says he's going to be in line for a promotion when he shows his bosses what he's got. Says charges will definitely be filed, just a question of what jurisdiction. And he says to tell the guy who his sister is all excited about to make sure he is really nice to her because she deserves it."

Joy. The perfect name.

"Another reason to get the story written as fast as we can," said Kempki, "because when they file charges, it doesn't belong exclusively to us anymore."

Nods came from all around.

"So?" said Kempki, not looking, but clearly aiming the word at Choy.

"What have I got?" said Choy. "Since our last meeting?"

Doing this did make him feel better. Focus on work, back in a routine.

"Well, we know the FBI knows who killed Wainwright, but we don't have a clue if the local police even care. I guess a meeting needs to happen, with the detectives and the deputy police chief, but ..."

"DD and I can do that," said Tait.

"But," said Choy, annoyed his friend assumed that was too big of a burden for him. "I'm still not sure which police we can trust, or if that even matters anymore. I'm guessing all the cops who were on Mason's side before, will be at the front of the queue wanting to help us now. Or at least once the news about ZZZFund being a Ponzi scheme breaks."

"That news should travel pretty damn fast," said Tait.

"Another reason to get the story written as soon as possible," said Kempki as Tait and Donicelli joined in with her to say "as soon as possible."

"I don't know," said Choy.

Again everyone else in the room looked at him.

"What do we write about George Mason? Good guy or bad guy? Is he cooperating with Homeland Security or has he been using the cover of cooperating with them? Have you gone through the files to see how many senior FBI officials have bought into the fund? And, it occurs to me that while you say the documents show tens of millions were skimmed off to go to the Committee of One Thousand, what if that was just a cover?"

"What do you mean?" asked Tait.

"Well, we know how fucking manipulative Mason is. What if he was using the Committee as cover for his own skimming? Or, and perhaps as well, what if hundreds of cops are part of this Committee of One Thousand? What if they were the original investors and got paid off with big returns? Or what if they were told investing in the fund was a way to send money indirectly to their favourite right wing cause? Wouldn't that be important news and shouldn't it be part of our story?"

"Yes," said Kempki.

"And while I was being untied by Tom Tennyson, I realized he, or maybe that guy he calls the 'Reverend', has been sending me these crazy right wing, racist Christian emails that I thought were just junk, but now I need to go through them."

"Probably means one of the Christian Identity groups is involved," said Kempki. "I've got lots of files."

"Bennett talked about bringing together Christians, states' rights believers, white nationalists, pro-lifers, constitutional militias, sovereign citizens," said Choy.

"That would be huge if she pulled it off," said Kempki. "The FBI would be very concerned."

"Ya," said Choy. "Holy shine the light on shit, I don't think we're finished digging in this steaming pile yet."

Thinking clearly about the story gave him another boost of adrenalin. He felt good enough to get back up on his feet and dance the Mambo.

2.

"Everyone but Waylon agrees we need to write the story now," said Kempki. "I say we go with what we've got. We have no choice."

They'd spent three hours going over this. They'd brought the class into the discussion and everyone agreed that the story needed to be written immediately, as is. Then they brought in the *Vancouver Sun* managing editor and editor-in-chief. Both agreed the story needed to be written immediately, as is.

"But it's my story," said Choy. "And there's still too many holes."

"It's not **your** story," said *Sun* Editor-in-Chief Arthur Morrow, on the other end of the Skype call. "It belongs to everyone who has worked on it and to the newspaper that pays your wages."

In his experience once management brought up the employer-employee relationship it was pointless to argue further. But he had to make his pitch one last time.

I owe it to… who? Celeste?

There was no doubt she'd be pleased that the possibility of her father being murdered would be made public.

Myself?

He would come across as the big hero. Morrow wanted a first person side bar about his two brushes with death —"make it dramatic and write as long as you want" — how often does a reporter get the opportunity to write something like that?

The public?

Readers deserved the whole truth, that's what a journalist promises to tell them. Fighting for the complete truth was worth it even though he knew defeat was inevitable because it was never truly attainable.

"The key to the story remains George Mason," said Choy. "And we don't know what to write about him. Is he a hero, risking his life to expose a right wing conspiracy? Or is he a bad guy, part of that right wing conspiracy, who just sold out his friends to Homeland Security? Or maybe even worse, did he set up everyone, Homeland Security, the Committee of One Thousand, rank-and-file cops, and us? Playing everyone off against each other for personal gain?"

"Interview the FBI or Homeland Security," said Morrow. "Ask them."

"But we can't, that's the problem," answered Choy. "We've uncovered a conspiracy that clearly involves some police, members of the intelligence services and the military. But we don't know who exactly. Some of them are probably players in the Committee of One Thousand, but which ones? Some of them are clearly victims of the Ponzi scheme, but which ones? So who do you suggest we talk to? Who the hell is not spinning us?"

"You write the story, based on what you've got," said Morrow. "You expose the existence of a conspiracy to defraud tens of thousands of investors through a Ponzi scheme and this so-called Committee of One Thousand. You write that, at this point, it's unclear exactly where all the money went, but at least a portion of it went to the alt-right group. You tie in Vancouver Police Chief Wong, who suspiciously 'commits suicide' right after he accumulates files proving the existence of the conspiracy. You add the murder of a veteran journalist who was working to uncover the conspiracy and you've already got one hell of a great story. But hey, we've got more. We've got a first person sidebar by one of our own reporters who was kidnapped and held hostage twice. Saved from certain death by a gymnast turned FBI agent. And another sidebar, an exclusive interview featuring the great-looking — with pictures— leader of heavily armed right-wing militias that want to take over the government of the United States."

The story does sound pretty good.

But Choy's entire being resisted. He felt used by Mason. This was exactly what the man who spun everyone wanted: A story with lots of shady characters, but no definitive answers; no big picture; no challenges to the system. But surely the facts that had been uncovered so far pointed to a story that involved Christian fundamentalism, biblical literalism, the politics of cops, intelligence agencies interfering in domestic affairs, rich people funding right-wing extremism and domestic fascism. He just needed more time to dig deeper. Mason was counting on journalism's superficiality and Choy had to do everything in his power not to be that man's patsy.

"Waylon, even if you get nothing more, and no one is arguing you stop digging, this will get you nominated for every award in the business," said Morrow, as if this would be the argument that finally convinced him.

Choy knew it was time to follow orders and it was usually better to do that by pretending to get onside. "So, you're committing to give me, us, the resources to continue digging?"

"Yes," came the quick reply. "But I'm not going to bullshit you Waylon, you know how company finances are, so it won't be carte blanche."

When someone in management says 'I'm not going to bullshit you' it always means they already are bullshitting you, but what choice do I have?

"You'll give me back all the vacation time I've used up on this story so far?" He had to take advantage of his backing down in order to secure exact details of what was being promised. "And at least another two weeks to keep working exclusively on this story?"

"Of course."

"All our expenses so far — gas, hotels a few flights — nothing has been really expensive."

"Yes."

"A ten thousand dollar yearly scholarship in the name of Adam

Wainwright to one graduate student in the school of journalism at the University of Nevada, Reno?"

Choy got thumbs up from around the room.

"Well, I can't promise that one, but I can tell you I'm pretty sure Toronto and the money boys in New York will go for it," said Morrow. "I'll certainly make the pitch."

"Okay," said Choy. "When do you want the story delivered?"

"As soon as you can," said Morrow. "Tomorrow by deadline at the latest."

"So, I guess we better get to work," said Choy.

"Yes you better," said Eileen Daily, the managing editor. "Good work Waylon."

"Hey, there's a whole room full of us here," said Choy.

"Good work all of you."

"Good-bye everybody," said Morrow. "Eileen will keep in touch."

"Good-bye," said Choy, ending the computer connection.

He looked up to smiles all around.

"I have to follow orders and write this story, but I don't have to feel good about it," he said. "And I don't."

"Not even a little?" said Donicelli.

"A wee bit?" said Kempki. "Come on, you have to feel a wee bit good."

"It is a great story," said Tait. "Even what we have so far."

"Adam would be proud of us," said Donicelli.

"Be happy," said Kempki. "You never get the whole story. That's just journalism."

But he wasn't happy.

It is a great story and Adam would be pleased, but there's too many missing answers.

Worse, thanks, to Kempki, it now occurred to him that journalists almost always only get part of the story, which led him to another existential crisis.

Is that all journalism can ever be? Bits and pieces of the truth?

Which, in turn, raised the question of what is the truth?

Perhaps, by its very nature, verifiable truth can only be bits and pieces of a larger unknowable bigger picture. Maybe all a journalist can do is search for the bits and let the bigger picture reveal itself as the sum total of many little pieces. Maybe that's what seeking the truth is really all about.

Despite, or maybe because of, this realization, Choy felt diminished.

"So, is everyone ready?" said Kempki. "How are we going to divide up the writing?"

"Well, Waylon has to write two sidebars, so I'll work on the lede of the main story, plus the part about Adam, while Doug digs into the data and other details," Donicelli said. "Which leaves you to coordinate again. I know I'm going to need a lot of help with fact checking, so assign some of the students to me. Doug will have the toughest job, synthesizing all our files into a story and probably a bunch of fact boxes and other graphic elements, so I'd say most of the students work with him."

Choy managed a smile. Donicelli was a good section head because of his ability to assign work to those best capable and it was good to see he hadn't lost his touch.

"Sounds like a plan," said Kempki. "Choy gets my office, Donicelli the broom closet, Tait the small space beside the control room, which becomes my office and the rest of you stay in here."

It always felt good to start writing. The gathering of thoughts, the emptying of his mind to find the perfect lede, concentration and creativity, a tight deadline, he loved it all. There was a time, maybe it only lasted a few weeks, or more likely a few months, back when he first started as a reporter, that a deadline caused panic, but now it was like a heroin fix – he longed for the rush that came with it.

"Is everyone ready for an all-nighter?" said Kempki. "We keep at this until it's done!"

Just then Choy felt the phone in his pocket vibrate. He would have ignored it, but walking into the office with his stuff, he looked at the screen. He recognized the number immediately. It was George Mason.

"Hello?"

"Choy?"

"Yes."

"I need your help. They've got Ertha."

"Who?"

"You know who. It's your fault."

"Amanda Bennett?"

"You were the one who told her I'm working for the feds and she's pissed. She's got Ertha and wants a very big ransom."

"And?"

"I need your help. You've got to come down here."

"Where are you?"

"Las Vegas."

"Why?"

"She's your girlfriend's sister. Celeste is frantic."

"Celeste is not my girlfriend. Are you going to swap me for Ertha? Is that your plan?"

"No."

"Then why me?"

"I trust you, said Mason. "I can't say that about anyone else."

Bullshit.

"I can't talk on the phone."

"I don't think so. Twice bitten, forever shy."

"I'll give you an interview, reply to any questions you have, full, open, forthright disclosure," said Mason. "You can finish your story. It's the only way you're ever going to get answers. But you need to get to my place in Vegas as soon as you can."

Answers, but not necessarily the truth.

"I don't think so," he said. "I'm interested in the truth and you don't have a clue what that is."

He pressed the "end" button and smiled. It felt good to break free from Mason's manipulation. He enjoyed the moment, then opened the laptop and as he stared at the computer screen to think about a lede for the story that had to be written quickly, his phone once again vibrated. He should have simply ignored it, but there was always the possibility it was Joy or Ben or Sam calling. Instead, it was Celeste, or someone using her phone.

"Hello," Choy said carefully.

"Waylon?"

"Yes."

"Please help us rescue my sister," said Celeste, or possibly Ertha — he certainly couldn't tell them apart on the telephone. "I know I told you she and I don't get along, but that was only to protect her from the people listening. She … I can't imagine life without her. Do you know what it means to be a twin? We are two halves of a whole. I don't exist without her."

This isn't fair.

"Waylon, please, we need you. I won't survive."

Not fair at all.

3.

Choy could not remember ever being so tired as Mack, a very polite young student who was well over six-feet tall and built like an NFL linebacker, along with Emmanuel, also from Kempki's class, who seemed kind of a nerd, volunteered to drive him down to Vegas. During the seven-hour trip south the two students took turns behind the wheel while Choy sat in the back seat working on his laptop.

"Focus on writing the two sidebars and send them to us as soon as you can," Kempki had said before they left. "Don't worry, we'll deal with the rest."

Don't worry? Impossible.

He worried about being set up, again. He worried Mason and Bennett had a plan that involved pretending to be on the outs with each other. He worried that Mason and Bennett were at each other's throats and he would be caught in a shower of bullets between them. He worried that he had been sweating with one sort of worry or other for most of the past fifteen hours and desperately needed a shower. He worried about what would happen to Celeste if her sister were to be killed. He worried that Mason was lying and wouldn't really answer all his questions truthfully so the story would forever remain unfinished. He worried that he wouldn't finish the two sidebars because he was so damned worried.

But after an hour of numerous false starts, the desert sun disappeared over the edge of the earth, the air cooled and the breeze in the convertible's back seat stimulated, rather than stifled, his creativity.

Once the words flow writing is the best job in the world.

He wrote about his adventure in the old mine first. Given how vividly fresh his memory was, all he had to do was close his eyes and the smells, sounds, sights, feelings all flowed back into his brain. The fear he felt flowed through his fingertips to the keyboard and screen in front of him. The certainty he was about to die, his thoughts at the moment when he lost all hope, then the emotions unleashed by that unexpected, miraculous leap across the chasm of despair all became digital zeros and ones that were represented on his screen by just over two thousand words. As he typed the last words of the first story he looked at his cellphone to discover he had finished it in not much more than two hours.

After a quick stop to pee by the side of the road under an intense star-lit sky Choy began the second story, one that was newsy and traditional in form. But, he was in the writing zone and it too came quickly. He punched out a dozen good quotes captured on his recorder, then filled in the spaces around them with observations, descriptions and more than a little analysis. He played around a little with the order of her quotes, then closed his eyes and the lede came to him almost instantly: "Sex sells, pushing products from cars to underarm deodorant. Amanda Bennett is betting it can also sell her extreme right-wing vision. In an abandoned Reno casino the five-foot eleven, expert marksman, dressed in a low-cut designer dress that reveals many of the 'assets' she is counting on to gain the attention of a Republican-leaning segment of the population, describes her politics and how she'd like to change the world." Then right into the quote about how America must crush its opponents at home and around the world. A few more tweaks and this story was done as well. About 1,400 words in not much more than an hour.

Almost 3,500 words in less than four hours, even with the stop for gas! Done in the middle of the night with only a few hours sleep the day before. But was it any good? He thought it was, but as he handed the laptop to Emmanuel in the front seat, he suffered his usual "is it really any good, I think it's good, maybe I'm missing something important, I think it's good" moment.

As Emmanuel began reading, Choy couldn't help closing his eyes. The temperature had fallen from its 111-Farenheight daytime high to the low seventies and a chilled wind gently stroked his face like a mother soothing her child. He felt calm and content. It was the first time in days he was settled, completely at ease with himself and his surroundings. He slept.

The car was pulling into a strip mall parking lot with an all-night Starbucks when he awoke.

"Where are we?" he asked.

"Las Vegas," said Mack, still at the wheel.

"What time is it?"

"Just before four," said Emmanuel.

"I got a couple hours of sleep?"

"You handed me the laptop and then crashed like an old mechanical hard drive. You were sleeping pretty deeply, even through your ringing phone. It was Marianne. She wanted to talk but I told her you were completely dead to the world."

"I feel much better," said Choy, who then remembered why he had handed Emmanuel the laptop. "What did you think of my stories?"

"They're fantastic," said Mack. "Especially the one about the mine, you had me in there with you."

Choy realized he must have slept through them stopping the car twice to switch drivers, if both young men had read his work.

"How can you write so fast and so well?" said Emmanuel. "I couldn't do a quarter of the words you did, let alone great ones, in the time it took you."

"It was pretty fast, even for me. It must have been all the adrenaline from everything that's happened. But I've done close to that volume in four hours before. I covered hockey, the Canucks, for a season, a long time ago. You get used to writing fast or you crash and burn when the gamer and a sidebar have to be punched out within an hour of the final buzzer."

"Don't know if I could ever learn to do that," said Emmanuel.

"I'd love to cover hockey, any professional sport really," said Mack.

"It's a really good beat to learn how to write fast," said Choy.

Feels good to write fast and well. These guys want to be just like me. Show-off.

"So, we thought we'd stop at this Starbucks to use the wireless," said Emmanuel. "Send the stories to Marianne."

"Good idea. I'll feel better knowing they've been filed. I wouldn't put it past Mason and Bennett to have cooked up this whole come-down-to-Las-Vegas plan simply to keep us from publishing the story for another day."

They got out of the car and Emmanuel handed Choy his laptop and phone.

"Soon as I send the stories and we talk to the team, we'll find a place to stay," said Choy. "I think there was a casino I saw driving out of here a few days ago, that was advertising $19 per night. Pretty sure my editor won't complain about three rooms at that price. I'll get a few more hours sleep and then we'll … I don't have a god-damn clue what Mason or Bennett have up their sleeves."

The two young men looked tired and perhaps a little concerned for their safety.

Choy felt surprisingly refreshed, almost enthusiastic about what the day would bring, and, as a result, once they checked into the Santa Fe Station casino and hotel and he had taken a shower, sleep was not possible. At 6:15 he called Mason.

"Okay, I'm in Las Vegas. I can be at your place in 15 or 20 minutes."

"You came in your car?" asked Mason. "By yourself?"

"Yes."

"Find a safe place to park — that asshole Davis has eyes for your car — and take a cab to my place right now," said Mason.

Manipulating me again, thought Choy. Pretending to be concerned about my car. He put his keys on the stand beside his bed, called the front desk with a message for Mack and Emmanuel and asked that they be given a card to enter his room when the two of them woke up. Just in case he needed them, they would have access to a vehicle.

The cab ride only took 15 minutes in the very early morning traffic. As he walked up the sidewalk to the front door Choy noticed Mason sitting alone in the living room.

He knocked and the door opened. Mason motioned for him to come inside, as he looked both ways on his street. "Go straight to the kitchen and we'll make you tea."

Choy retraced his steps from a few days earlier, through the dining room into the kitchen. Celeste, or maybe it was Ertha, stood in front of the table. Choy stopped, his mouth open. She stared for a moment, then tentatively smiled.

"Waylon."

He managed an insignificant smile but remained silent.

"Thank you so much Waylon for agreeing to help," said Celeste, as she threw her arms around him.

She stepped back, reacting to his tentativeness. "You're not happy to see me?"

"Happy?" said Choy.

"Sit down and we'll explain everything," said Mason.

Judgment

Dear WaylonChoy@yahoo.com,

You are not of the Elect. In fact you are of the evil ones. You are of an existing being known as the Devil or Satan and called the Serpent (Gen. 3:1; Rev. 12:9), who has a literal "seed" or posterity in the earth (Gen. 3:15) commonly called Jews today (Rev. 2:9; 3:9; Isa. 65:15). These children of Satan (John 8:44-47; Matt. 13:38; John 8:23) through Cain (I John 2:22, 4:3) who have throughout history always been a curse to true Israel, the Children of God, because of a natural enmity between the two races (Gen. 3:15), because they do the works of their father the Devil (John 8:38-44), and because they please not God, and are contrary to all men (I Thes. 2:14-15), though they often pose as ministers of righteousness (II Cor. 11:13-15). The ultimate end of this evil race whose hands bear the blood of our Savior (Matt. 27:25) and all the righteous slain upon the earth (Matt. 23:35), is Divine judgment (Matt. 13:38-42, 15:13; Zech. 14:21). Your end is near.

Jefferson Davis

TANGO

1.

Mason is a professional liar and Celeste was born with a penis, so why should I believe anything they say?

Their story was that Amanda Bennett kidnapped Ertha and brought her to Las Vegas to swap for a ransom. But why not do it somewhere more isolated, somewhere easier to get away? And why would she demand a reporter be present at the exchange?

To kill me?

The only plausible explanation was she hated that reporter and wanted to kill him. But again, wouldn't that be easier in a more isolated location rather than a big city full of thousands of tourists? And why the hell would the reporter be willing to go along with possibility of being killed? Something other than what he was being told was going down, but what exactly? Unfortunately he was curious, usually a reporter's strength, but in this circumstance a vulnerability that could be exploited.

When in doubt, bluster.

"I don't care about your problem with Amanda Bennett. As far as I know you two could still be partners," he said after Celeste had left the house.

"I guarantee you we are not."

"The bottom line is I'm not going to help, unless you answer my questions first."

"Which questions?"

"Who are you really and what have you done?"

As Mason paced to the back door and then returned, Choy thought of Celeste, who reminded him of a wounded bird. She cared about her sister's predicament. She had flown down from Vancouver, to be here just in case she could help. He was glad that

Mason had arranged for her to be taken to a safe location. That was an act of kindness.

"Who am I really and what have I done?" said Mason. "That's a bit deep wouldn't you say? And we've only got a few minutes before we get our instructions."

"Did you really cooperate with Homeland Security?"

"Yes," said Mason.

"Are you still cooperating with them?" asked Choy.

"With the FBI, yes," he answered. "In fact, they're listening right now."

Mason raised his eyebrows and moved his head sideways a tiny bit as if to indicate this was the reason he couldn't answer Choy's questions.

"So anything you tell me now would not only be on the record, it would be recorded by the police? And maybe others?"

Mason nodded.

"Convenient," muttered Choy, mostly to himself.

The perfect excuse for not answering self-incriminating questions.

"I do assure you I will keep my promise. I will truthfully answer all your questions at the appropriate time and place."

How about answering one of the important questions remaining to complete the story.

"Is it true there are members of the FBI, Homeland Security, the military and other government security forces who are part of the Committee of One Thousand?"

Mason tried not to smile, but couldn't control his facial muscles quickly enough and Choy knew immediately this was one question the man wanted to answer.

"Yes."

"Including some very-high-up-in-their-organization officials?"

"Yes."

"Including people who might be listening now?"

"Yes."

This ought to get the foxes inside the hen house fighting amongst themselves. And it gives Mason another excuse not to answer more questions. The man is a genius at turning a situation to his advantage.

"You're not just saying this to avoid answering my questions?"

"No. I know for a fact that Amanda Bennett has people inside the FBI, the CIA, the NSA, Homeland Security, the U.S. military, the Canadian military, the RCMP, CSIS, many local police forces and numerous other government agencies. Is that a direct enough answer for you?"

Choy made a show of opening his backpack, taking out a notepad and writing down Mason's quote verbatim. When finished he looked up and smiled.

"What would you say is the most common motivation for someone in the police or intelligence or military to cooperate with Ms. Bennett?" said Choy.

"Because they agree with her right wing views about the world. They're not fond of democracy and would prefer the police and military to have a much bigger role in running the country. They think our current government, with its foreign-born Muslim president, is weak and ready to fall apart. They want to be part of a group that is ready to pick up the pieces. Your usual fascist, neo-Nazi motivations. That and some guys just want to get into Amanda's pants."

Mason smiled again as Choy took down what he said.

"Would it be fair to say that certain police forces are riddled with Committee of One Thousand sympathizers?"

"No. That would not be fair to say. I'm talking scores of people, maybe a hundred or two at most. Of course, police forces, intelligence agencies, the military are riddled with people who have been trained to follow orders and not to think for themselves, so you only need a few well-placed sympathizers to take over organizations like that."

A ring of truth — not to mention a good quote — and unsettling to the cops listening in.

"Do you want another cup of tea?" Mason asked.

"Sure, and a glass of cold water. The desert air, I feel like drinking a lot."

Mason opened a cupboard to take out a box of tea bags, then unplugged the electric kettle and took it to the sink to fill with water, before putting it back onto its spot on the counter. He seemed to be having trouble getting the plug back into the wall socket.

"Waylon, there's a container full of filtered cold water in the fridge. I need to play with this plug a bit."

"Sure," said Choy, standing up. "This is interesting about the police, but you still haven't offered me one good reason to risk my life by going to this exchange with Bennett and her crazy friends. You said I'd get answers so I could finish my story ..."

"You will," said Mason, handing him a glass. "I promise, but please be patient."

There was a piece of paper in the glass. Choy glanced at Mason, who looked up at the ceiling, as if to indicate someone might be watching as well as listening.

Choy opened the fridge door, pulled the paper from the glass and looked at what was written on it. "You will be safe. If you want to learn the truth you can't miss this." He filled the glass with water and crumpled the paper as he did so.

Certainly knows how to manipulate a reporter.

He closed the fridge door and dropped the crumpled piece of paper onto the counter beside Mason.

"If you're not going to give me anything more, I'm leaving," said

Choy, who had already decided to accompany Mason, but thought it best not to reveal his intentions immediately.

He stared at Mason, then turned, as if to leave.

"Okay, I have one more piece of information I can give you here. Amanda Bennett and a very senior Republican have engaged in a little hanky panky."

"She's sleeping with a senator?"

"I never said a senator, but it might be."

"A senator or a congressman?"

"That would be a reasonable assumption. And I'll tell you his name after we get this exchange done."

Got to admire someone who does his job so well. Even if it is spin and manipulation.

Mason's phone buzzed and he looked at the screen. "It's her. Are you in or out?"

What choice did a reporter chasing the juiciest and maybe last story of his career have?

"You already know the answer to that goddamn question," said Choy, shaking his head in disbelief at himself, rather than at the smugly smiling man holding the cellphone.

"Everything is a go on our end," said Mason into his cell. "Okay. I understand. Okay, we'll be there." He put the phone into his pocket and said, "the MGM Grand monorail station, 20 minutes."

2.

They each bought a day pass and walked onto the almost empty last car of the monorail that ran alongside the Las Vegas Strip.

"She's going to meet us in here?" asked Choy.

"All I know is what she told me, 'get on the monorail at the MGM Grand station, back row, last car '," answered Mason as he studied the other two people in the car. "I'm guessing this will be a first step. She will make it difficult for anyone following us."

As the train pulled into Bally's station, Choy was feeling the butterflies that bred on the nervous churning in his stomach. Everyone who got on the train looked like a typical tourist, rather than an angel of death or an FBI agent. Not that, after Melissa Fung, he had any good idea of what an FBI agent might look like. A half dozen more people got on, and a couple got off at the Flamingo and the same at Harrah's. All 16 seats in the car were full and another half dozen people were standing. When the train picked up speed as it ran along the edge of a golf course, Choy half expected the muscular guy two seats ahead to turn and say, "you got the money?" but instead a few minutes later they pulled into the convention center station where almost everyone got off.

"Where is the money?" Choy whispered as he realized Mason wasn't carrying anything but the phone in his pocket.

Mason put a finger over his mouth to indicate silence.

"Are you going to trade me for her?" said Choy, again verbalizing his bad feeling.

"Calm down, I have this under control."

A former CIA agent would have likely done this before, an almost reassuring thought, until Choy realized "this" could very well be a double cross or worse.

In and out of the Westgate Station and then to the final stop at the SLS casino, the train began its return journey with only two passengers in what was now the lead car.

"I don't like this. There's something wrong."

"There's nothing wrong," whispered Mason. "They're watching to make sure we don't have anyone with us."

"Do we?"

Mason shook his head, more in exasperation than as an answer.

"Stay calm, we could be riding this for hours."

Every time someone got on the train Choy studied him or her carefully. He looked for signs such as a bulge suggesting a concealed gun, or something in their ear, but using this criteria only revealed the high proportion of tourists using the monorail at this time of day who were obese, old and hard of hearing.

Back at the MGM station where everyone had to exit, the two men walked to once more get on the last car, which again filled up as it neared the convention centre; this time it was standing room only as the train made its loop around the strangely-green-in-a-desert golf course. A man standing in front of them fumbled with something in his pocket and a piece of paper fell to the floor. Mason picked it up and handed it back.

"Thank you," the man said.

Choy was certain the paper was a message and sure enough at the last stop, the SLS casino, Mason stood up.

"Where are we going?" asked Choy.

"The sports book in the casino."

They walked out of the station, over a short pedestrian bridge, then down an escalator, through a construction zone, around to the front of the hotel, past some shops and into the casino. The almost empty sports book, doubling as a restaurant named Umami Burgers, was at the far end of the casino. They sat on a leather sofa, pretending to be interested in the horse racing on TV screens on walls half surrounding them. After about five minutes a waitress approached, asking if they wanted to order anything. When they said no, she handed Mason a piece of paper. He read it and handed it back.

"Back to the monorail," he whispered.

They rode the train back to their starting point and repeated the whole route again, then again. Choy became all too familiar with the parkades and parking lots that lined both sides of the monorail line. Las Vegas from the other side of the Strip looked like some science fiction dystopia built for automobiles rather than people.

It was on their sixth trip back towards the MGM Grand that a thirtyish well-built man got on at the Harrah's station, walked directly to the back of the car and showed Mason a piece of paper. The man kept the paper and walked away, getting off at the next stop a minute later. Mason held a finger over his mouth to indicate silence. As the train pulled away from the Flamingo, he stood up and Choy followed. By the time they reached the door the train was pulling into Bally's station. They exited the car and walked quickly.

"Where are we going?" Choy asked, as he followed Mason along a walkway toward the casino.

Again a finger to his mouth. They exited the station and entered a long hallway lined with shops that eventually came to an escalator at the top of which was Bally's casino. Rather than enter the main hall they veered right into another long hallway that was lined with meeting rooms. At the far end of the hall, they stood in front of a closed door with a sign that read "Director's Room". They entered.

The two big men who stood on either side of the door had guns drawn. The third man, Mr. Davis from the mine, immediately locked the door, then stood in front of Mason and indicated silence.

There's been a lot of this today.

Davis held up a small sign that read: "Strip. All your clothes off and on the floor."

Given the guns pointed at them, it did not seem an entirely un-reasonable request, so they complied. Once they were naked the two goons patted their clothes, grabbed their cell phones, wallets and keys and put these personal items into a small brief case that was lined with metal, then closed it. One of the goons put their clothes in a plastic bag and carried it out of the room.

"Where's the stuff?" Davis finally said.

"You think I'm an idiot?" said Mason. "You really think I would so easily walk into an obvious trap, Jefferson?"

The two men made their dislike for each other obvious. Choy suspected this had something to do with Amanda Bennett.

Davis approached Mason. "Mouth open," he said and looked inside. "Spread your legs and bend over."

Choy endured the same degrading routine, before each of them was given sweat pants, T-shirt, a pair of flip-flops, a baseball cap and sunglasses.

"Are we going to do this exchange or are we going to a beach party?" said Mason, once the two of them were dressed in identical loose-fitting clothing.

"A beach party," answered Davis. "Let's go."

The four men exited the meeting room, walked down the long hallway back to the casino, where the goon who had taken their clothing re-joined the party.

"Your shoes and clothing are in a car that's headed out of town. Along with the FBI."

"I'm going to need my cellphone if you want the stuff," said Mason.

The goon pointed to Davis, who lifted the briefcase to indicate where the cellphones, wallets and keys were.

Lined with lead, which stops radio signals. Another precaution to make sure no one is following.

The five men walked through the casino to an escalator that led up to an outside walkway, then down an escalator into an area of outside shops on the other side of which was a walkway across Las Vegas Boulevard. The intense sunlight and heat was almost unbearable. Choy was certainly happy to be wearing sunglasses, even if they were too tight. On the other side of the bridge, jammed with pedestrians, was a line of casinos. They entered the closest one, or at least an indoor "street" of expensive brand name shops leading to the Bellagio, a faux Italian palace and one of the fanciest casinos in Las Vegas.

"Keep those glasses on," said Davis as they entered.

It took at least 30 seconds for Choy's eyes to adjust to the much lower level of light. As he walked, almost blind, he was pushed from behind. They headed across another huge casino floor, again dominated by the caterwauling of electronic devices beckoning tourists from all over the world to part with their cash.

Just beyond the hotel's reception area a short hallway led to ornate doors with a sign beside it reading "Spa and Salon" and another smaller sign on the glass informing passers-by that the facility was currently unavailable because of a private party. They entered anyway and Davis told a smiling young woman they were members of the Latvian delegation.

"Will you be having any of our spa treatments today?" she asked.

"I don't think so," said Mason. "But if we change our minds we'll let you know."

"There are slots available for all our treatments."

"That's good to know," said Mason as he grabbed Davis's arm and pulled him to the other side of the reception room.

"Tell Bennett to fuck off, I'm not doing this with you and the other goons around."

"You think I'm scared of you?"

"You're too stupid to be scared."

The two men glared at each other for a moment.

"We're leaving," Davis finally said.

"Now," said Mason. "Or this whole thing is called off."

There was a little more staring down and then Mason said: "Outside in that garden with my guys. And give me that briefcase."

His guys? Mason knew all along where the exchange was going to be held?

Choy could feel the discomforting caterpillars in his gut digest themselves to become flying butterflies.

After handing over the briefcase, Davis and his two goons left.

"What's going on?"

No answer.

As they approached the young woman on the other side of the room, she smiled and pointed to the elevator. "The other members of your party are already upstairs."

They rode the elevator up and when they got off Mason said, "in here," entering the men's change room.

"You knew where the exchange would be taking place all along?"

"Of course I did. You think I'd agree to this solely on her terms?"

"But, all that back and forth on the monorail? These clothes?"

"It's in no one's interest to have the FBI blow this thing. Now clothes off."

Choy gave Mason a look of exasperation.

"We're doing this in the steam room at Ms. Bennett's request. She says it's because the steam makes surveillance impossible, but the real reason is she enjoys making men uncomfortable. She believes nakedness gives her an edge."

Naked in a steam room with Amanda Bennett? An edge! That's for sure.

"Everyone will be naked?" he lamely said.

"Everyone in the steam room will be naked. Those are the ground rules."

"Ertha?"

"Everyone in the steam room."

Naked and at risk of being killed by a beautiful woman. A memorable way to go.

Sex, murder, money were the perfect ingredients for a good story, but all he could think about was how to avoid staring and … Not that Choy was embarrassed by his body — he looked after himself — but nudity had always made him uncomfortable. The few times he had been to Wreck Beach in his late teens and early twenties had been more the result of youthful bravado than any real desire to enjoy a nudist experience. As Choy pulled down the sweatpants and stepped out of them he told himself to focus on details, be calm and loose. Be sophisticated. It was important to minimize distractions. But he couldn't stop himself from looking down at his parts that were no longer going to be private and wonder how they would stack up.

3.

As the door opened, steam billowed out and the smell of eucalyptus overwhelmed Choy's senses. The scented steam was cleansing, opening his nasal passages and all the pores of his skin.

"Are they in here?" said Choy.

Time to tango.

"Amanda?" said Mason, as a thick cloud reduced visibility to near zero.

"George, my dear," came a voice from the other side of the room.

They walked a few more steps until the outline of a naked Amanda sprawling on a wooden bench in the corner became visible.

"So good to see you both," said Bennett, making a point of looking at both men, from head to toe and then back to the middle.

Her gaze was both intimidating and sexual, an extremely uncomfortable blend that had Choy involuntarily crossing his hands in front him.

Beautiful.

Her skin was smooth and glistening. He should have been worried about her pulling a gun from somewhere and shooting him but was distracted by legs and breasts that were perfectly proportioned, her pubic hair … in the shape of SS lightning bolts.

Am I staring?

"What you are looking at," said Amanda to Choy, "is the work of an artist, a master of sugaring, possessor of a most gentle touch, the world's best bikini waxer."

She spread her legs so that the two men could appreciate her work of art better. Choy was mesmerized. He was incapable of diverting his stare as she looked down and touched herself nonchalantly as if demonstrating the beauty of her latest pedicure.

"Mostly you feel nothing but a warm, somewhat ticklish sensation," she said. "The moment of pain is brief and simply exquisite. She is truly amazing."

Choy was officially distracted. The last time he felt anything even remotely like this was when he froze on stage at the Grade Nine oratorical contest after imagining everyone in the audience was naked, a strategy that he had read would help combat nerves, but which in reality simply magnified them.

"Where is Ertha?" said Mason, focusing on the task at hand.

"Where is my package?"

"It's nearby."

"So is she."

"Do we bring them in together?"

"I'll show you mine if you show me yours," said Bennett.

Mason put the briefcase on the bench beside Bennett. "You understand that once I open this briefcase, we can only count on 20 minutes before the FBI arrives."

"As we agreed."

Mason opened the briefcase and picked up his phone. "Now," he said.

Choy caught himself looking at Bennett's breasts then pubic hair again and understood how effective a distraction nakedness could be. She could get away with almost anything undressed like that. He forced himself to look away, to fix his gaze towards the entrance.

"You're not calling anybody?" Mason said.

She held out her hand and he handed her his cell.

"Now," she said into the phone after tapping in a number.

About 10 seconds later a naked Tom Tennyson and an equally in the buff Ertha Wong entered the room, accompanied by a burst of steam.

"George!" said Ertha.

"Are you okay?"

"Yes."

"Keep her over there until we get the package," said Bennett in a stern, almost angry voice, that Choy assumed was a legacy of Tennyson's earlier fuck-ups.

Tennyson held a tight grip on Wong's arm as they sat on a bench on the other side of the room beside the door. While the steam made it difficult to see clearly, Ertha seemed at least as beautiful unclothed, something that Choy knew was not true of all women. Unlike Amanda, Ertha was discomforted by her nudity; it made her seem frail, less in charge than she had been in their previous meeting at the research facility. Tom, on the other hand, looked more intimidating. His muscles were everywhere and he clearly enjoyed showing them off.

"I want her over here, by herself," said Mason, pointing to the left.

Tennyson looked toward Bennett.

"When your package arrives."

"Tell him to take his hands off her."

"Ah, isn't that sweet. Jealousy."

"He's a psychopathic murderer," said Choy and everyone immediately looked his way.

Best to be careful when talking to a psychopathic murderer.

Tennyson let go of Ertha and stood up. As he did so the door behind him opened, once again accompanied by a billowing burst of scented steam. At first Choy couldn't make out who had entered but could see that Tennyson turned toward them, then quickly looked back towards Ertha, who had taken advantage of the distraction to move away and was in the centre of the room.

As the cloud of steam diffused, the new person was revealed. It was Ertha's twin, Celeste! Or possibly the other way around, how could you really tell, since, at least in all this steam, they still looked identical, despite their nudity and one of them being born with male parts. Whoever she was, the newest entrant to the room immediately went to her sister and they hugged each other in the centre of the room. In the process they turned a few times so it became impossible to tell them apart. Tennyson was confused.

"What the fuck!" said Bennett. "Grab them both!"

As she said this, the sisters split apart to opposite sides of the room, leaving Tennyson in the centre, looking first to one then the other and then to Bennett.

"What are you playing at?" Bennett said to Mason. "Where's the package?"

As everyone else looked at Tennyson and the two sisters, Choy noticed Bennett reaching behind her back. Her right hand reappeared holding a silver plated pistol. She pointed it at Mason.

"Where's my package?" she repeated.

"What are you playing at?" Mason repeated Bennett's words. "We agreed no weapons."

"My package!" she said pointing the gun at Mason, then at the sister to her right. "Now."

The sister to her left took a step forward and emptied the contents of a cloth bag onto the floor of the steam room. Scores of gemstones scattered across the ceramic tiles.

"My diamonds," shouted Bennett, getting down on her hands and knees to pick them up.

"Your package," said Mason, standing. "As agreed, my collection of pink and blue diamonds, minimum 50 carats each, worth $80 million. And now we will be leaving."

Bennett looked up and pointed the gun at Mason. He glanced at the weapon but continued walking towards the door.

"I would advise using the time you have left before the FBI

shows up to make sure you find all the diamonds, but if you prefer to shoot one or all of us instead …" said Mason, carrying the briefcase.

Choy and the two sisters followed quickly as Tennyson and Bennett knelt and ran their hands along the slippery floor to feel for diamonds.

"You fucking bastard!" shouted Bennett as Choy held the door open for a moment to produce another large burst of steam.

When Choy was on the other side of the door, he reached down to brush off whatever was caught between his toes. When he saw the colour and the size of the stone he immediately put his hand to his mouth and made himself cough. While he did so he slipped the diamond into his mouth.

Mason was at the entrance to the men's dressing room looking back at him. "You may want to get out of here before she decides to put a hole in you."

Choy walked quickly, glancing back once at the steam room. In the dressing room, the two men quickly put on the sweatpants, T-shirts, flip-flops and sunglasses, grabbed their cellphones, wallets and keys and made their way to the elevator. Ertha and Celeste, dressed exactly like them, were waiting. The elevator door opened and they got on. When the door opened again they walked through the reception area, past the same young woman who asked: "Leaving so soon?"

"A family emergency I'm afraid," said Mason.

"I am so sorry to hear that."

On the other side of the entrance to the spa the four of them joined a small crowd of people headed towards the hotel check-in area, but then thirty feet on, made another right into a parkade where a black minivan was waiting for them.

"Drive," Mason said to the driver as soon as they were seated.

The two sisters sat beside each other holding hands in the back seat. Mason opened his wallet and handed Choy a card. "Call this guy at the FBI 15 minutes after we let you out on the Strip."

"What just happened?" said Choy, finally able to speak.

Mason looked at the two sisters in the back seat then turned to Choy. "The Committee of One Thousand got what they wanted, my collection of 58 coloured diamonds worth a minimum of one million dollars each, over $80 million in total, possibly a lot more. And I got what I wanted as well."

"So everyone is happy?"

"Are you?"

"I have as many questions as answers," said Choy.

"You have all you're going to get today."

The van pulled over as it came to Las Vegas Boulevard.

"Remember, 15 minutes of walking in crowds before you call that number."

"Will I see you again?" said Choy, as he climbed out of the vehicle.

"Do I keep my promises? What do you think?" he said, slamming the door shut.

Choy had to find something to drink. His throat was very sore.

Judgment

Dear WaylonChoy@yahoo.com,

You shall return to the land of the race traitors and mud people who have no souls that can be saved. Do you understand? The United States of America fulfills the prophesied (II Sam. 7:10; Isa. 11:12; Ezek. 36:24) place where Christians from all the tribes of Israel would be regathered. It is here in this blessed land (Deut. 15.6, 28:11, 33:13-17) that God made a small one a strong nation (Isa. 60:22), feeding His people with knowledge and understanding through Christian pastors (Jer. 3:14-15) who have carried the light of truth and blessings unto the nations of the earth (Isa. 49:6, 2:2-3; Gen. 12:3). North America is the wilderness (Hosea 2:14) to which God brought the dispersed seed of Israel, the land between two seas (Zech. 9:10), surveyed and divided by rivers (Isa. 18:1-2,7), where springs of water and streams break out and the desert blossoms as the rose (Isa. 35:1,6-7). I shall remain in this blessed land. Through your stories and attempts to condemn us you will give our message the strongest voice it has ever had. So who has won?

Jefferson Davis

WINNER'S DANCE

1.

After four hours of questioning by the FBI, Joy Lee took Choy to her place where he called his Reno partners to update them. Everyone agreed that despite the strange events of the day, it made no sense to attempt a rewrite of the story that would be released by the *Vancouver Sun* in a few hours.

"We still don't know if Mason is a good guy or a bad guy, or somewhere in between," said Donicelli.

"He's not a good guy," said Choy. "Trust me on that one."

"While it's another great story involving the kids of the former Vancouver police chief," said Tait, "there's going to be sensitivities. You'll have to take care writing it. Probably best if you get a good night's sleep before tackling this one."

Choy immediately thought of SS pubic hair and assorted other issues involving lesser private parts. Given the events of the last few days he was definitely not up to writing this story immediately.

"This will be a great follow to the package that will go online at 9 p.m.," said Kempki. "And it's not as if the FBI is going to release anything about such a botched operation."

So far Choy had said nothing about the diamond he had swallowed and was inclined to continue on that course, unless he had to seek medical attention to get it out. He did ask Joy if she had anything that could help with constipation and received a sympathetic reply. "Stress can cause you to hold everything in. I've got Metamucil and All-Bran. Help yourself."

The two of them enjoyed a relaxing evening, including a light supper of raw vegetables, after he called the Santa Fe Station to arrange for Mack and Emmanuel to stay an extra night. They went to bed early and Choy woke up at 5 a.m. with a story bursting to come out, but not the diamond. He consumed a very large bowl of All-Bran and yogurt while he used Joy's desktop computer to write and by 7 a.m. had emailed fifteen hundred words to Tait and Donicelli. Just as he was about to climb back into bed his cellphone buzzed.

"About a mile south of the Mandalay Bay on the east side of Las Vegas Boulevard there's a Rebel gas station. Meet me there in an hour and I'll answer all your questions. If you let me drive your car while we're talking."

"I'll be there as soon as I can, but I have to go pick up my car first so I may be a little late."

"I won't wait around for long."

Fortunately, Joy offered him a ride to the Santa Fe Station and pointed out the fastest route to the rendezvous spot. The traffic was light so he pulled into the gas station at exactly the appointed time and parked at the pumps.

My baby is definitely thirsty.

Twenty gallons later Mason was sitting in front of the steering wheel. Choy tossed him the key as he entered the passenger side.

"This is the perfect car for a ride down the Strip. You restore it yourself?"

Choy nodded.

"How much is this baby worth?" Mason said as they left the service station and turned north onto Las Vegas Boulevard.

"It's not for sale."

"Everything, everyone is for sale. It's simply a question of price. How about a hundred thousand dollars?"

"You said I get to ask the questions if I agreed to let you drive my car."

"Yes I did. But before you start, I promised you this," said Mason handing him a large envelope. "Taken at the recent Trump coronation."

Choy opened it and pulled out explicit photos of Amanda Bennett and a man who looked vaguely familiar. The senior Republican politician.

"Thank you."

"I do keep my word. So ask away."

"Did Police Chief Wong commit suicide?"

"I very much doubt it."

"Did you kill him or order him killed?"

"No, of course not."

"Who killed him then?"

"Tennyson would be my first guess. He may or may not have been acting under orders from Amanda Bennett and/or Jefferson Davis."

"Why was he killed?"

"Because he discovered the Committee of One Thousand and the financial irregularities. As you know he confronted me a few days before his death."

"Did you tell Bennett?"

"I didn't have to tell her. Her people were, are everywhere."

"So you accept no responsibility for his death?"

"Why would I?"

"And I suppose the same goes for Adam Wainwright?"

"You know who killed him. You discovered an eyewitness."

"You were in no way responsible for Tennyson's actions?"

"I was not."

"Not even for enabling him by offering him a job and all the power that went along with that."

"I never hired him. Jefferson Davis did."

"And who does he work for?"

"Amanda Bennett."

"Even though he was being paid by ZZZFund?"

"He wasn't. He was being paid by SSSecurity."

"Which is owned by ZZZFund," said Choy.

"The fund has a controlling interest, but Amanda's people run it."

"So you're not responsible?"

"Certainly not in any legal meaning of the word."

"Why has Davis been sending me those crazy religious emails? I recovered them from my Trash folder and they use the Bible to justify everything from murder to racism to the overthrow of governments."

"I have no idea what you are talking about."

"You have no responsibility for enabling the right wing, racist, religious nut bars either?"

"If you play in the pigpen you're going to get slop all over you."

"What's that supposed to mean?"

"I couldn't very well work with the Committee of One Thousand but draw the line at Amanda Bennett's most trusted adviser."

"Davis?"

Mason nodded. "The prophet of the white race who will part the Atlantic Ocean and chase dark skinned people all the way back to Africa, or some other such nonsense."

"So you were just bullshitting when you told me before that you thought Amanda Bennett might become president of the United States and that some very rich people were backing her?"

"No, that was true."

"They support her despite Jefferson Davis?"

"Many of them support her because of Davis," said Mason. "As I told you and your friends, rich doesn't mean smart."

"But surely someone that extreme could never be elected president?"

"They said Donald Trump couldn't win the Republican nomination and he's not half the politician that Amanda is."

"And that doesn't scare you?"

"Why should it?" said Mason with a smug smile on his face as he drove in the centre lane of the Strip.

"Because you know how to manipulate her, right?" said Choy.

Mason looked over at his front seat mate and winked. "I know how to manipulate everyone."

"Okay. How about the Ponzi scheme that has stolen hundreds of millions of dollars from investors? Do you take responsibility for that?"

"That's more complicated than could possibly be answered by a simple yes or no."

"Did you design the scheme?"

"I helped. Amanda Bennett came to me with an idea. The FBI was eager that I participate."

"Did you personally benefit?"

"From the Ponzi scheme? I suppose there might be a paper trail that would suggest the answer is yes, but the truth is I had already made more money than I will ever spend. Just over $400 million. You saw where I prefer to live. I do not have expensive tastes."

"So, your motivation for participating in the scam was entirely noble?"

"If you believe working for the FBI is noble."

"What about Ertha and Celeste?"

"What about them?"

"You knew all along about Celeste contacting me?"

"Yes and so did Bennett. Once their father was killed we knew Ertha was also at risk. Celeste devised this plan to get a journalist involved."

"Celeste? To distract Bennett?"

"Yes."

"And whose idea was it for Celeste to show up at the exchange?"

"Hers."

"Another distraction?"

"Yes."

So Celeste has been using me all along. Her frailty a perfect disguise.

"You, Celeste, the FBI and Amanda Bennett all had reasons to get a reporter involved and have the story told?"

"Yes."

"Are you still working for the FBI?"

"It's complicated."

"Are you a member of the Committee of One Thousand?"

"It's complicated."

"Are you a true believer?"

"In the committee?"

"Or Amanda Bennett?"

"I believe in serving my country and myself."

"What sort of answer is that?"

"I believe in a country that enables some of its citizens to get rich. I'll do whatever it takes to ensure that continues to be true."

At that inconvenient moment the All-Bran began working. The traffic was moving slowly as they passed the MGM Grand with New York New York "entertainment complex" across the street and Choy considered saying he needed to use a bathroom, but decided against it.

"Frankly, I expected more sophisticated questions from you," said Mason. "What you've asked me so far are mere details of a more important bigger picture."

"Which is"

"Who is Amanda Bennett and what does she represent? Why would elements of the FBI be working for her and others against?"

"Okay," said Choy, alternately thinking about the stone inside him, his desperate need to expel it and salvaging whatever remained of this interview. "Tell me about Amanda Bennett and why elements of the FBI would support her."

"She's a shrewd politician who is willing to act to get her way. She understands the necessity of sometimes using force. She oozes sexuality, unlike that damn Clinton — an asexual woman leader comes across as bossy, even to other women. And while many would consider Amanda's views extreme they are in fact mainstream within certain communities."

"The police?"

"That's one, but certainly not the most important."

"Which is?"

"That part of the ruling class who consider themselves American patriots, those who are willing to fight for this country's interests to be put ahead of the interests of the international ruling class, the people that Donald Trump is speaking to in the current election campaign. When he loses think of the opportunity she will have. The Republican Party will be searching for scapegoats and certain sizeable parts of the right will be looking for a new home."

"What if Trump wins?"

"That's not going to happen," said Mason. "But if he did, it's even better for Amanda. Many of her supporters are among what the news media is calling the 'alt-right' that is running his campaign. If the buffoon actually wins the election she will be one of the most powerful behind-the-scenes politicos in America."

If Mason is right, American politics is about to get even weirder. If that's possible.

"She speaks to the people who believe a strong authoritarian figure is exactly what is needed to solve the problems of contemporary society; for them Amanda Bennett is a very attractive figure."

"They're fine with her Nazi sympathies?" said Choy.

"She has rough edges, but with time these will be polished smooth."

"How will her supporters and the cops react when they discover she ripped them off?"

"You underestimate Amanda and overestimate her followers."

"What does that mean?"

"It means she learned PSYOP from me. It means you are assuming that what you understand to be true is the only possible narrative."

"She has a plan to blame someone else for the Ponzi scheme?"

"Most certainly."

"Who?"

"Well, she's never told me, but it does not take a genius to figure it out."

Choy thought for a moment and then realized the answer was obvious.

"You?"

Mason nodded. "And, I expect, the FBI, the federal government and assorted other usual suspects."

"And you think she'll get away with that?"

"It's a plausible enough version of what you journalists like to call the truth."

"Come on, really?" Choy had difficulty believing people could so easily be fooled.

"I tell you she came to me with the Ponzi plan and I only went along with it because the FBI wanted me to and you are willing to believe that. But what if she came to you and said it was the other way around?"

"Would I believe her or you? Now that's a good question."

"But also completely irrelevant."

"Why? Because there's no such thing as the truth? There's only spin?"

"People believe what they believe for many reasons other than an appeal to reason or citations of some 'objective reality' that you call facts," said Mason. "Look around you. We're in the heart of the Strip. More than any other place on earth this is proof that spin works."

Choy looked up at the casinos lining both sides of the street, but had difficulty thinking about what Mason was saying, because his primary focus was on controlling his urge to defecate.

"A Potemkin village, illusions inside of illusions, magic in a Mirage," said Mason. "Yet millions of people come to spend billions of dollars. And you know why? This place works because it is built on the understanding that 90 per cent of what we do is determined by our lizard brain. Food, sex, bright lights, the many forms of intoxication and luck — all of these appeal to our non-rational selves."

"People come for a week or a weekend to have a little fun," said Choy, thinking a debate might ease his discomfort. "They understand this place is an illusion. They go home to the real world when their vacation is over. Las Vegas is hardly proof that we are governed by our lizard brain."

"I was making a point about the power of basic instincts, about the factors that determine what people believe. And it's clearly not verifiable facts, to the exclusion of everything else."

"So?"

"Until you accept the essential primacy of the lizard brain you will never understand the appeal of politicians like Donald Trump, Amanda Bennett or the raw power of propaganda."

"Propaganda?"

"The word sounds bad in English, so we call it advertising, marketing, spin or simply the media, but it's all the same damn thing. Armies do it. So do governments, corporations, political parties, charities, advocacy groups, newspapers ... it's simply people trying to manipulate the way other people think for various ends."

"Newspapers are propaganda? They try to manipulate how people think?"

"Of course they do. What is this 'gatekeeping' you are taught in journalism school? Filtering. Letting people know what is important by positioning, headline size and repetition. Influencing people."

He may have a point.

"Owners of newspapers manipulate the way their readers think," Mason continued as they drove past a partially built casino that seemed a remnant of some post-apocalyptic zombie attack. "To sell something, whether it's civic pride, a political party, cars or the local football team. Am I wrong?"

This man is making sense and I have to go to the bathroom.

"Newspapers are propaganda providers, prostitutes selling themselves to the highest bidder. And you know what the so-called death of newspapers is really all about? Just like happens to a high class hooker when she gets old, newspapers have lost their top customers, who have moved on to the younger and sexier prostitutes — Google, Facebook, Twitter."

That was it. Choy finally tuned Mason out. Instead he thought about his need for a toilet to do a diamond dump. Mining for this precious gem was not going to be pleasant, but if it was worth as much as Mason had said, it would mean he could take the buyout, leave the newspaper and do whatever he wanted.

"A journalist's job is not to tell the truth, " Mason continued to babble. "It is to tell people what to think, so the system functions as smoothly as possible."

Choy had no choice but to hold it in. There was a risk Mason might have noticed something in the steam room and 10 minutes in the bathroom could raise suspicion.

"Civilization is more fragile than we realize. Go to Iraq or Syria and you will see. Most of us here have it good and the journalists' job is to make damn sure it stays that way."

If it comes out in my pants? Think about something else.

"What good is freedom if it leads to chaos, car bombings and the end of order?"

Were there any other questions he wanted to ask Mason? A few occurred to him but they involved ways of selling diamonds discretely. Choy was tired of this man's company, tired of his constant manipulation, tired of the crap that spewed from his mouth. Why bother asking for answers from a man who didn't believe there was any such thing as the truth?

Primal urges, the lizard brain — more powerful than we think.

Just when he thought it was impossible to control his sphincter any longer Mason stopped the car in front of the Las Vegas Review-Journal building, less than a mile on the other side of downtown from the Strip.

"Well, I hope you got what you wanted," Mason said as he opened the door. "I have a meeting here with an old friend. The publisher and I go way back. He wants to discuss Donald Trump."

All Choy could manage was a grunt.

"Watch your back," Mason said, walking away. "Maybe I will see you around."

Choy carefully got into the driver's seat and looked up at the nearby downtown casinos. A few minutes later the car key was in the right hand of a doorman in front of the Union Plaza hotel and Choy was headed to the nearest toilet stall.

2.

Choy was pretending to sleep as Donicelli drove the car north to Portland and Tait sat in the front seat beside him. The past 10 days had been the most intense, the scariest and maybe the best time of his life. He had risked his life and survived. For the first time he felt like a real journalist, one who confronted power, with fear sure, but not favour.

I found Joy. I have the diamond.

What happens in Vegas stays in Vegas.

It was both a marketing slogan and good advice, given the circumstances.

I can't tell anybody. No one. Not Doug or Dominic or Joy or my kids. Am I capable of that? If Bennett ever finds out, she'll kill me for sure. Or kidnap one of my kids and hold her or him for ransom. Maybe she'll kill me anyway, just because I annoy her. Although while she's on the run from the FBI killing me would be an unlikely priority.

Kempki was convinced that Bennett would eventually surrender to the police because a trial, with all its publicity, and potential martyrdom, was exactly what she wanted. If that were so, the murder of a journalist would be counter-productive — unless he had stolen something from her, something worth a lot of money.

Mason had said each of the 58 stones was worth at least a million dollars, but that some were worth a lot more. Near as Choy could calculate from Google searches his might be one in the "lot more" category. First of all, the colour, deep blue, was rare. And the size was around 50 carats, which was very large. Bennett may not have known exactly how many diamonds were in the bag and even if she did, it was entirely plausible that one, or more, had fallen down a drain or Tennyson had taken it. Or maybe she would think Mason or Celeste and Ertha had ripped her off. If Waylon Choy exhibited no suspicious behaviour, he would not be a prime suspect. And he did have some insurance — the photos and recording of Bennett with the senior Republican.

How long to keep the diamond secret? A few years. Then on a European vacation, I visit Amsterdam and sell it at a deep enough discount that the buyer will ask no questions. Not a bad plan.

If he took the buyout, sold his house and started writing books, money wouldn't be an issue for a decade or so, at least. And maybe he'd be successful enough that it wouldn't be necessary to sell the diamond. Maybe the blue stone would be a mysterious family heirloom that his grandkids find in an old shoebox after his and Amanda Bennett's death.

He did feel guilty about leaving out parts of the story. It felt like lying. On the other hand, had he ever written a story that told the whole truth? How could anyone even know the whole truth? And it was common to purposely leave out part of a story because something could not be proved to the satisfaction of the newspaper's libel lawyer.

No reason to share the diamond with Donicelli and Tait. They didn't have two near-death experiences. Wainwright though.

It was depressing that Wainwright's mother refused to acknowledge her son's death. Religion could be a terrible thing.

What if, when I do sell the stone, I dedicate a significant part of the proceeds to remember Adam Wainwright? Some sort of prize named after him. Even better, what if I dedicate the rest of my career in writing to Adam Wainwright? Having the diamond, even if it's never sold, gives me independence and the ability to choose the stories I work on. How about, from now on, every time a project comes up I ask myself: Is doing this something that would honour Adam's memory? And only pursue the ones that do.

Choy felt like a real, honest-to-goodness investigative journalist, dedicated to uncovering the truth, willing to stand up to the rich and powerful on behalf of the poor and powerless. The last two weeks had taught him he could. And he could do it even better if he were no longer limited by working for a conservative, mainstream newspaper. He'd write for magazines and publish books instead. Without fear or favour. A crusading journalist making a meaningful contribution to building a better world, that would be something Adam would have respected.

Why had he never seen journalism in this way before?

Maybe I have, sort of.

Even though he'd always primarily wanted to entertain his readers, he did have some vague sense of journalistic integrity and responsibility. He had always known journalism was essential to democracy. How could citizens be informed voters if there were no reliable sources of information? And he did care that what he wrote was true.

It was cynicism that had blinded him to journalism's real possibilities. It was impossible to be a journalist employed by a big corporation and not be cynical. He had survived the real world of an actually existing newsroom by ignoring the shallowness, the subservience to powerful interests, the dependence on advertising, the pathetic pursuit of positions of power, the benefits that could accrue personally if you learned to live with all the bullshit, and the invisible chains that accompanied actually getting paid to do a job you loved, by wrapping himself in a cocoon of cynicism.

Now it will be different. I'll do whatever is right. I'll be free to decide what stories to pursue.

This was a pleasant thought, one that allowed him to feel okay about himself, one that allowed him to sleep.

3.

The funerary urn sat in the middle of a corner wooden table, surrounded by pints of beer in an almost empty Portland brewpub around the corner from where Wainwright had lived. Choy, Tait and Donicelli had spent the night in the apartment and were at the door to this establishment when it opened.

"Getting drunk in the morning," said Donicelli, staring at the urn. "We're doing this for you my friend."

Choy and Tait nodded.

"Okay, who is going to start?" asked Donicelli. "I want to go last."

Choy and Tait looked at each other.

"Okay," said Choy, picking up his beer. "To Adam Wainwright, who taught me to be brave enough to take a buyout. I learned from you that journalism should be more than a job. It should be a way of life, a commitment to truth."

"A commitment to truth," repeated Tait and Donicelli, as each man downed three or four substantial mouthfuls of brew.

"To Adam Wainwright, a journalist who died doing what he did best: Comforting the afflicted and afflicting the comfortable," said Tait.

"Comforting the afflicted and afflicting the comfortable," repeated Choy and Donicelli, as all three men drank again.

"To Adam Wainwright," said Donicelli, "who loved to tell stories, we promise never to forget how and why you died. We will remember and tell your story far and wide."

"Far and wide," repeated Tait and Choy, as each of three men repeated the ritualized toasting.

"To a dying craft and the journalist who preceded its ultimate demise," said Choy. "Adam, you were a whiz with the 5 Ws and a special genius with the last one. You knew when to get out."

"The 5 Ws," repeated Donicelli and Tait.

"To typewriters, terminals of mainframe computers, copy run-ners and wire editors when there were still wires," said Tait. "To copytakers, stereotypers, platemakers and typographers with sharp knives. Adam, you outlived them all, even if your life was cut much too short."

"To Adam Wainwright, proof of the critical importance of newspapers and journalism to a functioning democracy and the sad realization that they are never going to be the same again," said Donicelli. "To the death of newspapers. Long live journalism."

"To the death of newspapers. Long live journalism."

"Ninety-nine journalist scum on the wall — Take one down, smack him around — 98 journalist scum on the wall," sang Choy.

They toasted. They sang. They drank.

And they drank.

The End

About the Author

Gary Engler is a former journalist, local union official, marine engineer, apprentice millwright, postal worker, truck driver, playwright, audio-visual technician, and assembly-line worker. Earning money from writing while attending St. Francis High School in Calgary in the late 1960s got him hooked on literary endeavours even while he worked at various real jobs. His first professional theatrical production was Sudden Death Overtime at Factory Theatre Lab in Toronto in 1974. His first published novel was The Year We Became Us (Fernwood 2012 and Spanish language translation, Cuba 2016). He also spent 20 years as a reporter, feature writer and editor at the Vancouver Sun.

Made in the USA
Columbia, SC
22 July 2020